The Creative Lower Being

Praise for the Author:

'Riotously comic' - The Sunday Times

'Highly entertaining ' - The Guardian

'Pure joy' - The Daily Telegraph

'Unique imagination at work' - The Sunday Tribune

'A storyteller like no other' - Time Out

'Surreal and witty' - The Observer

'Non-stop invention, high level of wit'
- The Irish Times

'Intelligent humour, careering comic visions'
-The London Independent

The Creative Lower Being

Karl MacDermott

Killynon HouseBooks

This novel is entirely a work of fiction. The names, characters and Incidents portrayed in this book are the work of the author's imagination. Any resemblance to actual persons, living or dead, events or localities, is entirely coincidental.

First published 2007 by Killynon House Books Ltd.

ISBN: 978-1-905706-09-9

Cover design and text layout by Agnieszka O'Toole

Printed and bound in Denmark by Nørhaven Paperback

KILLYNON HOUSE BOOKS
Killynon House, Turin, Mullingar, Co. Westmeath, Ireland
Website: www.killynonhousebooks.com
Email: khbooks@iol.ie

About the Author

Karl MacDermott was born in Galway. A promising comedy career in the 1990's was cut short by a bizarre water polo accident. He is currently writer-in-residence at his home in Dublin. This is his first novel.

To Mrs. Chadwick

November 22nd 365 days to go

I wanted to go to the cinema by lunchtime because I figured it would be quiet and I could relax. So I left the house by late morning and had walked into town by one o'clock. Sadly, when I arrived at the multiplex, there was a large queue. I hate that multiplex. All multiplexes. They are the cinematic equivalent of fast food restaurants. People turn up, scratch their heads, look up at the menu and wonder what they will have. I don't understand that approach. I never enter a cinema without knowing exactly what I am going to see. And today I was planning to see a movie I felt I could relate to, about a loner with a rich imagination who doesn't sleep very well. As I looked around, I noticed that most of the cinemagoers ahead of me were signing up for the mega-pass deal the multiplex offers. The deal entails seeing all the movies you want over the course of a month for only €12.50. Or over the year for €150. Economically, it's a great bargain, but I would never do it. Because then they will own me.

Me: Manus Mannion. A Creative Lower Being. Obsessed by the past. Former stage actor and comedian. At present a screenwriter. A committed melancholic and non-viveur. Interests include going to the cinema, searching for the correct remote control, and acquiring rare Memphis Minnie recordings. Born on 22nd November,1963. A day of worldwide grief.

**Mannion's Personal Fact No. 1*

And any time I planned to go to a movie in the future,

I'd check if it was on in the multiplex first, to make the best of my deal. And I would keep going up there all the time, and supporting this emporium of hard sell crassness, dodgy frankfurters and pop-corn. So with a feeling of moral superiority, I paid my €6.50 for just the one screening. I made my way up the stairs. I entered the half full cinema. The lights went down. I was bombarded by all sorts of ads I could not relate to. Neither the young beautiful people who appeared in them nor the young beautiful products that they were promoting. And I'm only 39. Today.

Then the trailers began. What is it with today's movie trailers? They all last about five minutes and give every minor plot detail away. The big movie companies try to get you to go see their movie but after sitting through the trailer you don't need to, because you already know exactly what is going to happen. A trailer came up for a movie I planned to see. I had heard that there was an interesting plot twist in this movie so, fearing they might reveal it, I immediately closed my eyes and put my hands over my ears. The sound system was so loud I could still clearly hear the dialogue, so I secretly started to hum and sway until it finished. A couple in the next aisle, slightly alarmed, looked over at me. The trailer finished and the 'please switch off your mobile phone announcement' appeared. Just as the opening credits rolled, three 17- year-old guys in tracksuits walked in laughing, accompanied by a girl around the same age. Most definitely D.L.T.'s (Dodgy Looking Types). I'd spotted them in the queue debating which of the three twenty past one shows they would go to. Just my luck. They ended up going to a movie they half wanted to see because it's part of the mega-pass deal. They were holding their oversized cola containers and their plastic tortilla chips and sat two rows behind me. The movie finally began.

Donnie Darko (2001) 122m. * D: Richard Kelly. Jake Gyllenhaal, Drew Barrymore, Katherine Ross, Patrick Swayze. A mixed up troubled teenager at a 1980's high school suffers from visions that could be premonitory. Engrossing psychological thriller that ultimately disappoints with a muddled conclusion. [R]**

After two minutes though, the running commentary, the 'insightful' queries and the jokes from behind began. I immediately tensed up. The other members of the audience didn't seem to mind. One woman, in front of me, kept taking out her mobile phone. The tiny green display screen distracted my eye as she continually checked her text messages. Ten minutes later, things had gotten worse. The D.L.T.'s behind me were still at it, slightly louder than before. They especially found Donnie's imaginary confidante, Frank, the six-foot demonic rabbit, particularly hilarious. Some of the other members of the audience were starting to notice and began to sigh disapprovingly, but no one was actually bothering to confront the Tracksuit Four. I decided to bite the bullet. Momentarily turning into my father admonishing his offspring, I turned round, glowered and said, "Could you please keep it down, I'm trying to watch the movie!" My request was met with a giggle. Then a "Fuck off". Then another giggle.

Two minutes later, one of them, who I shall refer to as Tracksuit No.1, got up and walked down the aisle. As he passed me, my heart jumped into my mouth, and I worried that this may be some delayed form of physical retaliation, but he just walked by. He was gone for ages. The other three just kept up their low chat. In the meantime a confused looking Chinese student came in late. He sat in the row in front of me. He had dyed chestnut hair and after a moment took out his mobile phone and checked for text messages. After fiddling with it for a while he put it away and shuffled in his seat. He watched the movie for ten minutes, got up and left. He wasn't losing out because it's just another movie he can be disinterested in, as part of his mega-pass deal. As he left, Tracksuit No.1 returned and made his way energetically up the aisle. More jokes and giggles ensued.

I'd reached breaking point. Donnie's bizarre odyssey was complex enough to follow without all these distractions. I decided to seek out an usher. I rushed out the door. No sign of an usher. I scampered down the corridor past Cinemas Seven, Six and Five. Still no sign of an usher. I hurried into the main merchandising area. People were sitting, chatting, and picking at various cardboard buckets of popcorn, whilst others consumed assorted disparate junk in the various retail areas.

I eventually spotted a figure of authority holding a torch. I approached him. He was spotty and no more than 14. He looked up at me. And I am only five foot four. Before I opened my mouth I knew how futile it all would be.

"There are a few 17 year olds, messing around in Cinema Eight," I said.

I looked at the fear in his eyes.

"How many?"

"Four."

I knew what he was thinking. He was thinking, does this sad, near middle-aged guy, in an anorak, honestly believe that I, a 14-year-old, am going to ask four 17-year-olds to keep quiet.

I looked at him. "Well?"

I started to head back to the cinema, coaxing him along.

He walked meekly behind me. Whatever happened to the old ushers, I wondered. Those frightening figures in navy uniforms and peaked caps wielding their torch like some secret weapon. They would have a trouble maker by the ear and out of the cinema in no time. But now they are all gone. And all you have is some terrorised, acne-ridden kid whose voice has yet to break, trying to make some extra pocket money. We re-entered the cinema. I led him to the Tracksuit Four. He stood behind me. I stood aside. He moved with me and still stood behind me. Peering his head around my shoulder, he eventually cleared his throat.

"We've had some complaints from the customers, could you keep the noise down?" he asked, his voice cracking with the tension. His request was met with a giggle. Then a "Fuck off". Then another giggle. What a way to spend a birthday.

November 23rd 364 days to go

364 days to go to the big Four O. Much of that time will be spent looking back, re-evaluating and trying to make sense of my life to date. I have decided on a suitable format.

"Manus Mannion's Incidents and Memory Guide."

Key to Incidents and Memory Ratings:
***** **Brilliant.**
**** **Good.**
*** **O.k.**

****   Not Great.**
***   Awful.**

The Mannion Guide rates with the following symbols.

G   General Audiences: All ages allowed.

PG   Parental Guidance Suggested: Some material may not be suitable for Children.

PG-13   Parents strongly cautioned. Some material may be inappropriate for children under 13.

R Restricted: Children under 17 require accompanying parent or adult guardian.

NC-17   No Children Under 17 allowed.

I was at a loose end after getting home from the cinema. I felt depressed. It was my birthday after all. My mother always jokes that she remembers vividly what she was doing the day President John F. Kennedy was assassinated. Having a caesarian. And since my girlfriend,Kirsten, was away on that business trip, I was all alone. I turned on the television and ironically John Hurt was on appearing in a version of 'Krapp's Last Tape'. While watching the play, I imagined videotaping myself watching the play and in thirty years time re-playing that videotape of myself watching 'Krapp's Last Tape' and as I would watch myself watching 'Krapp's Last Tape', I would ponder over my own intervening thirty years.

Suddenly, the phone rang. It was Kieran. He didn't know it was my birthday, he'd just rang on the off chance. Which is surprising because he never does. He wondered did I want to go out for a few drinks. I jumped at the idea.

Glum and Glummer (2002) 140m. ** D: Richard Linklater. Kieran Finn, Manus Mannion. Two depressives, a struggling screenwriter and failed rock star, go on the tear in Dublin City, lamenting the way their**

lives have turned out. Heavily influenced by Cassavetes, a surprisingly engaging and truthful two-hander. [PG]

Kieran is another Creative Lower Being. He's a session musician in the music industry. He also plays in a tribute band called The Counterfeit ZZ Top, although they have taken a career break recently, ever since that gig last June, when an audience member suffering from pogonophobia set fire to their false beards. With that lugubrious demeanour and endless sighing, Kieran is a dysthymic bohemian zombie sleep-walking through a life of endless disappointment. He always wears black.

"Why do you wear black, Kieran?" I asked him once, after five years of us drinking together. "To paraphrase Chekhov, I'm in mourning for my dreams," he replied. He must have stolen that line from somewhere because he's only ever read two books in his life, 'The Commitments', by Roddy Doyle and a discounted Neil Young biography. In fact, I don't know why I hang around with him because he doesn't know anything.

He claims to be a film buff but when I asked him awhile back, what his favourite film noir was, he looked up from his pint, stared at me for a moment and then in all seriousness, replied, "'Shaft'." Kieran likes to drink. A legend in his own liver. He always laps me. My limit is five pints. His limit is limitless. He needs at least four pints just to get the batteries whirling and then he doesn't stop. He's one of those guys whose face dons a crazed, demonic expression when he takes a big gulp from his pint glass. You look at him from the corner of your eye in amazement and shudder slightly. After three gulps from his pint he is already getting fidgety and restless about ordering another round. By the time he has to get in the last orders he practically has a nervous breakdown from the stress. He has a mobile phone. He is always trying to convince me to get one. I refuse to do so because that would give him an excuse to be late for our appointments. He could always contact me in the last minute then, if he hadn't got himself organized and was running behind schedule, to tell me he would be late or worse still that he had to cancel. I prefer waiting in the pub for an hour staring at my pint, wondering will he show at all, rather than giving him the easy option of calling. I also feel a rare pleasure in his guilt when he eventually does rush in, all apologies, and insists on paying for an extra round.

We usually meet in Grogan's pub on Castle Street. A booze-fuelled den of artistic underachievers and modish young wannabes. I'm not crazy about the place. Especially the toilet situation. I don't like the gents toilet in Grogan's. There is very little pee leeway at the urinal. Pee leeway is very important. Especially in Grogan's, with the amount of pints drunk there. Who devised the whole urinal concept? Why are men expected to widdle up against a wall? Women don't have to. Why can't we have a bit of privacy? I, personally, have always hated that sphincter tightening moment when I am forced to pee next to someone. And so does Bob. He loses his happy go lucky, carefree shape and tensely shrinks to the size of a paper clip.

Bob: Affectionate term for penis. Coined in mid-adolescence as a consequence of said organ always living in hope.
** Mannion's Personal Fact No. 22*

Kieran doesn't have that problem. Because he never seems to have to go. He drinks three times as much as me yet I'm always the one timing my anxious trips to the gents, hoping the cubicle will be free.

Certain women are attracted to Kieran's jaded hangdog presence and he has this theory that if a woman smokes, she goes to bed with you much quicker than if she doesn't smoke. He is a committed smoker. He also has the ability in a pub to talk complete shite with complete strangers. I could never do that. Most Irishmen can. And if I'm out drinking with him and some bearded scruff merchant, sits opposite us at our table and having nothing better to do, starts up a completely idiotic conversation, Kieran reacts in a very friendly manner and includes the intellectually challenged hirsute one in our conversation. I cannot stand when that happens. I don't want to listen to this whiskered nonentity's opinions on the war on terrorism or the situation in Iraq, because I have arranged to go drinking with Kieran tonight, and him alone.

Last night a different scenario evolved. We were sitting down and a young woman politely asked if she could sit on the stool opposite us. We told her there was no problem. The minutes went by, and I thought, at least she's quiet and is keeping to herself, as she sipped her glass of lager. Kieran noticed the Marlboro Light between her fingers. But then over the next half hour a whole gaggle of her friends gradually turned up. And within the next ten minutes, Kieran and myself were completely surrounded as wayward stools were located and our table space was quickly colonised. Evidently, it was somebody else's birthday. Somebody with a lot more friends than me.

November 28th   359 days to go

Like most Creative Lower Beings I spend a fair bit of my time walking pointlessly and aimlessly. My little catchment area is between Andrew Street, Suffolk Street, Grafton Street and Wicklow Street in Dublin 2. Sometimes I veer off towards South William Street, and take a left at Chatham Street whereby I end up back on Grafton Street. During my walks I ruminate on things I have ruminated on many times before.

In fact, I read recently, that a human being has 60,000 thoughts every day but 95% of those thoughts are the same thoughts he had the previous day. I believe this to be true. The things that have constantly pre-occupied my mind, over the years are a smorgasbord of random musings. Thoughts like, will I go for coffee? Why does no one watch showjumping on the television anymore? How come so many unhealthy looking people work in hospitals? I think I'll put the potatoes on at half past six. Whatever happened to Judge Reinhold? I wish I'd been a Beatle. How come movies with funny out-takes at the end are never all that funny in the first place. What do sheep count when they try and get to sleep?

Though in a deep contemplative state, I am still fully aware of my surroundings and am constantly keeping an eye out for unwanted accidental meetings. For I hate bumping into people. I hate small talk. And I get an extra thrill if I successfully avoid a person. It's my speciality. That and brooding. I sometimes tell people that this is what I studied in college. Brooding and avoiding people.

Most times if I see someone I know on the street, approaching in the distance, and they are not a very close friend who is in need of urgent medical attention, I literally run up a side road with my head in my ruck sack rather than face a conversation. Like the one I had with an old college acquaintance, Brendan Tynan last month.

"Manus. How's it going? What are you doing with yourself this weather?"

"Oh, you know, bit of this and that. Mainly screen-writing."

"Are you still doing the auld comedy?"

"No."

"Must be a hard old graft with the auld writing."

"Yeh."

"Still you're doing what you want."

"Yeh."

"Not much money in it, though?"

"No."

"As long as your happy."

"Yeh."

"Lovely seeing you. Listen keep in touch, give us a bell. I'm in the phone book, we'll go for a jar."

They always say, "Keep in touch." Why would I want to keep in touch with Brendan Tynan? Why would I want to go for a jar with Brendan Tynan? If I met Brendan Tynan in a bar we would have nothing to say to each other after five minutes. We had nothing to say to each other twenty years ago in college, after two minutes. Maybe, though, I should look him up in the phone book, and ring him and meet up with him once, for an evening of strained recollections. And then the following week maybe I should ring him up again. And again. And start harassing him, and insisting we meet regularly, and turning up at his house unannounced and freaking out his wife and young children. Maybe then that will teach him to stop saying "keep in touch" to people.

Last Monday was particularly bothersome. Within the space of forty minutes I had seen and circumvented three people I have known over the years. First off was Rachel. I noticed her coming towards me in the Stephen's Green Shopping Centre. She noticed me too. In a moment of weakness, I almost said hello to her, but quickly came to my senses and instead initiated that 'tacit synchronicity of avoidance'. 'The tacit synchronicity of avoidance' is that pre-meditated split second decision two acquaintances take, whilst walking towards one another, not to acknowledge each other, while at the same time feigning that they haven't actually spotted one another.

Rachel was more than happy to comply. I respected her for her maturity. I hadn't seen her for about ten years. She looked quite well. I met her on a Government sponsored AnCO Course in 1985. She came back to my flat once in 1987. Did she want to have sex with me? I mean she came back to my flat. She *agreed* to come back to my flat. In fact that night she'd invited me out to an Agnes Bernelle concert where some middle-aged businessman who'd had too much to drink kept shouting, "Sing us another song, Fräulein," trying to impress Agnes with his one word of German.

Later, Rachel and I went drinking with some other people and then we went back to my flat. I made her tea. Did she fancy me? I was never much good at spotting those things. And there she was yesterday. I didn't want to talk to her. She didn't want to talk to me. A Ghost of AnCO Courses Past.

Five minutes later, I see a guy in dark glasses who looks familiar but slightly more filled out. He sees me. Again, we do that lovely 'tacit synchronicity of avoidance' — this time he's the initiator, I am happy to be the initiatee, and as I join in this most sublime choreography of indifference, I recognise him. It was Peter. Another Ghost of AnCO Courses past. This time, one from 1986. He was trendy then with his post punk look and heroin diet. He still looks quite fashionable. I think he wanted to be a rock journalist. Drumcondra's answer to Lester Bangs.

About 20 minutes later on Chatham Street my mastery and technique is tested again. Walking with a bag of potatoes and a leek, I spot a familiar face behind another pair of dark glasses. I immediately recognise Miriam. She is with some tall guy. I knew Miriam years ago. We shared a kitchen together in a flat on Leinster Road. She saw me and I saw her. This time there was danger. You can't afford to look at them for more than a second or sentiment and nostalgia might overtake proceedings. Maybe *they* want to stop and talk. We can't have that. A quick movement of the head is essential. This time I am the initiator, she a reluctant initiatee.

It wasn't all plain sailing last Monday, though. I guess with all that stress, I had become tired, and had lost my sharpness and was no longer on top of my game. For suddenly I saw Helen at around quarter past four and it was too late to engage in 'that tacit synchronicity of avoidance'. It started off quite innocuously. I looked at somebody pushing a pram.

I hadn't recognised her immediately and then suddenly it was too late. Damn, she's seen me, I thought to myself, and we're too close. Shit, now I'll have to say hello. I then had to make some rapid calculations. Do myself and Helen have a 'stop and talk' relationship or a 'nod and grunt' relationship? For normally, there are two types of interaction you have with people, who for one reason or the other, you have inadvertently been forced to greet on your street travels. People you stop and talk to. And people you nod and grunt at.

After a moment Helen and myself both realised we didn't have a 'stop and talk' relationship anymore, just a mere 'nod and grunt' relationship, and with much relief, I nodded and she grunted. I met Helen years ago. She was a failed costume designer. I was acquainted with people she shared a house with. I did not fancy her. At all. But we started hanging out together. And I got it into my head that she fancied me. And then I started thinking maybe I fancied her. I then became obsessed with her. I worked myself into a frenzy. I'd monitor her every move. Wonder where she'd been and with whom. I couldn't let anyone else take her away. She was mine. I was crazy about her. I couldn't eat. I couldn't sleep. I had to tell her. I was in love with her. I waited until the time was right. "I love you," I said, sitting next to her on that couch as she was getting off with some theatre director guy at that house party in Ranelagh. I repeated my declaration loudly over the Talking Heads song 'Psycho Killer' that was blaring in the background. "Did you hear what I said, I love you!" She continued to purr pleasurably as he placed his hands inside her blouse.

December 7th 350 days to go

How does anyone survive in this world past the age of four? That's what I was thinking this morning as I was lying in bed recovering from a hangover of cranium drilling intensity. Being a child up to that age is like being a star. Everybody wants you. You are the centre of attention. Your every move is noted and applauded but then, all of a sudden, it's over. You are all washed-up. Career as cute, lovable kid is finished. And the next batch of kids come on the scene to be adored.

How does anyone survive that? It's simple. We are programmed not to remember. Some device is triggered and all those experiences on that early infancy hard drive are deleted. Our memory only starts truly functioning when we are five. Which is just as well. Because if we remembered all that love and undying attention from those early years when we were older and unhappier, and insignificant and unsuccessful, we'd all probably do what a lot of ex-stars do and consume copious amounts of drink and drugs to help us live in a self-induced haze, recalling a litany of past glories. "I was something when I was two! I'd walk into a room, heads would turn, I'd smile, they'd all laugh, and the women, always picking me up... it was incredible."

Unfortunately, I consumed copious amounts of drink last night. Which caused me to get violently ill. Or maybe it was that new Ben Affleck movie, 'Changing Lanes', I'd seen earlier. He *really* irritates me. Later, I had a most embarrassing scene. On the street. As I was just about to get sick, some English tourists approached me looking for directions to the Abbey Theatre. I proceeded to point them in the correct direction as I was throwing up. They had some difficulty in deciphering my instructions and persisted in getting me to repeat the information. Now prostrate in a corner and heaving powerfully, I apologised profusely and between bouts of retching, and sent them on the proper route.

Still vegetating in bed by lunchtime, I began recalling those days I would miss school when I was younger. Usually because of a stomach bug. I remembered vividly how much I used to hate vomiting when I was growing up. I still have a detailed record of those dates I vomited as a child.

On September 16th, 1972, I devoured a packet of wine gums too quickly. Threw up. On October 31th 1973, I had a meal of steak and onions and chips that not only kept repeating all night but talked back to me loudly, raised its voice and engaged in some lengthy argumentative discourse. Threw up.

On November 24th, 1974 started burping up the taste of hard boiled eggs. Always a dangerous sign. The much feared 'eggy wind'. If one got 'eggy wind', without having recently consumed an actual egg, one was doomed and might as well organise a one day lease of the toilet. Burped that putrid flavour for over seven hours. Then threw up.

But let us examine February 4th, 1977 for a more detailed re-enactment of what would occur. It was a windy night. Stomach bug nights always seemed so windy. I was woken by my younger brother Colm, rushing to the toilet and getting sick.

Colm Mannion: A successful estate agent. Only sibling of Manus Mannion. Second born of Eddie and Cora Mannion. Date of Birth: 25th September 1966. Born in Galway the day the county won the All Ireland Gaelic football championship for the third time in a row. A day of much joyful celebration.

**Mannion's Personal Fact No. 6*

Oh no, I thought. Then he came back to bed, and I reasoned, well if he only gets sick the one time, maybe it was just something he ate that didn't agree with him. So I lay awake and waited, to see if he'd get back to sleep. Forty five minutes later, he jumped out of bed again. My heart sank as I heard that distant echo-like intermittent sound of someone throwing up in the toilet. Again. Then I heard another door swing open as hurried slippered footsteps traversed the landing. Bedraggled, hair askew, commando father, in yellow pyjamas, had belatedly turned up at the scene of the incident.

After finally spewing up his last drop of technicolour chunder, for now, Colm returned to bed. At this stage, I was worried, I needed reassurance. The next morning I asked mother, "What's wrong with Colm? Is it just something he ate?" Then I uttered those four words I hated most as a child, "Or is it contagious?"

She tried to comfort me by replying, "Don't worry, pet."

Of course two nights later she threw up. Oh, sweet Jesus! It is the dreaded familial stomach bug! The succeeding days were always the same in this situation. I'd just have to wait. Wait for the bug to hit me. I'd start rationalising. "I'll give it three days. It usually takes hold in three days. If I survive the next three days, I'll be fine." I would stop eating. My logic being that if there is nothing in my stomach, I can't throw up. Perversely, of course, by not eating I would be lowering my resistance. I'd walk around school starving and tired, surviving on cream crackers and water. Waiting, just waiting to get sick. The three days would soon be up. Everybody at home would be well on the road to recovery.

Relief. Missed that one. Just to be on the safe side I'd give the cream crackers and water diet another day. Then I could relax. The time would pass. At last I could enjoy my first big meal in four days. Moussaka. Mother just couldn't stop making it for a whole year after that holiday in Corfu in 1976. At the best of times mother's moussaka was filling. At the worst of times it was positively leaden. This was one of those 'worst of' times. An acidic basketball nestled in my stomach. As the night progressed I felt fuller and fuller. Being prone to fatalism even at that early age, I knew there would only be one outcome and it wouldn't be pretty. Cue commando father in yellow pyjamas. I'd be in bed for three days. I'd miss school. Trouble is, all mother would give me would be cream crackers and water. That would mean my sole diet for six days would be cream crackers and water. So I'd sleep. The most incredible deep sleep. And listen to the radio and read books about long-dead Hollywood film stars.

Carole Lombard (1908-1942) *"Vivacious, attractive leading lady and wonderful comedienne. Appeared in many screwball comedies of the 1930's. Married to Clark Gable. Killed in a plane crash."*

If the Curse Of The Stomach Bug wasn't bad enough, I was further exposed to barfing incidents every time we went on a trip, for Colm also suffered from car sickness. Not always.

But that didn't help. Because one was always aware of the *possibility* that he might get sick in the back of the car. So I never enjoyed travelling, especially with father driving. Father wasn't a complete psychopath in the car, but I would go so far to describe him as psycho-lite and father cleaning up vomit from the back seat of his new Datsun, is not one of those childhood memories that comes basking in a warm glow of nostalgia. It was always the same routine. Each Sunday after lunch, the parents would brightly say, "Let's go for a spin!" It is one of those expressions that sounded perfectly normal in your childhood but in hindsight sounds totally absurd as one visualises a family of four cramming into a washing machine.

The Spin (1974) 100m. D: Vincent McEveety. Manus Mannion, Cora Mannion, Colm Mannion, Eddie Mannion. A flustered father takes his wife and two sons, one of whom suffers from travel sickness, on an outing in his new car. Undemanding family fare remembered for an infamously graphic vomiting scene which subsequently influenced 'Monty Python's Meaning of Life'. [PG-13]**

We'd all get into the car. Parents in the front, children in the back. Colm and I would start arguing about who would sit in the middle. Me, Colm or his imaginary friend, Rufus. When that would be resolved by U.N. negotiator mother, the journey would commence. I would look at my brother. "Are you o.k.?" I'd ask lowly.

"I'm fine!" he'd reply defensively. Five minutes into the journey on the way to Athenry, I'd look at him again. Colm's face would have donned a slight shade of green.

"Are you sure you're o.k.?" I'd enquire.

"I told you I'm fine!" he'd respond tensely.

The journey would continue. As I kept observing my brother, I would marvel at the different shades of green that could be displayed on one freckled human face. I would also be, at the same time, filled with a profound sense of unease.

Eventually, I would mumble to him, "Are you sure you're o.k.? Because you don't look o.k.!" He would take in a nervous breath and just nod. His eyeballs would be bigger and he would just stare ahead. He'd be in the process of entering that higher plane of nausea. Now I'd be getting really apprehensive. Then he would turn white and stay ominously silent. This would always be the signal. For volcano alert. My brother would throw up. Then I'd feel nauseous, because at the end of the day, vomiting is like singing. Once someone starts, others feel the impulse to join in. The car would pull to a halt amid a symphony of expletives. Colm would be bundled out by crack commando father. I would be advised by level-headed mother, to get out of the car for a few minutes to stretch my legs and remain calm. The sweet smell of sick would fill the country air. I'd dread getting back into the car. Once in the back seat I'd look at my brother. He'd still be white as a sheet, but he'd be over the worst. My nightmare would just be beginning as my innards would start to rumble.

December 11th 346 days to go

I had to go and pick up Kirsten's coat at the dry cleaners this morning. She wants to bring it down to Galway over the weekend, when we get our Christmas visit with my parents out of the way. She wasn't due into her office until lunchtime and had some paperwork to do at home so she asked me to collect it. Always glad to get out of the house, I agreed.

I arrived at Price's Dry Cleaners on Pembroke Road, the one place she trusts in Dublin to do a proper job and I presented the shop assistant behind the counter with the correct docket. She searched the railings and eventually found the cream coat on a hanger, nicely wrapped in cellophane. She asked for €30, and I handed over the money. Then she put the coat in a paper bag. That annoyed me. This woman probably thought I had a car parked outside — myself and Kirsten don't own one — however I didn't want to be walking around town with a newly cleaned coat in a paper bag wrapped under my arm for the rest of the morning looking like an extra from some drama set in the garment district of New York circa 1924.

"Don't you have one of your plastic bags with a handle?" I asked.

"We don't use them anymore," the woman replied. "But hang on, I might have an old one lying around."

She eventually found a slightly crinkled green plastic bag under the counter. This bag was completely dissimilar from their normal range of plastic bags. I have picked up Kirsten's laundry many times before and am very familiar with their plastic bag set-up. I felt uneasy. The bag looked worn. This will cause trouble ahead, I thought. Kirsten won't like the idea of a newly cleaned coat in nicely wrapped cellophane put in a rogue green plastic bag of indeterminate lineage. She is, after all, the only woman I know, who questions the pedigree of plastic bags. I was in a dilemma.

Just as the shop assistant was about to place the coat in the rogue green plastic bag I said "Hold it, I'll take it without the bag, thanks anyway!"

I left the shop, newly cleaned coat, cellophane wrapped, in paper bag under my arm. It started to rain. I re-entered the shop. The shop assistant smiled at me. She removed the newly cleaned coat in the nicely wrapped cellophane from the paper bag and packed it in the rogue green plastic bag after all. I went for a cup of coffee. Over the coffee, I planned my return to the house. If I removed the newly cleaned coat out of the rogue green plastic bag, as I get off the bus and just walk in with the coat on the hanger, Kirsten will be suspicious.

"You brought it home like this?" she'll ask in her slight Germanic accent.

However, if I walk in the door with the coat in the rogue green plastic bag, there will be even more trouble.

"Where does this bag come from?" she'll ask. "And who

knows what's been in this bag before," she'll say. Then I might try to reason with her.

"But it's wrapped in a layer of cellophane anyway."

But I know Kirsten would immediately dismiss that argument and continue:

"You know how much I hate it when newly cleaned things are put in old plastic bags!"

As I paid for my coffee, I mused how much the Germans are obsessed with the accumulation of bacteria, and that the name of their country, in the English language, is a summation of their worst nightmare. Germ. Many. Then I wondered why was I thinking about Germany, in the first place? Kirsten is actually from Liechtenstein.

Kirsten Offenbach: Liechtensteiner. Has been in a consensual unit with Manus Mannion for eleven years. Into hiking, self-improvement and not being ripped off. Slightly neurotic.

**Burke's Personal Fact No. 3*

December 12th 345 days to go

The problem with the coat eventually resolved itself yesterday. I finally decided to kill a few more hours away from the house and only arrive home with the coat by the time Kirsten had left. Anyway, the siren song of the pint of plain was calling. Arthur's lament. I walked into my local. The Royal Oak is a small cosy pub – like one of those down the country – off an old lane near Rialto where I live. The pub was almost empty, yet I still couldn't attract the barman's attention. Eventually I placed my order.

As I sat down, delicately placing the newly cleaned coat on the seat, I started ruminating on the fact that although I have been coming to this compact little pub for three years, I still didn't know the barman's name and he didn't know mine. I was never much good at that easy rapport with barmen that other Irishmen excel at. You hear it, day in, day out, that guttural self-assured bark of, "Two pints Francis, whenever you're ready!"

Once, many years ago, I tried it. I'd been drinking in Tobin's, a famously rundown hostelry off Grafton Street, on and off for six months, and one day in a moment of courageous abandon while collecting my pint of Guinness, I said to the barman, "Oh by the way, my name is Manus, and yours is... ?"

"John," he replied.

The following Saturday I walked into the bar. Just before shouting confidently "John, a pint!" I looked around. John wasn't working that night. I meekly ordered my pint from another barman.

A few days later, I was there again. Still no sign of my new pint pulling friend. I debated whether to introduce myself to the other barman. I decided against it. John must be on holidays, I thought. The weeks passed by. One afternoon I went in for a quiet one, and as I waited for my pint, I noticed a plaque on the wall behind the bar. In memory of John. I read the inscription.

"To John. He may be gone, but he'll be forever in our hearts."

"John's dead?" I asked the other barman incredulously.

"Yeh, he got depressed one night after work, and threw himself into the Liffey. Very sad, so much to live for," the barman replied, sadly.

I looked around at the various yellow faced craggy afternoon barflies, the peeling paint work, and the ancient cigarette stained tables.

"Too true," I said, nodding sympathetically.

When I first arrived in Dublin, at the age of twenty-one, I would go into various drinking establishments and order a glass of Guinness with a drop of raspberry juice to sweeten it. Rugged barmen would give me the evil eye. After much deliberation, I decided an urgent overhaul of my drinking habits was required. I resolved to change tack and soon afterwards ordered my glass of Guinness with a drop of black current juice instead. I needed that dash of black current juice to kill the taste of the hops, for I had never acquired a taste for alcohol before I left Galway.

When I was growing up most Irish adolescents had their first drink the night they received their Inter Cert results. That day was considered a landmark event. From that date onwards, you were considered a grown-up. You were expected to fit into a suit. Joke in a semi-jocular fashion with adults, while still showing them the proper respect. Maybe get a part-time job and earn money outside school hours. Learn to drive a car. And get drunk. None of the above applied to me. I was 15 going on 12 to paraphrase Rodgers and Hammerstein. I got six honours in my Inter Cert. After all the work I put into the exam, and all the congratulations at home, I felt a slight anti-climax on the day. Mother detected this.

"Aren't you going out this evening with your classmates?" she asked.

I looked at her. I hadn't planned to go out. I had an interesting evening lined up, listening to records I'd listened to a hundred times before and watching a repeated wildlife programme about the proboscis monkey from Borneo on the television. But some of my classmates were going out to have a few drinks, alcoholic drinks, and go to a disco later, to try and meet some girls. Maybe I too, should venture out into the real world.

"Go on, it's a once in a lifetime occasion, just don't stay out too late," mother continued.

I decided I'd go out. Firstly, I met my classmates in some dingy bar in Salthill.

Salthill: Place of Birth. Galway's premier tourist resort, notable for its incessant rain and ongoing sewage problems.

** Mannion's Personal Fact No. 15*

They looked so mature, in their jackets, sipping their pints at the bar. I ordered a Fanta. I tried to join in with the raucous banter but felt completely ill-at-ease. I clung to a few fellow ill-at-easers, Austin and Michael. Swots in jumpers, with their shirts buttoned up to their Adam's apples, incapable of relaxing. We played table soccer and pool, while the others filled themselves with pints of lager, to build up their courage for the disco. Suddenly it was nine thirty. Time to leave and go across the road to one of Salthill's primary night spots — San Fran Disco.

San Fran Disco (1979) 110m. ** D: Bill Forsythe. Manus Mannion, Michael Farrell, Austin McLynn, Tom Lawless. Three sensitive school boys go to their first disco. Cliched teenage story, enlivened by a great soundtrack of disco favourites from the 1970's. [PG-13]

Music pounded from inside as sixteen expectant, and three anxious, school boys paid their admission. The door man gave me a look. "Sorry son, you can't come in, this place isn't for kids."

This night was becoming more rite of non-passage than rite of passage. Tom Lawless immediately sprang to my defence.

"Ah no, he's with us, he's 16!" shouted Tom.

"16! You have to be 18, to get in here, what age are you?" the doorman asked Tom.

Tom paused. "Uh."

"Ah, come on, it's our Inter Cert night," Adrian Madigan piped up. The doorman looked at the woman behind the ticket booth. She nodded.

"O.k., but no messing, I'll be keeping my eye on you lot!" he warned.

We went inside. At first with the flashing lights I couldn't see very much but when I got my bearings, all I could see were girls. Loads of them. Since leaving Scoil Íde, at the age of seven, to go on to St. Enda's boys only National school, I hadn't really been exposed to them.

And here they were jumping up and down joyfully keeping beat to 'Disco Inferno' by The Tramps. Then to my surprise, some of my classmates approached some of these girls, and from their interaction it was quite obvious that they knew one another. They started to dance to 'Cars' by Gary Numan. I stuck to Austin and Michael. Not wanting to feel completely left out we started half-hopping together in strained unison to the synth-driven back beat. Austin started getting really into it. Fifteen years of repression and being called a swot were being exorcised manically on the dance floor.

Alarmed, myself and Michael looked at each other. Burgeoning hormones and sweat filled the air as the D.J. announced the start of the slow set, with Rose Royce's 'Love Don't Live Here Anymore'. Boys furtively circled prospective dance partners, and took the plunge. "Can I have this dance?" they asked. Most girls would accept coyly and a three-minute rhythmic embrace would begin. Myself, Austin and Michael stared at the proceedings. It would be frowned upon, nay suicidal, for the three of us to keep time to the slow set, however much we kept our respective distance.

So we just stood there, rendered immobile by our lack of courage. I was overcome with a sense of nausea and fear. I didn't know any of these girls. I didn't know how to talk to any of these girls. With the music this loud I wouldn't be able to talk to any of these girls even if I knew how to talk to any of these girls. And now I'm expected to *dance* with one of these girls? I wanted to go home. I saw a fogged up mirror beside me and with my right forefinger printed the word 'Help'. If this was the real world, could I have my place on the living room sofa back please?

December 16th 341 days to go

The weekend went o.k. Kirsten travelled down on Friday on her own. I had decided to go down a day early, on the Thursday. Took nearly five hours to get there. Roadworks outside Kinnegad. When the bus finally arrived in Galway I noticed father sitting in his car waiting. Had been there for an hour and a half. He was not a happy camper. After a five-minute rant about the weather and the traffic situation, he eventually said gruffly "So how are you anyway?" trying to say he was glad to see me but not wanting to give too much away in case I might think he was going soft.

"I'm fine, I'm doing well," I replied and then quickly ran out of something to say. I quickly glanced down on my "What to talk to dad about" list, and sadly crossed out "Traffic situation" and "The weather".

"So, eh, your Auntie Maisie's got the shingles," he mumbled trying to think of some useless piece of family information to pass on.

"Really? Maisie? Shingles!" I feigned interest and concern.

There was a long pause as he stopped at some traffic lights.

"I've got that old coat of yours cleaned at the laundry," he said almost as an aside. I smiled. He always uses that one. In his own ham-fisted manner it was his way of saying he loves me. There was another very long pause between us. Then we both had an idea. We both thought of that sentence two men always use when they have run out of things to say to each other.

"Did you see the match?"

We both felt a palpable sense of relief. We were five minutes from home but an intricate exchange of views on the previous night's soccer match should eat up the time, and then once back in the house we could seek out our separate corners. I secretly reprimanded myself for forgetting to write "soccer" on the "What to talk to dad about" list.

"Yeh!" I said. Then in a deflated tone, "Nil-all."

I cursed the heavens that the match we were referring to was nil-all.

I mean if it had been one-all or two-all, we could have said something like "Do you remember that goal in the last 10 minutes?" or "Do you remember that penalty? There's no way that was inside the box!"

I desperately tried to find something else to say.

"Did you see the Sky match on Sunday?"

"No, I was at the rugby game," he replied.

"Oh, let me see. How's mother?" I asked, clutching at straws.

"You know your mother," he said briskly.

We were stuck in traffic. Two minutes to Glenard Close.

Two minutes of excruciating, unbearable silence. Then I remembered something. There was a big game coming up. Everyone was talking about: Third Round of the F.A. Cup. United versus Arsenal.

"Who do you think is going to win between United and Arsenal?" I asked enthusiastically.

He perked up. "I dunno, could be tight!"

"Yes, but United will have the home advantage," I continued.

"Yes, but you can never write off the Gunners!" he said keenly.

We got some momentum going. "But it's not easy going to Old Trafford!" I chipped in.

"Yes, but the Gunners are a great cup team," father added wisely. We were lost in the midst of conversation.

"Yeh, but United will have Keane back after injury," I added, sounding like some overpaid, overrated, underwhelming telly pundit and not caring.

"Yes, but Arsenal will have Viera back after suspension and they are always a different team with Viera," he said with conviction.

The car pulled up outside the house. We both felt a quiet sense of satisfaction for we had communicated. The conversation had taken a bit of time to get going but it had built to a steady, memorable pace. We smiled weakly at each other and got out of the car.

December 21st 336 days to go.

I'm writing this in our nice hotel in Rome at eleven thirty at night. We'll be here for a week. Like all sensible people, myself and Kirsten always try and get away for Christmas. It's been a long day. The morning started off in quite a fraught fashion as we debated how much money to leave lying around the house in case it got burgled while we were away.

"I read it is always best to leave some spare cash lying around, in case burglars come in. They look around, they can't find anything, they'll get pissed off, and they'll mess the place up," Kirsten announced in a flustered tone as she squatted on her suitcase on the living room floor in an attempt to get it to close properly.

"How much do you want to leave?" I asked.

"What do you think?" she said, still pressing down on the suitcase.

"€20?" I replied.

She nodded. I placed the €20 next to the television. Kirsten told me to put it on the televison, so the hypothetical burglars would definitely see it. Then, after a while, we both decided to move the €20 to the kitchen table. I wondered should we leave a note. "Dear Burglars, we're out at the moment, here's some money for your trouble."

Then the taxi pulled up. There is a golden rule when getting a taxi to the airport. If you are not ready, the taxi pulls up early. If you are ready, the taxi pulls up late. We weren't ready. For Kirsten was undecided if €20 was enough.

"Well, €20 isn't £20. And with inflation, I mean like two years ago maybe you could have left twenty quid, but now with inflation and everything, maybe we should leave €30? With twenty they might go 'is that all'?" she continued.

"You mean index linked?" I said, baffled that a term I picked up during my ill-fated college studies was making a rare appearance in my vocabulary.

"Yes!" she replied.

I took out another ten euro note and placed it on the kitchen table. The taximan, still waiting outside our house, beeped his horn. We checked everything was in order one more time, set the alarm, grabbed our suitcases and got into the taxi.

We both hate taking taxis. No matter how friendly the taxi driver is, we are always under the impression he's going to try and rip us off and as he talked to us in an informed manner about his holiday in Sardinia last May, we nodded tensely, our eyes glued to the taximeter. We eventually arrived at the airport. To our relief, he didn't charge too much.

We checked in. Bought newspapers, passed duty-free, and waited anxiously for our flight to be called. We showed our boarding passes and stepped on the plane. I fastened my seat belt and breathed tensely. I just want to categorically state that I am not scared of flying. I'm scared of crashing. If I had my way they would convert every aeroplane into a giant airborne black box recorder. Then if the plane did crash, it would always remain intact. The plane didn't crash. The first potential disaster of any holiday-going experience had been averted.

Once we landed in Leonardo Da Vinci Airport, we then apprehensively confronted our next potential disaster when travelling: Waiting for our luggage in the baggage reclaim area. The longer you wait the more worried you get. Eventually though, our two identical organically leather-bound green suitcases turned up. We arrived in Rome's Termini Station on an airport shuttle service early in the evening.

Our accommodation was near-by, but we accidentally left the train station through a different exit route and ended up lugging our baggage in a circle for half an hour before finally locating our hotel. Pressing the buzzer we announced ourselves, and walked up the three flights of stairs to the desk. The nice, friendly Italian woman told us our room number, gave us the key, and asked for one of our passports. I handed her mine.

We went up a further flight of stairs and reached the door. Now, another potential disaster loomed. The moment before opening that door is always an excruciatingly nerve-wracking ordeal, on any holiday. Because if the accommodation is inadequate, a nagging dissatisfaction will overshadow the whole vacation.

We opened the door. Kirsten, as she always does, walked warily to the bed and checked the bed sheets and mattress. I sighed tensely as I hoped it would get her seal of approval. She then smelt the pillows. There was a pause. She nodded. Relief. I didn't feel like checking out immediately and walking around Rome looking for somewhere else.

Then, like some meticulous botanist, she cautiously entered the bathroom. The bathroom, in whatever accommodation we have, is always a prospective source of grief and unhappiness. Kirsten walked around it tentatively. It seemed clean enough. To me. She went over to the towels and felt them. She thought about it intensely for a moment. They were slightly old. I held my breath. But they were clean. I sighed calmly. She then turned on the shower to check the water pressure. "It could be stronger," she said in a slightly disapproving fashion. I'm Irish, I mused. Things like that don't bother me.

We returned to the bedroom. She admired the tiled floor. Another good sign, I thought. Carpets, those dust mite graveyards, are always frowned upon. So, the third obstacle for any pleasant holiday, after plane remaining intact and luggage turning up, which is quality of accommodation, had been overcome.

We both showered and bravely faced our next hurdle. A nice place to eat. We walked into the cold, Italian night air. It was eight thirty. By my calculations, given our track record, we would be sitting down in a restaurant to eat by quarter to eleven. You see, for myself and Kirsten, choosing a restaurant while on holidays is one of the most difficult and frightening decisions one has to make. Armed with the street map given to us by the hotel and a reputable guide book we set off on our quest. We passed by one place. It looked nice but it was a bit dead. We passed by another place. That was packed. I proposed we go in.

"No," she said, "It's full of tourists."

"Right," I said. Then she noticed a lively sounding place down a laneway. But as we were just about to enter we realised it had been booked by a private party for the evening.

We headed back to the nice place that was a bit dead. It was still a bit dead. Maybe we could take the tram and check out the Trastevere area on the other side of the river, she suggested. My stomach growled. I really wanted to eat. Who knows how long we'd wait for a tram? I thought. Given my extreme state of hunger, I had of course, momentarily forgotten that I wasn't in Dublin but in a highly civilised capital city in Europe which actually adhered to stated transport time tables. I insisted we find somewhere in the locale.

She said,"O.k., it was just a suggestion." A slight irritation crept into her voice.

We continued our elusive trek. It was now past half nine. Only another hour and a quarter to go. We passed by another place. It seemed like a nice place but then eagle-eyed Kirsten spotted a bored Indonesian youth sitting alone, on a high stool, looking out from the kitchen.

"No. It's a wine bar. All the food gets micro-waved," she said.

We kept walking. We both agreed that what we wanted to find was a moderately priced, family-run trattoria, which was packed with locals, and where maybe momma or poppa were in the kitchen cooking their secret recipes which had been handed down through the generations, and their son and daughter served the tables with efficiency and pride.

We decided to head back to the nice place that was a bit dead. It was, even now, still a bit dead. We were now post hungry. And near nauseous. In desperation, we looked across the road and spotted a small supermarket. We nodded at each other, went over to it and bought some bottled water, ciabetta bread, cheese and salami and headed back to the hotel room.

December 29th 328 days to go

Got back yesterday. I enjoyed it. Sort of. I learned some interesting facts. For example, boxing was very popular in ancient Rome. I realised this by looking closely at all those statues in one museum, and noticing that they all seemed to have broken noses. Also, in another museum, I found out that during the Neo-lithic period, people had a tendency to drop an awful lot of cups and plates and vases. All the exhibits on display were just cracked or smashed items of china. I figured maybe mankind hadn't yet developed a strong enough grip by that stage of its evolutionary journey. In fact, I was surprised by the amount of museums that were actually open. I had hoped that over the Christmas period they might all be closed but there was no such luck. Generally I'm not a museum person. Maybe, I'm not a holiday person. Three days into the holiday, I was already psychologically preparing myself to go home. I don't like to be separated too long from my routine back in Dublin. The walking around the streets aimlessly, the looking for bargain C.D.'s and all the while, trying to write the odd screenplay.

I like short holidays. A week, ten days maximum. That's why I appreciated this one. And I didn't get too restless. Kirsten prefers longer holidays. Three weeks, a month. So she feels a bit dissatisfied now, and slightly deflated, maintaining it was pointless going somewhere for such a short time. Actually, it could be said that myself and Kirsten are not a completely compatible holidaying couple. She likes to go to museums, I like to read the paper. She likes to go on day trips to rare archeological sites, I like to read the paper. She likes walking that extra four miles to check out that seventeenth century hermitage up that hill, I like to read the paper. She likes the sea, and loves to swim. I like to read the paper. I sometimes ask myself, what is she doing with me? But she knew what to expect.

When Manus met Kirsten: (1991) 94m. ** D: Nora Ephron. Manus Mannion, Kirsten Offenbach, Irene Dolan. An unlikely couple, he from Ireland, she from Liechtenstein, meet and fall in love. Likeable romantic comedy, with impressive performances from the unknown leads. [PG]**

The first time she saw me, I was reading a newspaper. I was standing in Eason's of O'Connell Street at the time. I've always loved reading the newspaper. In previous years, when even poorer, I spent much time flicking through newspapers and magazines in various retail outlets throughout the city. However, in the early 1990's, there were not as many quality newsagents as there are today and if you wanted to spend a good chunk of your afternoon browsing, the shop with the greatest selection of magazines was Eason's on O'Connell Street. Sadly though, Eason's was largely staffed by what I termed 'The Browsing Police', that group of humourless uniformed middle-aged harridans employed by large newsagents who, if they spotted you picking up a magazine in their place of employment immediately come over to you and harass you verbally. There was one particular employee, the name on her tag was Ms. Irene Dolan, if my memory serves me correctly, who always had it in for me. She'd be on the lookout every time I entered Eason's. As I confidently sauntered over to the magazine section and picked up my morning's reading she'd appear out of nowhere, standing behind me.

"Are you going to buy that magazine?"

I wouldn't answer her.

"Well, would you like to buy a magazine that someone else has picked up and gone through?"

"Uh..."

"Put it back. Now. There's no reading of the newspapers or magazines!"

This went on for years. Weekly humiliation. One day, after another dressing down, I decided to devise a plan. A devious, vengeful plot. I got up early and bought the Irish Times in my local shop. I asked the shop keeper for a receipt and in those pre-receipt times, slightly puzzled he wrote one up for me. I put the receipt in my pocket, the newspaper in my rucksack, and I stepped on a bus and got off at O'Connell Street.

I entered Eason's and quickly went over to the newspaper section. While Ms. Dolan was not looking I removed my Irish Times from my rucksack. Standing there, I opened it widely and started to read it. And I waited. And waited. I looked over. Ms. Dolan was busy with a customer. Slightly exasperated, I finished the Sports section. I looked over again, she was stamping the price on some school books. I half read that special feature on that failed coup in Moscow. I was becoming disheartened when, suddenly, there she was.

She said, loudly and with conviction, "There's no reading of the newspapers or magazines."

The array of fellow flickers standing next to me, muttered a little and gradually put back the various publications. Ms. Nolan walked away. I stood still defiantly, and continued to read about Mr. Gorbachev's fate.

She noticed this and approached me again, "There's no reading of the newspapers or magazines," she repeated, a slight nasty assertiveness creeping into her voice. She left again. I remained unfazed by her display of petty authority. As she went about some other business she kept an eye on me, waiting for me to put back the newspaper. I just turned another page nonchalantly. Finally she had enough. She stormed over to me. "Are you deaf?" she inquired. "I'll only say it once more. There is no reading of the newspapers and magazines."

She then upped the ante. "Or I'll have you thrown out"!

I looked at her and with a triumphant smile said, "But this is my newspaper."

She looked slightly puzzled as I produced my receipt and waved it in front of her face. She took hold of it and examined it. After a moment, she said, "This is a bus ticket."

I grabbed it from her and realised it was the bus ticket. I frantically looked for my newspaper receipt, but couldn't find it. Had I thrown it out, mistaking it for the bus ticket? Ms. Nolan looked at me witheringly. And waited for me to put back my newspaper.

"Actually, it really is my newspaper," I mumbled, "but I'll put it back to avoid a scene."

"Is this the receipt?" An attractive foreign woman, wearing a multi-coloured goretex jacket, and oddly framed glasses, possibly Swiss or German, had bent down and picked up a bit of paper from the ground with the aid of a small white tissue. She handed it to me. I looked at it.

"Yes it is. Thank you," I said.

I gave Ms. Dolan the receipt. "There. I told you it was my newspaper!"

Ms. Dolan for once was speechless. I folded my newspaper under my arm in a victorious manner and smiled at the foreign woman.

"I'm Manus," I said. "How do you do"?

"I'm Kirsten," she said returning a smile.

January 2nd 324 days to go

Time to shape up. Set deadlines. Make resolutions. No more wasting time. No drinking for four weeks. Over that period I plan to have the new draft of 'The Shamrock Sumo Club' completed. My producer Ben Devlin from Rosebud Productions is right. I have to get my act together. But will a story about a group of farmers, from Mountbellew in Co. Galway who set up Connacht's first

Sumo Wrestling Club strike a chord with the cinema going public? Ben is very hopeful. When he meets prospective money men he sells it as a cross between 'Fight Club' and 'The Full Monty'. He is convinced it will be made.

January 6th 320 days to go

January sixth. Little Christmas. How did Jesus, Mary and Joseph end up so poor? Whatever happened all that gold, frankincense and myrrh they got from the Three Wise Men? That was enough to set them up for life. I have three theories.

Theory Number One: It was all a big misunderstanding. Joseph and Mary thought the Three Wise Men were really bandits on the run who under pretence decided to temporarily leave the stolen valuables with them. They also presumed that the Three Wise Men would come back later, when it was safe, kill them and collect the valuables. Convinced of this, they buried the valuables near-by, and the following morning left Bethlehem, with the baby Jesus, forever.

Theory Number Two: It was a miracle gone wrong. From the very beginning Jesus could perform miracles, but being only a baby, he sometimes got the proportionality of things confused. At two months old, longing for a plaything, he turned the gold, frankincense and myrrh into a rattler.

Theory Number Three: Private Investigation fees. Joseph hired a private investigator to find out how his wife really got pregnant. After twenty years of paying this individual with the gold, frankincense and myrrh, the investigator still hadn't solved the mystery.

January 15th 311 days to go

Trying to write today was a complete disaster. Maybe I'm just tired of working on 'The Shamrock Sumo Club'. I came up with the idea five years ago when Sumo Wrestling was still seen as something new and novel in the popular imagination. I read an article about the lack of new Japanese Sumo Wrestlers being trained and how the Japanese Sumo Association were looking for competitors from other countries. That's how the main character, Sean O' Brien, came into being. But after five drafts, 'The Shamrock Sumo Club' is still no closer to being filmed. I am living in Development Hell. Bursary Purgatory. How can I inspire myself to move forward? What I need is methodology. A means of just getting down to the work. I decided to do some research on the net and find out how other writers went about the daily grind of actually writing.

Each evening, after Ernest Hemingway finished his day's writing he would break the nib of his pencil, place it on the desk, leave his study and go about his business. The next morning he would go into his study refreshed, pick up the pencil he broke the day before and slowly sharpen it with a penknife. As he sharpened the pencil he would think about what he had written up until that point and when he felt the pencil was sharp enough to use, he would commence his day's writing. So the secret is to write only with a pencil, I thought. For twenty minutes I tried to find a pencil. Eventually I found one in the kitchen with no nib. Wonderful, I thought, I can be all-rugged and Hemingwayesque and try sharpening it. I got out our small vegetable knife from the drawer and proceeded to whittle away at the pencil.

Within a minute I had cut my finger and was bleeding profusely. Having eventually found a band-aid and still stinging from the TCP I had administered, I looked up Somerset Maugham instead. What was his method? I found out that each morning, Maugham would go into his study and before he got down to work, on his blank sheet of paper would write 'Somerset Maugham, Somerset Maugham, Somerset Maugham, Somerset Maugham'. Eventually he would come up with an idea and continue on the work he had done the day before. I tried the Maugham Technique. I wrote the words 'Somerset Maugham' over and over again with my good uninjured hand. Still nothing came. William Faulkner was no help either. He just got drunk or kept going home to Oxford, Mississippi.

The day went from bad to worse. I work at my upstairs window and I became distracted by looking out and spotting my neighbour across the road sitting by her upstairs window. After a while, she kept looking up from her desk, now and then, and I began to feel slightly unnerved. What's she working on? Maybe she's writing a novel. Does she use the Hemingway Method or The Maugham Technique? Maybe she's writing about me in her novel. I decided to move downstairs and work from the kitchen at the front of the house. Then she moved downstairs, came out her front door and was sitting by her front porch for half an hour getting some early afternoon winter sun. I was keenly aware of her presence as I tried summoning Scene 62.

After ten minutes I moved upstairs again. Twenty minutes later the sun had gone in and I noticed she was back at her desk once more. Trying to put all distractions aside, I closed my eyes for a moment, took a deep breath and concentrated very hard.

Suddenly I started to type. As if a switch had been turned on. Things just started to flow. I got into an amazing groove. Even my injured finger felt no pain. Scenes spurted out. Act Two was finally taking shape. I was surfing on a creative wave heading for Final Draft nirvana. Nothing distracted me anymore. I was lost in my own world. I was in, what they call, the zone. Then my computer crashed. Amidst the delirium I had neglected to save.

January 26th 300 days to go

I came off the wagon last night. I was invited to a launch party. I was amongst my own. Surrounded by hundreds of other Creative Lower Beings. Let me explain the term. It is my theory that people involved in the creative sphere can be split into two distinct categories. Creative Higher Beings and Creative Lower Beings.

Creative Higher Beings are people like Samuel Becket, Louis Armstrong and Pablo Picasso. Artists who have that original signature. Creative Lower Beings are everybody else. People working in that vague, amorphous, precious, Darwinian world known as 'The Arts' who strive to have that unique essential brilliance, but are basically condemned to a life of self-delusion and derivative mediocrity.

Sometimes they can be people who dreamed of a life of success and affirmation in a particular creative sphere when young. But as they got older and more desperate they ended up half doing something else, in a completely different creative discipline. Former lead singers in rock bands who end up writing the theme music for television soaps, for example, or failed novelists who teach media studies and do dissertations on topics no one is interested in. Then there are the actors who branch out into running sweaty overpriced theatre workshops, and esoteric poets who end up as television script editors.

On the other hand, some other Creative Lower Beings can be people who are quite happy with their lot as they impress assorted liggers with what they 'are up to', or 'have lined up' at some swanky media gathering where the free drink runs out by eight thirty. The bottom line though is that Creative Lower Beings are ultimately stuck near the lowest rung of the creative ladder and somewhere in the back of their minds they still aspire to moving up that ladder and becoming Creative Higher Beings.

With further examination, this hierarchical creative universe can be broken down into additional sub sections. The Creative Higher Being can be divided into the Successful Creative Higher Being, for example, Seamus Heaney, and the Unsuccessful Creative Higher Being , for instance somebody like Vincent Van Gogh. Conversely the Creative Lower Being can be split up into the Successful Creative Lower Being, which is basically all the people involved in film, T.V., comedy and the theatre who make a living, and the Unsuccessful Creative Lower Being, people involved in film, T.V. comedy and the theatre, who don't make a living. Like me. There are further subdivisions, for example, the Creative Lower Beings who think they are Creative Higher Beings.

Then there are the people who think they have talent but are completely devoid of all creativity and are simply known as the Lower Beings, but at the moment we will just discuss the Creative Lower Being. He inhabits all the major cities of the world, London, New York, Paris, Madrid and some of the lesser ones too, like Vilnius and Dublin. He is usually in his mid-to-late thirties. It is essential for his survival that he has an understanding, high-earning, hard-working girlfriend.

Between various commissions, or before the next contract work, or while waiting for that agent to call, he passes his days checking for bargain C.D.'s in record shops, re-reading the same books in the same bookshops that he has read a thousand times before, flicking through magazines in various newsagents, and meeting fellow Creative Lower Beings for coffee. They will rant against the world, the price of coffee, their stalling career and how unfair it all is. But they will vow not to let it get them down. But it will already have got them down. For they will be beyond down. They will be dead. Inside. But they will keep up appearances. They won't let the gradual decomposition of their spirit show. For image is all. And as long as you look successful, you are successful.

Let us now examine the appearance of the Creative Lower Being. The Creative Lower Being is easily identifiable in shops, bars, on the street, or at parties because of his very distinctive 'look'. Observers of the species have noticed however, that over the years, this 'look' has changed. In the early 1990's, pig-tails and black leather jackets were *de rigeur*, the odd cravat was ill-advisedly on display, hair gel was also a dominant feature as were red doc martens and black trousers pulled up slightly too high. I would describe it as a post-Morrissey look. But by the late 1990's that look had been replaced. And a sort of early

1960's casual preppy look came into vogue. Now, every Creative Lower Being worth his salt walked around in chic navy trainers with the obligatory white stripes, light brown slacks, fashionable beige zip-up jacket, perfectly coiffured sideburns and stylish, yet slightly faded, brown leather shoulder bag. The slightly faded quality was most important, for the bag needed to imply that it was being opened and closed regularly, continually picked up and carried everywhere as its owner endlessly spewed out new, essential, groundbreaking ideas to increasingly impressed industry figures.

Though belonging to the Creative Lower Being breed, all this adherence to image has bypassed me. In fact, I've always had a serious image problem. My main difficulty over the years, is that although deep down, I believe that I have the personality of a goth, sadly I have the dress sense of Val Doonican.

All my life I have remained a wooly jumper man and have never owned a fashionable beige zip-up jacket. Wearing wooly jumpers, though, is also an economic decision; for with my wooly jumper I don't have to change my 'look' every three years. I just have to keep wearing it until it looks like it's been run over by a tractor. Then I purchase a new one. Also, wooly jumpers are excellent for hiding my alarmingly expanding beer gut. Because like most Creative Lower Beings who secretly long to be a Creative Higher Being, I am predestined to increase my intake of alcohol the older I get. After all, my life is empty but my bladder is full, and drink is the food of the unfulfilled.

February 1st 294 days to go

February the first has always been a big date in my life. It was on this day 29 years ago that I became acutely aware of mortality. It is all Rudolf Valentino's fault.

My Night with Valentino (1974) 260m. * D: Newt Arnold. Manus Mannion, Colm Mannion. A frightened school kid becomes obsessed with the ghost of Rudolf Valentino. Overlong but truly eerie tale. [PG-13]**

Myself and Colm were alone in the house, mother and father were out at some function and a documentary came on the television about the life and times of Rudolf Valentino.

Rudolf Valentino (1895-1926) "Smouldering Italian-American silent screen star. A cultural icon of the 1920's."

I wouldn't usually have watched a programme at eight o'clock in the evening, but this particular night I had finished my homework early because we'd had a half day. This programme scared me enormously, especially the last twenty minutes with the details of Valentino's unexpected painful early death due to acute appendicitis and a perforated ulcer. The programme also contained graphic photographs and grainy news reel footage of him lying in his coffin.

I went to bed that night gripped by fear, waiting for the ghost of Valentino to appear at the curtain. I don't know what he would have said, maybe he would have just gesticulated wildly in silent movie acting manner. But he didn't appear.

Morning arrived, all was well. I got up, went to school. The night before seemed unreal in a way, as if it hadn't really happened, but as darkness fell, thoughts of Valentino started to dominate my mind once more. I tried staying up as late as possible but eventually was ordered to go to bed. I was in my own private torture dome. I tossed and turned, trying to get to sleep wondering would he turn up this night. Again, he didn't. But that wouldn't matter because every night, come bed time, I'd get the same petrified feeling again. It went on for months. There was always a certain safety while my parents hadn't yet gone to bed and I could see the light from the landing at the bottom of my bedroom door. I would always try and will myself to sleep before that landing light was turned off, because when I heard that switch, I would be filled with a new level of unremitting panic.

As a result of all this, I developed a morbid fascination with the past and old movies. The older, the better. I'd watch an old movie with mother and ask "Who is that actor?"

She'd reply, "Humphrey Bogart."

I'd feel compelled to ask another more important question, "Is he still alive?" If she answered yes, I'd feel safe, slightly relieved, but if the answer was "No, he died years ago," I'd get that spooky feeling, another potential member of the 'The Rudolf Society', to hang out with Valentino beside the bedroom curtain. If the actor or actress had only died recently and had lived to a good age, like Edward G. Robinson for example, I didn't mind too much, but if an actor or actress had died years ago, violently or mysteriously – Thelma Todd comes to mind – I'd be pretty spooked by that.

Thelma Todd (1905-1935) "Zany, blonde comedy actress of the early thirties, a willing foil for many legendary screen comedians. Allegedly murdered by underworld figures."

I became especially obsessed with the silent era. They didn't show many silent movies on the television apart from the odd Chaplin film but I got my hands on a cinema book covering the period. Turning the pages I was both enthralled yet terrified. Some of the make-up in those days was very macabre. The images left an indelible mark on my imagination. Early D.W. Griffith biblical extravaganzas interspersed with farcical Mack Sennett slapstick comedies and World War One propaganda dramas.

I was also aware that there was a greater chance that all the people referred to in the book were dead. Long dead. This gave me an extra little frisson of excitement and terror. One actress who scared me a lot at that time was Theda Bara — The First Vamp who was a big star around 1916. In her exotic black eyeliner make-up, white silk dress and mysteriously evil pose, Theda made an unwelcome appearance in many a nightmare. Though billed as someone foreign and dangerous she was in reality the daughter of a wealthy respectable Jewish family from Cincinnati, Ohio.

Eric Campbell also preyed on my mind. A Scottish actor who had played the heavy in many of Charlie Chaplin's early two reelers, he had died in a car crash in 1917. With his large frame and frightening stare, he had fulfilled both criteria for being a member of 'The Rudolf Society', sudden violent death and aeons since his date of expiry. Then there was Virginia Rappe, a starlet of minimal profile, whose bloody death was purported to have been caused by rotund, silent screen funnyman, Fatty Arbuckle, in 1921. Other members of 'The Rudolf Society' included comedy star John Bunny, who died in 1915 from Bright's Disease, leading man Wallace Reid, who died of drug addiction in 1923 and the unfortunately named Larry Semon, a long-forgotten silent screen comedian, who died of overwork and stress in 1928.

February 3rd 292 days to go

On my afternoon wanderings around Wicklow Street today, I was confronted by at least seven individuals trying to sell me lines for various different charities. Finally, exasperated, I stopped and asked one of them, if I buy a line from him, what does he have to do in return. He didn't understand what I meant. I then told him he had it easy. I reminded him that when I was a child and tried to sell lines, I couldn't just sell the lines and collect the money, I had to do something else as well. Like go for a run. A long run. In the rain. For hours. He looked at me incredulously. I told him I'd buy a line from him if he went on a six-mile run at the weekend. That shut him up. I walked away triumphantly and reminisced.

Rainy Sunday Afternoon: (1977) 91m. ** D: Tony Richardson. Manus Mannion, Austin McLynn, Adrian Madigan, Tom Lawless, Victor Higgins, Leonard O' Sullivan. In a town in Ireland, school children are forced to run endlessly for charity, by a sadistic teacher. Bleak tale, a curious cross between 'Chariots of Fire' and 'Kes'. [PG]

The sponsored run occurred at least once every three

months. Br. Leonard would enter the class room in his own inimitable, repressed, psychotic way, holding a folder. He would inform the class that they were to go on a sponsored run on Sunday to help send some sick children to Lourdes the following Easter.

As he would walk past our desks, he would pull at the odd ear or thump the odd head, just for the fun of it and would hand out the sponsored line forms from the folder. He would tell the class that each line cost 50p, and would warn us that he wanted all these lines sold and all forms completed by Friday because it was for a good cause.

I detested trying to sell sponsored lines. Especially on a day that rained. If it rained I would not have brought my bike and I would have to get the bus home. I would have to wait until twenty-three minutes past four, for the bus to pass down Dominick Street. But school would have ended at five past four. Some of the my hardier classmates would already be on their way home. They would have a head start in carpeting the neighbours and the houses from the surrounding areas with their sponsored line requests. But I knew by the time I got home at ten to five, sponsored line fatigue would have set in and nobody would want to buy a line from me.

Finally my bus would pull up. The route home was a long and arduous one. The bus would go to the bottom of Dominick Street, take a left, trundle on to the Fr. Griffin Road Technical College, making all the necessary stops along the way, turn right, go past The Crescent, and then turn left on the road to Lower Salthill. The bus would drive all the way towards Upper Salthill, past run-down amusement arcades, one-star hotels, the odd chipper, and the Church of Christ the King. Then it would turn right at the bottom of Daly's Fort Road and make its way slowly up the hill passing Salthill Park on the left and those slightly faded, elegant, old grey houses on the right.

Eventually the bus would take a left at the bottom of Daly's Fort Road and go up Dr. Mannix Road. And would arrive at my stop outside the Pearse Stadium. I would jump off, and lugging my oversized school bag on my back, like some miniature misplaced foreign legionnaire, would cross the road and run up Glenard Close. As I did so I would pass countless door bells being rung, and see smiling mothers signing their names on forms for some of my triumphant classmates. I would arrive home deflated. What could I do? At first, I would try the odd house, beginning across the road, at Mrs. Lally's.

"You were very slow off the mark, Manus, I've bought three already!" she would say.

Next door it would be the same story at the O' Toole place.

"Sorry, I sponsored one of the Armstrong boys," Mrs. O'Toole would say shouting over Trouble's animated barking. Even Mrs. Harrington, who was always quite supportive, would not be giving any money this time. "I've used up all my change, sorry Manus. Must rush, I've something in the oven, bye!"

Teatime would arrive. I would look at the sponsorship form. The still blank sponsorship form. It seemed almost a shame to have to deface such a pristine, nicely designed form, I would think. But I had to. Or I would face the wrath of Br. Leonard. Br. Leonard was that evil Brother from Central Casting. Short, stocky and built like a pit bull terrier, he was prone to violent rages whilst teaching us his beloved Irish.

At other times, he'd be remarkably placid and loquacious, as he'd indulge in the odd embarrassing 'light' moment and try to amuse us. We would laugh along with him in an attempt to keep up his good mood and defer prospective beatings.

The two words 'prospective beatings' helped concentrate my mind as I continued to stare down on those twenty unfilled lines. I knew I had to start filling it out somehow. In desperation I would buy a line myself. I would practice my autograph, celebrity style, and would write my address. I would bemoan the fact that 50p was one tenth of my pocket money but justify it by remembering it was for a good cause. My own self-preservation.

Next, I would wheedle mother to buy a line. She would also buy one for Colm. Then I would come up with a master stroke. I'd do a deal with my next door neighbour, Mrs Flynn, wherein she would buy a line from me if my mother would buy a line from her son, my classmate, Noel. Now I would have four lines. I would make sure the lines were spaced out in a certain manner in an attempt to give the impression that more than four lines had been sold. But no matter, from what angle I looked at it, at the end of the day, there were still sixteen lines to be bought. Then father would come home. Another potential sponsor. I would approach him sheepishly.

"Dad, will you buy a line from me?" I would ask.

He would turn around, and stare at me.

"No. I never sign my name to anything." There would be a pause and then he would murmur enigmatically, "because then they'll have me."

He would leave the room. In desperation, I would check my pocket money. Two pounds left until Saturday. I knew I would have to sacrifice it. I would have to buy four lines myself and fabricate four totally believable neighbours. 1. Elvis Gandhi, 23 Dr. Mannix Road, Salthill. 2. Groucho McCartney, 73 Daly's Fort Road, Salthill, 3. Sue Ellen Rossiter, 13 Dalton Drive, Salthill. 4. Ziggy Swarbrigg , 46 Devon Park, Salthill.

The Monday after the run each of us would have to stand up in class and announce how many lines we sold. "15 lines, Brother," Tom Lawless would proclaim confidently. "Well done, Tom." "19 Lines, Brother," Adrian Madigan would say. "Let me see," Br. Leonard would say. Enthused, he'd rush over to Adrian and examine his form.

"That is the kind of perseverance I'm looking for!" he'd announce.

I'd stand up, my knees buckling with fear. "Eight lines, Brother," I'd say meekly. There would be some assorted giggles in the class.

"Eight lines!" Br. Leonard would thunder, sticking his nose into my face. The saliva around his mouth taking on a rabid foam like quality.

"Sure what sort of number is that? You couldn't even send a wheelchair to Lourdes on that!"

I'd desperately try to come up with some excuse.

"I didn't feel well Brother, I couldn't go out that much."

He'd look at me with contempt and would point his finger at me.

"I've my eye on you Mannion, and you better start pulling up your socks or else!"

My heart pounding, I would stay rooted to the ground.

"Now sit down!" he'd bark dismissively. Then Hugh Cunningham would get up.

"Three lines, Brother." Br. Leonard would nod, and say understandingly:

"It's o.k., Hugh, you had rugby training." Hugh, would smile and sit down. I'd look over at Hugh in disgust.

Similar to the present education system in this country, my old school, St. Joseph's Patrician College, operated a two tier system with different rules applying to the haves and the have-nots. But in this case the haves were the ‘have an ability to play rugby’ and the have nots were the ‘have not an ability to play rugby’. I was one of the latter. Father, who had gone to St. Joseph’s in the 1940’s, and having played rugby for the school, had for years tried to interest me in taking up the sport.

Being small in stature and nifty on my feet, he figured, I could have made a tricky scrum half. I was vehemently opposed to the idea. I found it difficult to understand how any father could wish for his son to have his testicles randomly grabbed by jersey-wearing testosterone-fuelled neanderthals. Because it makes you a man? Well the way I saw it, if you got your crotch arbitrarily clutched continually over a prolonged period of time, chances are, medically, that this could possibly make you less of a man. It wasn’t just the genital gripping, or the gratuitous stamping, or the psychotic punching, that turned me against rugby, although obviously that had a major bearing on my decision, it was also because, I thought, aesthetically as a sport, rugby was such a grinding tedious spectacle. A muddied war of attrition, each army comprising of 15 squat, raucous, ear-bitten thugs.

With its emphasis on rugby, St. Joseph’s produced its share of novice sociopaths over the years. But oddly, I seemed to have been the only one who noticed this. One of the books we had to read for our Leaving Certificate was William Golding’s ‘Lord of the Flies’. One day at break time, after an English class where we discussed the book, I looked around our school play ground. To the left, I noticed some older boys bullying some younger boys. Under the gym I saw two other boys squaring up for a meaningless skirmish, with the cretinous chorus of “Fight!” “Fight!” “Fight!” coming from the enthralled circle that had gathered around. On the tarmacadam to the right, a few others were engaged in the ‘poling’ of some unlucky pupil, a pastime the more sadistic boys partook in, which involved grabbing an unfortunate victim, forcing his legs apart, and propelling him towards a basketball pole and ramming his genitals against said structure. Then in a moment of blinding lucidity I thought to myself, this is 'Lord of the Flies'!

February 4th 291 days to go

According to the Taoists the thighs are the storehouse of motivation and an antidote to writer's block is incessant pummelling of your thighs. Tried this for half an hour this morning. End result? Sore thighs. Filled with self-loathing at my inability to move forward with the draft, and with my access to the internet curtailed by service provider problems, I headed into town to do some alternative research on Sumo Wrestlers. Flicking through a book on the subject in Hodges&Figgis,

I found out that women are banned from the sumo wrestling ring, the doyho, because their menstrual blood might upset the Shinto Gods. This might help me with that scene between Sean and his girlfriend Dympna. It might be a cause of friction. And friction causes conflict. And conflict is drama. And drama is good.

I hate doing research. In an ideal world, I'd fly to Japan and hang out with a few Sumo Wrestlers. Find out about their lives. Share buckets of seaweed stock, prawns, vegetables and tofu with them. But I have an excuse. I don't have the resources. If I had, I don't think I would go anyway. All writers hate research. That's why in so many books the main character is a writer because then the writer doesn't have to get up off his arse and worry about what the main character does. I mean, given my psycho-sociological problems, how can I be expected to pick up a phone and ask a complete stranger about his life, when I have enormous difficulty picking up a phone and talking to people I know? Also research can be dangerous. This writer acquaintance of mine was working on a crime novel, and a minor Dublin criminal figure agreed to meet him in a pub in Kimmage.

At the end of the evening, in the car park outside the pub, after getting some very funny anecdotes from the criminal, the criminal decided on the spur of the moment to take the writer's wallet, steal his car and even confiscate his notes. He then warned him not to go to the gardaí or he'd be shot. So, not only was the writer left penniless, stranded, and traumatised from the encounter but he'd got no material out of the evening.

Just as I was leaving Hodges&Figgis, it started to rain. I decided to browse some more and went over to the cinema section. There, I flicked through some books with stills of long dead movie stars like Leslie Howard and Veronica Lake.

Veronica Lake (1919-1973) "Born Constance Ockleman. Alluring, petite, leading actress of the 1940's, famed for her legendary peek-a-boo hairstyle."

Then I felt this overpowering feeling that as I enter my fortieth year, I will never change. And that things will never change. Football managers will just keep getting younger. And as the rain cascaded down, I was transported back in time once more to the 1970's, and those dreary wet Friday afternoons after school when I'd walk pointlessly and aimlessly around Galway's main shopping thoroughfare, the imaginatively named Shop Street. I'd spend hours in O'Gorman's Bookshop flicking through their movie books. Then I'd flick through the books in their rock music section. Then like a lot of my classmates, I'd head to the various record shops in town. It must be noted that I am using the term 'record shop' very loosely.

The Record Shop (1976) 68m. ** D: Waris Hussein. Manus Mannion, Austin McLynn, Tom Lawless. On wet afternoons a bunch of school kids hang out in a shop that sells the odd record but they never buy anything. Somewhat static, dialogue driven piece. Plays like a bizarre cross between 'High Fidelity' and 'Angela's Ashes'. [PG-13]

Galway city in the 1970's was a rain-filled backwater — an oasis of parochialism, crisp eating and dodgy show-bands. A kind of mid-market Albania on the Atlantic seaboard where everyone wore Farah trousers. And there were no proper record stores. You might find, if you were lucky, the odd L.P. stacked on some revolving rack in the corner of one or two run-down Electrical Appliance Shops, but that was it. And for a burgeoning rock music fan like myself, this was a shameful state of affairs. Philomena Begley on the same rack as the Beatles defied logic and good taste. At least there was the odd Fab Four album on display, because overall, the selection of post 1962 non-indigenous pop music was very limited. But we had to make do with what was there and most Friday afternoons after school, a large proportion of Galway's disaffected youth would hang out around that one revolving rack in Cunniffe's Electric, on Mainguard Street.

"Random Sample of records on rack of Cunniffe's Electric, October 1st 1976"

1. Charley Pride — "Country Feelin'."
2. James Last — "Classics up to Date Volume One".
3. Acker Bilk — "Acker Bilk and His Paramount Jazz Band".
4. The Dubliners — "Double Dubliners".
5. Dinah Shore — "Dinah Shore Sings Some Blues with Red".

If rock music in record shops was in short supply it was positively ignored on Irish television. There was absolutely no rock music on Irish television in the 1970's, except bizarrely, one Saturday night every June, when they would transmit 'Rockpalast', a live concert of a German rock festival that would always feature Cork's own rock guitar legend, Rory Gallagher.

So I would stay up and watch this and practice my air guitar and head-banging in my over-sized dressing gown and hand-me-down slippers. Other than that there was nothing. Rock music did not exist. Apart from one television advertisement. It would start off with a snippet of the Rolling Stones performing 'Jumping Jack Flash'. The camera would zoom in on Brian Jones, then it would cut to Jimi Hendrix looking resplendent in a saffron shirt playing a guitar solo, then as it cut to Janis Joplin singing 'Me and Bobby McGhee', a solemn public service announcement type voice-over would come on underneath the music and state, "Brian Jones, Jimi Hendrix, Janis Joplin, they took drugs... and they died from drugs. Don't take drugs".

I felt this advertisement was an excellent incentive to take drugs. I asked myself, would I prefer to be Brian Jones, Jimi Hendrix, Janis Joplin or the guy making the announcement in the ad? Eh, deceased rock icon, please. Brian, Jimi and Janis reminded me that there was a world out there, another world other than the crass, country music on a life support machine, showband universe of Roly Daniels, Margo and Big Tom and the Mainliners. Despite that name, Big Tom and The Mainliners definitely did not take drugs. Although with those big lapels, shiny suits and unnerving smiley faces, they looked like they were on something.

February 5th   290 days to go

Met Kirsten in town. We needed some cheese for the weekend. We hadn't decided what cheese to buy, and the shop assistant gave me a sample of a new cheese. We both tasted it and looked at each other, and then the assistant asked would we like some of it. So we looked at each other again and Kirsten asked me, "What do you think?"

Not knowing what to say, I nodded in a non-committed yet slightly positive manner. The shop assistant waited patiently. Kirsten then nodded at the shop assistant and asked for a small piece to purchase. So the shop assistant cut a piece, but it was more than we wanted but we took it anyway, and we paid the €7.58 and we left the shop. Outside we both realised that neither of us liked the cheese very much. But now we've got this lump of cheese, just sitting in the fridge that we have to eat.

February 10th 285 days to go

My journey as a Creative Lower Being all started because I was short in height. From the age of seven I had been the smallest in the class. Returning to school after each summer holidays was particularly traumatic for me, especially in secondary school, as I measured how much my classmates had sprung up in height, yet I seemed continually stuck at four foot one.

I even had to cycle, to my eternal shame, a girls' bike to school. Because with a girls' bike, I did not have to risk life, limb and my minutely developed scrotum sack with an unpredictable crossbar. As a result of all this, somewhere in the back of my mind, I felt the need to stand out, to be noticed, and to prove I was better than them and to make them forget about that crossbar free girls' bike.

After the Inter Cert I sat down with my parents to discuss my future career.

"What would you like to do?" father inquired.

"I don't know," I said.

"Well, the way we look at it, with the subjects you've been doing, you have two choices. Do you want to work in the Science area or the Commerce area?" mother asked.

"I don't know," I repeated, shrugging my shoulders. Given my physical size what I really wanted to be was a comedian. Or a dictator. For from what I could see, most short men ended up being comedians or dictators in order to compensate for their lack of height. So what would it be? Comedian or dictator. I weighed up the options. Being a dictator wasn't a very popular career choice in the Ireland of the 1970's. And the openings were quite limited. And the job itself had got a lot of bad press over the previous thirty years. Still if you played your cards right, the people might grow to grudgingly respect you and you could have a job for life.

Also you would have your own private army. I'd already decided the name of my one: 'The Hawaiianshirts'. To give fascism a friendlier sunnier face. But what would my platform be? The trouble is, I didn't have any strong political views apart from being vociferously opposed to Ireland's nascent Space Programme.

So after some deliberation, I decided to give the world of strong arm, hard man politics a miss. It would have to be a life in comedy. I had a passable ear for accents, had enjoyed my appearances in the odd school play, and even at this early stage had a wonderful natural ability to suffer and feel chronically depressed. Like all the great comedians. Yes, comedy it was to be!

I was pressurised by my parents to see my career guidance councillor, Mr. Sullivan, for some advice. I was quite sceptical of career guidance councillors because school managers always seem to give that post to the teacher who can't do anything else. Apart from teach that other most essential of subjects: Civics. To paraphrase that famous quote: Those that can, do. Those that can't, teach. Those that can't teach, teach career guidance and civics.

So you've got generations and generations of failures in checked jackets with elbow patches giving career advice to generations and generations of school children. So what sort of advice can these career guidance councillors give? They've proven particularly incompetent in their own chosen profession. So why should we listen to them? Also,

Mr. Sullivan had a peculiar speech defect. There were legendary stories of pupils in previous years going in to meet him, and being told they should become doctors. Misunderstanding his advice, they would come out afterwards having decided to become dockers. Prospective bankers ended up working on tankers, hopeful engineers became reluctant auctioneers. I entered the office. He told me to take a seat. Or to take some meat. I figured it was the former.

"So, what would you like to be?" he asked.

"A comedian," I said.

He laughed. That's a good sign I thought. For, from now on, I will be judged solely on the laughter I create. I tried becoming the Class Clown. Unfortunately there was already a Class Clown, Victor Higgins. I made a quip once in French class which got quite a good response, but afterwards in the corridor, Victor came up to me, grabbed me and said, "There's only room for one Class Clown in this class. I'm that Class Clown."

"Sure, Victor!" I said.

Victor could be the Class Clown, I thought, but no one said I can't try and amuse classmates in the school yard. So I started doing impersonations of various teachers during break-time. Victor found out about this. One day in the middle of a rather broad yet uncanny impersonation of Mr. Sullivan, Victor turned up with all the other Class Clowns. There were 25 Class Clowns in all, from all the various classes spread over the five years. He poked his finger into my under-developed chest-bone.

"Listen, we've got enough Class Clowns in this school. There's no room for any more. Isn't that right, lads?"

"Yeh, Victor!" the various masters of mirth mumbled.

"There's only so much laughter out there, Manus, and we don't want you stealing it. From now on, you are not allowed tell any jokes, do any impersonations, make any sarcastic asides or witty comments in the entire school complex or we will hang you by the hood of your coat from the basketball hoop after school..."

"I read you loud and clear, Victor," I said.

"I'm not finished yet. While up there, we will pull down your trousers around your socks..."

"Victor, you have my word that..."

He interrupted me again. "I'm not finished yet. Let me finish!"

"Sorry Victor."

"And place the teachers duster in your underpants after dipping it in a toilet bowl..."

"Uh-huh. I see."

" That I have taken a big squishy dump in. Understand?"

"I understand, Victor!"

After no deliberation, I decided I would accept Victor's ultimatum. Anyway, maybe I could by-pass the school and find somewhere else to hone my comic skills. But where? Where else could I learn the craft of stand-up comedy? The opportunities in Galway in the late 1970's were minimal. In those days there were no comedy venues and there were very few comedians. The odd dicky bow merchant, who in real life sold insurance, might be able to wrangle a gig doing hoary old jokes and a raffle at his local golf club once a month, but that was it. And it was impossible to break into that circuit.

But what about the other circuit? I thought. In those days, for entertainment in more rural areas, people would sit in, invite a few friends round to their house, have a few drinks around the fireplace and listen to an old Irish storyteller, called a seanchaí, entertain them. Desperate to gain experience in front of a live audience I came up with a novel idea for work. I would become a warm-up man for the seanchaí. My uncle Jim, mother's brother from Loughrea, knew a distant neighbour who was planning to have a seanchaí around to his house the following weekend. I pressurised mother to ask uncle Jim to ask his neighbour whether it could be possible for me to do five minutes of jokes before the seanchaí came out. Mother was very worried about my infatuation with the world of comedy.

Cora Mannion: née Lee, mother of Manus and Colm Mannion, wife of Eddie Mannion. The more innately balanced parent in the family, imbued with an admirable common sense. Not a disciplinarian. Spanked eldest son only once in May 1970 with a wooden spoon, but it subsequently took her ages to get those blueberry stains off his trousers. Excelled at the high jump in her youth.
**Mannion's Personal Fact No. 5*

"Why would you want to be getting up there making a right eejit of yourself ?" she asked. She told father to have a word with me.

"Why would you want to be getting up there and making a right eejit of yourself?" he asked. They both tried to dissuade me.

"You have your Leaving Certificate coming up, you don't want any distractions!"

But I persisted. Eventually, uncle Jim arranged everything. My very first gig was the following Saturday night. Mother would drive me there. I was set on my way. All I had to do now was come up with an act. I did not have the time to write five minutes so I would have to steal material. There was an Andy Williams T.V. special on that Sunday night. The special guest was manic American comedienne from the 1970's, Carol Burnett. That was not ideal. She was female and most of her laughs derived from pulling faces. Still I was desperate. I attached the microphone lead to our 1972 Philips tape recorder. I placed the yellow sticker that had been used many times over the previous six years on the living room door, which read, 'Quiet Please! Recording in Progress.' I stood nervously next to the television. When Carol was announced by Andy I switched the red button on the microphone and pressed down both the 'Play' and 'Record' buttons. Carol started her act. I listened intently for potential material. Completely ignoring the yellow sticker, father walked in.

"Have you seen your brother?" he inquired.

"Shhhh, I'm recording!" I hissed.

Carol continued with her act. A minute later the doorbell rang. It was Mrs. Tierney collecting the church dues. Father and herself decided to have a neighbourly chat. I had to go out to the hallway and ask them to keep it down for that microphone picked up everything. Then Colm entered the living room.

"Phone."

"Who is it?" I queried lowly.

"Auntie Philomena," he said.

"What does she want?"

He shrugged his shoulders. I whispered manically to him to take over the taping and instructed him that when Carol Burnett finished he could turn off the tape recorder. I walked into the dining room at the back of the house. We used to call it the dining room but it was more of an all-purpose room. We never dined there, except for Christmas Day when the expensive china and Waterford glass were released from captivity for an afternoon. I picked up the phone. Auntie Philomena was my godmother from Mayo. She was a very devout person whose whole sense of spiritual well-being had been irrevocably shattered in August 1961 when Saint Philomena's feast day was removed from all liturgical calendars. Philomena was a saint no more. They'd found out she'd been a slightly dubious character after all. Since then my aunt had become more insecure yet even more religious, feeling she had to make it up to God personally, for her namesake's demotion.

She had a radar system about churches. For example when she was on a bus and she'd be facing somebody, and talking to them, and the bus would pass a church and there was no way she could have seen the church for it was behind her, in mid-sentence she would dutifully bless herself and continue the conversation. And she always referred to her brother Joseph, my uncle Joe, as Joseph, the Lord have mercy on his soul. She'd say Joseph, the Lord have mercy on his soul, loved his turnips. Anytime his name was mentioned, this compulsive need to say very quickly, the Lord have mercy on his soul, would follow.

This would annoy Uncle Joe greatly because he wasn't dead. He would usually be sitting in the same room as her because they still lived together. Myself and Auntie Philomena hadn't had much communication since the day of my confirmation when I had said to her, incredulously, "One pound twenty-five pence. Is that all?"

But now she was going into the hospital for a hip operation and, being a superstitious old woman, was worried she mightn't come out alive. The phone call was her way of mending fences. Of course she didn't die and lived until 1998. In fact Uncle Joe, the Lord have mercy on his soul, outlived her by two years. Then he died. The Lord have mercy on his soul.

When the phone call was finished I ran back inside to the living room. Carol Burnett had finished her routine and Colm had turned off the tape recorder. Later that night, I played back what had been recorded. Leaving aside the incessant background noises, I realised I could use very little. Also half the country watched Andy Williams, the half that had only one television channel and nothing else to watch, and maybe some of my prospective audience on the following Saturday night might have seen it. I decided on another course of action. I would buy a comedy L.P. and nick the best jokes from that.

On the following Wednesday after school, I ventured up town. By the late 1970's things had improved enormously concerning record shops in Galway. At this stage, there were one or two retail establishments which one could enter, with the sole purpose of purchasing long playing records as opposed to electrical items. My favourite was Music City. It opened in the summer of 1977. I remember the first time I went in there. I inhaled a sharp expectant intake of breath as I surveyed the surroundings. Not a revolving rack or Larry Cunningham record in sight. Shiny new posters from the latest international releases on the wall. Hundreds of records. Artists listed in alphabetical order. More than one record from each artist in each section. Actual rock music being played in the shop. I had arrived in aural civilisation.

This particular Wednesday afternoon, I went over to the comedy section. Sadly, there wasn't that much to choose from. It was either Cheech and Chong, the Goons or George Burns. I decided against Cheech and Chong because I felt that hippy, drug related humour might not work with a seanchaí's natural audience. I'd heard the Goons on the radio the odd time and liked what I had heard, but they were English, and there were still many unreconstructed Brit haters out there, especially in rural areas. So it had to be the octogenarian Jewish American humour of George Burns.

That night I listened to the record. It was very funny. I was thrilled. Before going to bed, I replayed it many times and started feverishly transcribing some of the best one-liners. The rest of the week flew by. Suddenly it was Saturday teatime. I stared at the mirror in my bedroom and said the line, "People ask me do I have trouble having sex standing, and I say, at my age I have trouble standing!"

Somehow it seemed funnier with George saying it. I tried delivering it a different way. It still wasn't as funny as George. I then realised I had a serious problem. 90% of George Burns's act dealt with being 81. I was 16.

Clutching at straws, I looked on the bright side. Some of my audience tonight might be 81, I thought, so they will be able to relate to George's routine. But he's old and from New York and Jewish, and they are old and from Co. Galway and Irish. Same planet. Different worlds. Who am I kidding? I can't make these people laugh! I can't compete with Paudeen Dan, the seanchaí! They'll be expecting a certain type of thing. I was crazy to think I could succeed in the first place! I've got to call it off. I'll get mother to ring uncle Jim. To tell him I can't do it. I became hysterical. I ran downstairs and into the kitchen. Mother was setting the table.

"I can't do it, ring them, cancel it!"

Normally in a story like this, the mother would tell the cowardly son that he has to do it, he can't run away from things all his life. She would then add that it was his idea in the first place, and did he ever think he might be letting people down. Then she would say that at first she was against his dream of being a comedian, but now she realises it's what he really wants, but the only way he'll learn to be a successful comedian is to get out there in front of people, even if they are very old, deaf, senile people from Loughrea. Then she would finish her speech by telling him that she is disappointed in him and did he never hear the old adage 'The show must go on!'. But that speech didn't happen. All she said was "Thank God!" and ran into the dining room to ring uncle Jim.

Afterwards she came back in and said, "Now promise me, no more of this comedy carry on."

"I promise," I said.

February 17th 278 days to go

The best laid plans of mice and Manus. I had to cancel a meeting with Ben this morning. I haven't reached my deadline. I promised him definitely by the end of the week I'd have a completed draft of 'The Shamrock Sumo Club'. The trouble is, I've come up with another idea for a new screenplay. This is always the case when you have an old idea to work on. You come up with a new idea, a better idea, and you want to spend all your time on that idea rather than finishing the work you have to do. The idea is for a zombie movie. There is huge demand for zombie movies nowadays and I am convinced it is a worthy objective to start working on one. It's called 'Spud Zombie'.

Spud Zombie: [2005] 89m. ** D. Tadgh Jennings. Jerome O' Malley, Mary Dineen, Barry Mulrooney. Low-budget Irish zombie flick, set during the Irish Potato Famine, where zombies with potato shaped heads roam the countryside and terrorise the peasants. Gory, subversive, but at times hilarious sclockfest that is well worth a look.**

I've just completed the first scene.

FADE IN.

1. INT. OLD COTTAGE. NIGHT.

A woman Peg, her husband Paddy and daughter Nora, sit around an old table in a dark, run-down cottage and stare at a weakly lit candle. Gloom fills the air. A gale blows outside, rain pours down and the candle continually flickers. Stomachs rumble. Suddenly a younger man, soaked to the skin, holding an old fishing rod, enters with some fish. It is the son of the household, Pat.

PAT:

I caught some fish, dad. We can have that.

He proudly places it on the table. Paddy looks up at him.

PADDY:

Don't like fish, Pat.

Pat is incredulous.

PAT:

Ah come on, it's been a pretty bad year for the auld spuds, maybe if we just change our diet a bit.

Paddy is adamant.

PADDY:
I don't like fish.
Peg intervenes.

PEG:
He's right love, it stinks the place up.

Pat sighs. He picks up the fish and leaves the cottage. Nora looks forlornly into the distance. Peg turns to her.

PEG:
What did you do today, a stór?

Nora looks at her.

NORA:
I bought a raffle ticket.

PEG:
Oh, what's the prize?

Nora responds brightly.

NORA:
Two tickets on a coffin ship.

Paddy and Peg are interested.

PADDY:
Really? When's the draw?

Nora is about to answer when they hear a man scream outside. They react.

PADDY:
What was that?
PEG:
Sounded like Pat.

They all get up and look out the window. The wind and rain has stopped. It is ominously quiet. They then hear another scream.

NORA:
I'm scared. What's going on?

Paddy grabs a pike from inside the door.

PADDY:
There's only one way of finding out!

He opens the door and they all scream as they are greeted by up to nine Spud Zombies. Spud Zombies are Zombies with heads shaped like large potatoes. They force their way into the cottage. Paddy tries to kill one of them with his pike but to no avail as they slowly approach and overwhelm the helpless family. Much screaming and mayhem ensues. Fade to Black. Roll Opening Credits.

February 25th   270 days to go

Ben rang again this morning. I told him I'd made a breakthrough. I was lying. In fact the phone rang while I was engaging in some hurried auto-eroticism.

Emission Impossible: (2003) 8m. * D. Alan Smithee. Manus Mannion. A struggling screenwriter tries to masturbate whilst working on a problematic screenplay. Gratuitous, voyeuristic, and highly offensive. [NC-17]

Kirsten is away on business for a few days. After a restless hour in front of my computer this morning and feeling edgy and irritable, I entered the bathroom and tried to initiate 'Operation Release'. Feeling slightly guilty as always, during the actual process, I mentally tried justifying the act. I told myself that if I did not do this now, tomorrow I would be like a cat on a hot tin roof, incapable of work and severely irascible. So as to pre-empt that situation, I decided it was perfectly legitimate to discharge my accumulated seminal fluid to avoid any immediate restlessness.

Anyway, I figured by Thursday, when Kirsten returns, my supplies shall be replenished and I will be ready to involve myself in some joyous mating rituals. But somehow as I clenched Bob tightly and jerked him in a rhythmic fashion, I couldn't get into it.

Momentarily I felt my long dead Granny, Granny Lee, was watching me. Then I wondered can I really afford to waste my semen? I read recently that every time a man ejaculates he produces enough semen to impregnate the total female population of Europe.

But I am convinced I have a spectacularly low sperm count, so for me it would probably be just the female population of a small cul-de-sac in Lisnaskea.

However, I persevered with my wrist gripping motion. But Granny Lee and Lisnaskea were still on my mind. Then I started to ruminate on what would happen if I died during the middle of the activity from a massive coronary. Wouldn't that be the most embarrassing way to expire? With all these thoughts scurrying around my mind, Bob seemed to lose interest. And then the phone rang.

March 5th 262 days to go

Still struggling with the screenplay. Spent the morning pummelling my thighs. After lunch I just had to get out of the house. To get my mind on other matters, I decided to go to the movies and catch the latest Nicholas Cage vehicle.

Adaptation (2002) 130m.** D. Spike Jonze. Nicholas Cage, Meryl Streep, Chris Cooper. A troubled, insecure screenwriter enlists the help of his twin brother to complete a project. Highly imaginative, bizarre, and extremely funny journey into the world of screen-writing. Loses its way in the last half hour. [PG-13]**

Needless to say, it didn't help. Afterwards, I headed to

Tower Records to do some obsessive magazine flicking. The staff never bother you in Tower Records because they are too busy working on being dismissively cool and vacant. I picked up a magazine and started flicking, but after a few minutes I looked up and slowly realised that everyone around me, my fellow flickers, were twenty years younger than me. I put the magazine back furtively and, feeling increasingly uncomfortable by the age group of the shop's clientele and the choice of music pounding in the background, I made a speedy yet regretful exit.

Afterwards, I walked the streets, pointlessly, aimlessly and suddenly encountered the Dermot Butler problem. Dermot Butler is someone I know who is stuck in that obscure area between somebody you 'stop and chat to' and somebody you 'nod and grunt at'. I know him but how well do I know him? And he has an identical problem with me. Four weeks ago I saw him walking towards me on Andrew Street and because he spotted me and gave a little smile, I didn't feel comfortable engaging in that 'tacit synchronicity of avoidance'. So I decided just to nod and grunt at him and walk on by but he wanted to stop and chat. After prevaricating for a moment I eventually stopped out of politeness.

However, now he felt a little rejected, a little hurt, he realised he didn't really count in my scheme of things. He made a little joke to quell the awkwardness, "Oh, so you don't want to talk to me, huh, not important enough, huh?"

We had a little conversation and then we parted ways. Afterwards, to my amazement, I felt a little guilty. I thought to myself, maybe I should have stopped to talk immediately, that's what I'll do next time, he's a nice guy. But as Dermot was walking down the street he probably thought to himself — you know I'm never going to stop to talk to that person again, I'll say hello, but that's it.

So the next week we bumped into each other again. Now I decided, out of the goodness of my heart, that I wanted to stop and chat but he just wanted to acknowledge me and walk by. He stopped in his tracks reluctantly. We had a brief chat and parted ways. Now I was the one who felt offended. Fuck that, I thought, I was willing to talk to this guy and he seemed completely uninterested.

But Dermot was probably thinking, I should have stopped to chat after all, he is an o.k. guy, next time I'll do that. So when I bump into Dermot next, what will happen? Pissed off with him after our last encounter I'll probably just nod and grunt at him but he, feeling guilty, will probably want to stop and chat. So things will be reversed again, and this will go on ad nauseam until one of us dies or gets a job.

Then there's this other guy I keep bumping into as well. Alan something. He really is doing my head in. I met him about 17 years ago. He used to hang out with a bunch of people I knew. It was 1986 and we'd be in the same room at some late night party in a cold suburban house in Terenure, where people would drink cans of Harp and crash out on the carpet and slowly watch their drool freeze.

So I only know him very vaguely. I don't think I've ever had a proper conversation with him in my entire life. But what perplexes me is that every time I see him on the street he gives me a big smile and says hello. I find this so disturbing because Alan has messed with the natural order of things. He has stepped out of his designated area in my hierarchy of casual acquaintances. At best, he should be a 'nod and grunt' acquaintance. But to be honest he shouldn't even be a 'nod and grunt' acquaintance. He should be an 'ignore totally, you knew him vaguely years ago, and he was a bit of an eejit' acquaintance. But instead I get this big smile and hello on the street, and because of his complete mis-reading of the situation, I have to give him a big smile and say hello back. And I feel cheap afterwards. I mean if I'm giving Alan whoever a big smile and hello, in retrospect I should treat some of the mere 'nod and grunters' in my life a bit better.

I felt I had to head home. I decided to wait for a bus on Dame Street. This proved the agitated state of my mind, for I always try, if possible, never to wait for a bus. There are reasons for this. Sometimes there are about forty people queueing at the bus stop, or four different buses turn up all at once, since the bus stop serves six routes, and the one you are waiting for, the 123, unable to find space at the stop, just drives by. On other occasions, by the time the bus arrives at the bus stop, it is full so they can't take on any more passengers.

Then there is the occasion when a completely different bus, say the 77, stops at the bus stop. But it's not meant to stop at this stop. But the 54 is still stationary at the 77's stop. So, the 77 stops at your stop, and the bus that should stop, noticing there's nowhere to stop at the stop, stops half-way down the street. Ever alert, you have to rush, with nine other hapless souls, shopping bags in flight, half way down Dame Street, in the pissing rain, hailing the bus while holding your umbrella, hoping the driver notices you before he decides to move on.

This time, surprisingly, a half-empty bus arrived almost immediately. Manically searching for the correct fare, I got on. I only had €1.50. The bus driver told me in a very friendly tone that he couldn't give me any change for my €1.20 cent fare and instead gave me an extra long ticket. He told me if I had nothing better to do, one day I could go up to Dublin Buses' headquarters on O'Connell Street and with this extra bit of the ticket, Dublin Bus would reimburse me the 30 cents. I told him I had nothing better to do and looked forward to going up there the following day. He smiled.

I took a seat. I was depressed. Clouds enveloped us. A duvet of despair. It started to rain. Old people surrounded me with their smelly coats, hair loss and stale urine. I saw the future. It was bleak. Then I heard the bus driver say "See you, take care," to someone leaving the bus. I thought to myself, what a nice bus driver. Then he stopped at a corner between stops to let someone else off. I thought, this is the nicest bus driver in the world. Ever.

Another person got off. "See you, take care," he repeated, and I thought, this bus driver is too good to be true. There are nice people in this horrible harsh world, this bus driver has re-ignited my faded enthusiasm for humankind. I must stop avoiding people, I mused. I must stop indulging in that 'tacit synchronicity of avoidance'. I should talk to people. Like Dermot Butler. Be interested in people. Listen to people. Smile at people. Like Alan what ever the fuck his name is. Yes I will change.

Then the bus approached my stop. I pressed the bell. An African guy got off before me, "See you take care," the bus driver said. The African guy smiled. This is unbelievable I thought, and so wonderful. I had a near epiphany. The world can be good. The smallest gestures can renew one's hope. Then, to top it all, suddenly the rain stopped and the clouds dispersed and a brilliantly shining sun broke through. Feeling reinvigorated, on my way down the aisle I smiled at all the passengers. They looked back at me in a puzzled fashion.

Finally, the bus stopped. The door opened. I started to get off. I didn't hear a word. I looked at the bus driver for a moment but he still didn't say anything to me. I almost gestured to him, implying that I too, was expecting a friendly farewell.

Then almost as an afterthought, in a slightly bored manner, he said, "See you, bye!" I alighted the bus. The sun had disappeared again. I was troubled. "See you, bye!" I thought. All he said was "See you, bye." And it was the way he said it. Almost dismissively. "See you, bye!" Not "Take care," but "Bye." Why did he say "Take care" to everyone else but only "Bye" to me? "Bye" is a farewell of lesser worth. "Bye" is nothing. It's a throwaway. But "Take care" is "Take care". It means you are concerned for the future welfare of this person. Why did he do that? Why didn't he say "Take care?" This is the inconsequential trivia that consumes my day.

March 6th *261 days to go*

What should I expect? I spend my whole life avoiding people and when I am compelled to deal with them, I can be quite brusque. I then have no right to turn around and be slightly miffed because some employee of Dublin Bus said "See you, bye," instead of "Take Care."

Why can't I be friendlier? Why can't I send out the proper vibes. Up until the age of 14, I quite liked talking to people. But then something happened. All of a sudden the prospect of conversation filled me with utter dread. Especially with the relatives. I hated those Sunday nights when uncle Dan and auntie Maisie would visit.

Family Visit (1980) 205m. ** D: Pat O'Connor. Manus Mannion, Cora Mannion, Colm Mannion, Eddie

Mannion, Dan Lee, Maisie Lee. An unhappy teenager resents his relatives visiting. Overlong and slightly depressing with a lead character who is strangely dislikeable. [PG]

I would have been looking forward to watching that Jeff Chandler movie all week.

Jeff Chandler (1918-1961) "Muscular American action star from the 1950's".

But then father would announce, "Uncle Dan and auntie Maisie are coming around after tea." The Jeff Chandler movie would immediately be off the agenda, for relatives had to be entertained in the living room and it would be the height of bad manners to have the televison on when there are guests present.

I would go upstairs and, as a form of protest, hide under the bed in my bedroom. And wait. I'd smell that distinctive hardware shop smell one smelled being under that bed. Eventually I'd start feeling slightly claustrophobic, would crawl out and just lie on the thick new carpet. I'd feel comfortable and safe there.

I'd look at the sickly pink paint on the ceiling. I'd look at my posters hanging on the wall beside my bed. I'd have one of The Beatles and one of The Stones but pride of place would always be my latest work of Art. When I was about 15, and most guys my age were out at rugby training, or smoking cigarettes and drinking cider up trees, or gobbing spittle at passing cars, I went through a phase of making collages of old movie stars at home. I'd cut out old black and white photographs from movie magazines and television guides, paste the pictures together on a large white sheet of paper and hang the result up on the wall. I'd study my poster intensely and become lost in a bygone era.

Sample selection of stills from Movie Collage No. 5:

1. *Franklin Pangborn and Jack Carson from "Romance on the High Seas"1948.*

2. *William Bendix and Alan Ladd from "The Blue Dahlia" 1946.*

3. *Alice Faye and Adolph Menjou in "Sing, Baby, Sing" 1936.*

4. *Richard Conte and Valentine Cortese from "Thieves Highway" 1949.*

5. *Eleanor Parker and Hope Emerson from "Caged" 1950.*

6. *Edward Everett Horton and Fred Astaire from "The Gay Divorcee" 1934.*

7. *Paul Muni and Helen Vinson from "I am a Fugitive in a Chain Gang" 1932.*

8. *Bud Abbott and Lou Costello from "In the Navy" 1941.*

9. *Bob Hope and Lon Chaney Jnr. from "My Favourite Brunette" 1947.*

10. *Peter Lorre and Sydney Greenstreet from "The Mask of Dimitrios" 1944.*

Then the door bell would ring. I would break out of my tinseltown reverie. Slightly forced pleasantries would be exchanged as the front door would be opened. Uncle Dan and auntie Maisie would be ushered into the living room. Conversation and strained laughter would emanate from downstairs as tea and biscuits would be served on that silver tray for special occasions.

Eventually, I would hear father coming up the stairs. He would pop his head into my bedroom. "Come on and say hello to your uncle Dan and auntie Maisie, come on!" he would demand. I'd get up slowly and reluctantly follow him down the stairs. He'd open the living room door. As I entered the room, the first thing I would see would be the overhead light glistening on uncle Dan's bald head as he stood up. Tall, gaunt, joyless, and still wearing a three piece suit and pioneer badge, uncle Dan seemed three epochs out of date.

"Ah, there he is, how ya doing?" he'd say as he stretched out his large hand.

"You're getting fierce big this weather," he'd continue. "What age are you now, 13, is it?"

"16," I'd say wearily.

Uncle Dan would continue. "So, how are you getting on?"

"Fine," I'd say in a monotone voice.

I'd look at auntie Maisie. Having given birth to six children, auntie Maisie seemed shrivelled and exhausted before her time but she still could summon up enough energy for a meaninglessly irritating comment.

"How are you, jeez, we haven't seen you for ages, probably taking notice of the girls at this stage, are you?"

I'd blush and nod embarrassedly. There would be an awkward silence. Father would intervene. "Eh, you can go back upstairs again Manus, you probably are quite busy with your homework."

My uncle and auntie would smile as I'd leave and go back upstairs to my room.

Homework? How could one concentrate on one's homework after such an oppressive family experience? I'd feel an immediate urge to keep that long standing appointment my wrists had with my razor blade, a razor blade which still, I might add, hadn't been used for shaving one solitary bristle.

March 18th 249 days to go

Have finally finished the latest draft of 'The Shamrock Sumo Club'. I spent all day yesterday, St. Patrick's Day, working on it instead of going to the new fantastic 'Mardi Gras let's be flamboyant and colourful and get pissed for a week' Dublin City Patrick's Day Parade. I am meeting Ben next week.

Later, after five, myself and Kirsten arranged to meet up for something to eat in Shay Guevara's, our favourite vegetarian place. We walked in and were about to check the menu board when Kirsten noticed somebody she knew, whose name she couldn't remember, eating some mushroom and potato gratin. Fearing this person might notice her, and worried she would have to introduce me to this person and then have to recall this particular person's name, Kirsten suggested to me that we leave Shay Guevara's, walk around for half an hour and come back. This person will have finished her meal by then and will have left. I suggested, since I was rather hungry that we go somewhere else.

But Kirsten had her heart set on Shay Guevara's. The food is healthy, there are good-sized portions and it is reasonably priced. So we walked around for forty minutes. Then we came back. The person was still there. Her friend had turned up. They were deep in animated conversation. I looked at Kirsten. She looked at me. In desperation, we looked across the road and spotted a small delicatessen. We nodded at each other, went over to it and bought some bottled water, ciabetta bread, cheese and salami. We headed home.

March 22nd   245 days to go

Having finished the script last week, I felt so restless this morning I even did some hoovering. We have two hoovers. The old hoover and the new hoover. We have held on to the old hoover because of Orla, our next door neighbour.

Over the years, her hoover always seemed broken so she always popped in to borrow our hoover. Kirsten eventually became quite unhappy about this arrangement and started thinking Kirsten-like thoughts. Who knows what state Orla's carpets are in? Do I really want to use my hoover after that?

So last year we bought ourselves a new hoover. But we kept the old hoover. It was part of a master strategy. We'd lend the old hoover to Orla anytime she popped around. Now Kirsten would be happy. And Orla would never know and she would be happy. And I wouldn't care one way or the other.

But then one day, about six months ago, Orla knocked on the door asking to borrow our iron. She needed to iron her old curtains before donating them to Oxfam. Kirsten lent her the iron. The next day we bought a new iron. But we've held on to the old iron. It's becoming like a Noah's Ark for electrical appliances around here. Soon, we'll have two of everything.

March 28th 239 days to go

Not having being back to Galway since before Christmas, I have decided to visit the folks this weekend. Have just got in after another long exhausting bus journey from Dublin. There are certain rules for intercity bus rides:

1. Always place as many bags as possible on the seat next to you to prevent other passengers sitting beside you.

2. If it is getting close to the time of departure, always stare out the window and never catch the eye of a passenger who has just got on. If you are a book lover, now is the time to start reading. Large books like atlases, though difficult to transport through crowded cities, are particularly useful to hide behind.

3. By this time it is also essential to be wearing your portable C.D. player and playing your music as loudly as possible.

4. If feeling acutely tense about someone sitting down next to you at the last moment, a prayer at this stage might also come in handy.

5. If the worst case scenario does occur and somebody asks "Is this seat taken?", feign deafness, sigh and grumble and make a big scene about having to shift your bags. This will send out the signal, in no uncertain terms, that you do not want to be disturbed by unnecessary conversation over the next three and a half hours.

I thought I was safe, but just outside Heuston Station, an old farmer got on and sat next to me. Sitting on the edge of the seat, with an old 1960's sports kit bag pressed up against his chest, I noticed that he seemed tense about his day out away from home. He didn't want a conversation but he thought it impolite not to start one. So he persisted in hounding me with small talk. I kept my responses to a monosyllabic minimum. I made sure I never gave him an opening to expand the conversation and wore my sunglasses throughout to avoid eye contact. I'd stopped bringing my atlas on intercity bus rides four years ago after developing a hernia problem. Thankfully he got off outside Enfield.

At last I could stretch my legs, I thought, as I listened to my music. Suddenly my tranquillity was shattered because intercity buses have become more sophisticated with time. I looked up. The driver had put on a video cassette. 'Forces of Nature', with one of my pet hates, Ben Affleck. (While on the topic I have other pet hates. I hate newsreaders who never apologise and move on to another item, when there has been a cock-up in the news report. I hate people in motorised wheelchairs overtaking you in the street. I hate going to the newsagents on Sunday morning to buy the Observer and half the supplements are missing. I hate having to pay 20 cents to my bank every time I withdraw money from an A.T.M. machine. I hate people who confuse Fats Waller with Fats Domino).

The video soundtrack was intrusively loud. I called over the young ticket collector.

"Hello. Can I tell you something? I don't want to watch this video, for it is an example of crass, formulaic, mainstream American cinema. Now maybe a few other people don't want to watch it either. So why don't you put it to a vote, on the bus, and being a democrat, I will abide by the decision."

He was confused. I was the first person ever to complain about the playing of a video on a bus. "That's a bit strange," he said. "I'll ask the driver. It's usually his decision."

The ticket collector went over to the driver. They consulted for a minute. The driver nodded. The video was momentarily turned off. Some of the passengers reacted. The ticket collector stood in the middle of the aisle.

"Maybe some of ye don't want to watch the video. So we're going to have a vote on it. Who wants to watch the video?"

All the passengers put up their hands. 41 in all. The ticket collector smiled and mischievously inquired, "And who doesn't?"

I raised my hand slowly and took it down again.

March 29th 238 days to go

Slept in my old room, Number 2, last night for the first time in many years. When myself and Kirsten are down we usually sleep in room Number 3, the guest room. For years I wanted that room as my own room but my parents insisted myself and Colm stayed in room Number 2.

Quick Change (1981) 2m. ** D: Terence Davies. Manus Mannion, Colm Mannion. Not to be confused with the Bill Murray vehicle , this is a very slight tale of the nightly tension and embarrassment two brothers feel when having to change into their pyjamas. [PG]

Most nights Colm would be in bed before me, but as I got older, he'd be up at the same time.

That meant we would go to bed at the same time. That meant that we had to undress around the same time. Remembering that we weren't Swedish, and what a terrifying condition nakedness was, this nightly moment led to mutual awkwardness and shame. Eventually we devised a system, and a delicate co-ordination of timed exits and averted gazes came into play. Sometimes other strategies were tried. I remember, for about six months in 1974, employing 'the removing your pants under your bed-sheets while trying to get on your pyjamas' manoeuvre.

This proved far too much effort, and for a while I contemplated just walking around for the rest of my life in a giant quilt to save the hassle.

Other times Colm would forget our little arrangement as we would talk about some soccer match, but then I would always say bluntly in mid-sentence, "Eh, I'm removing my trousers now, could you turn around?"

He'd nod and turn to the wall as I would feverishly try to remove my underpants over my ankles, losing balance in the process and manically looking for my pyjama bottoms under my pillow. Then he reached puberty. He seemed to be out late more often. I was the one tucked up in bed. And someone must have told him there was no need for this furtive undressing any more.

One night I was reading a biography of Louis B. Mayer when Colm came in as usual and removed his clothing. I immediately became engrossed in the book. After the requisite time allotted, usually about three paragraphs on the machinations of M.G.M. studio politics of the 1930's,

Norma Shearer (1900–1983) "Lady like, Canadian born actress of the 1930's. Married to producer Irving Thalberg."

I looked over and there he was, buck naked, sitting on his bed. I wanted to look away demurely, but like a passer-by in the aftermath of a car crash, I could not help but stare. For comparison purposes. I gasped. There is no God,

I thought. He was bigger than me. Or he seemed bigger than me. He got into his bed, still naked, asked was I finished reading, turned off the light and said goodnight. I laid awake. "This can't be true. He is three years younger than me. He looks more sexually developed than I am. He's swanning around like some extra in a porn film. He's probably already got laid. He's got laid first?! Empty a guy's potty when he's four years old and this is the thanks you get. Humiliation! He is humiliating me. He's getting laid first!"

Then I heard some frenzied rhythmic movements. Or I thought I heard. I wasn't sure. I continued my inner dialogue. "Oh, brilliant, he's got laid tonight and now he comes home and he's wanking! I'm sharing a bedroom with a semen factory! That's it, I want my own room!"

The next day I asked mother could I move into the spare room, room Number 3. I explained that since myself and Colm were getting older, maybe we needed a bit more space for ourselves.

"That's out of the question," she replied. "Number 3 is for guests."

"But we never have any guests," I protested. "That room lies vacant 365 nights a year!"

"Well, in case, on the off chance. Your cousin Carol turned up there not so long ago," she said.

"That was the spring of 1975," I retorted.

"Was it?" she said, surprised. "How time flies," she continued wistfully as she left the room.

I went to father. He was in his usual place, sitting in the car, parked inside the garage, reading his newspaper. Father used to devise strategies to get out of the house. This was one. Here in the sanctuary of his own Datsun, with the car radio on low, tuned into BBC Radio 3, he could read his newspaper, smoke his pipe and have a bit of peace and quiet. I tapped on the windscreen. He raised one of his dark eyebrows and glared at me, not wanting to be disturbed. "Can I have my own room?" I said. He pulled down the car window.

"What?"

"Can I have my own room?" I repeated.

He looked at me for a moment. "Ask your mother," was his reply. He went back to his paper.

"Who is this man?" I thought.

Eddie Mannion: Retired. Husband of Cora Mannion. Father of Manus and Colm Mannion. Swarthy in complexion. Short of stature and shorter of fuse. For party tricks, balanced items of furniture on chin. Always liked Perry Como and never rated Sinatra.

**Mannion's Personal Fact No. 7*

April 7th   229 days to go

I had a meeting with Ben this morning. He has read the latest draft of 'The Shamrock Sumo Club' and has certain suggestions.

"Why don't you introduce a Japanese company into the town?" he said with semi-enthusiasm, while keeping an eye on his mobile phone placed on the coffee shop table.

"What do you mean?" I replied in a puzzled manner.

"No. No wait. Or maybe have the company there already in the town for ten years, and now, this is good, and now have them pull out of the town. And then the townspeople start resenting all things Japanese as Sean O' Brien and his farmer friends continue to become more obsessed with

Japanese culture while attempting to set up their Sumo Wresting Club. This creates friction. And friction causes conflict. And conflict is drama. And drama is good. It also gives the piece a zeitgeist issue," he continued, running with the idea.

"A what?" I queried.

His mobile rang. He checked who was calling. He stood up. "Hang on. I've got to take this." He talked important business for twelve minutes. His coffee went cold. He didn't seem to mind. The call ended, he mumbled an apology then took up where he was.

"A zeitgeist issue. Globalization. Multinationals. Economic recession. A bigger issue that underscores the movie. A zeitgeist issue. What do you think?" he asked, very satisfied with his contribution as he sat back down in the oversized comfy chair.

"I don't know," I said weakly.

"I think it would really give it an extra dimension," he replied in a slightly persistent tone. His mobile rang again. He checked who was calling. "Hang on, I have to take this!"

After incorporating Ben's many ideas over a five year period, I now have to figure out how to introduce a Japanese company into the script. I don't think Ben realises how difficult it is to just parachute a Japanese company into the middle of Mountbellew. And why should I have to listen to Ben tell me how to improve my idea in the first place? Ben doesn't know anything. He can't create himself. All he can do is comment on my creativity. You see, he's done the film courses. And he's read the screen-writing books. He hasn't paid for any of it, mind you, he's scammed some faceless semi-state body to bankroll everything. And loving the sound of his own voice, he makes what sounds to him like valid points about character A's back story or character B's motivation. And you nod and take notes. And you try to put the fact that Ben has never written a sentence in his life to the back of your mind. Or produced a successful movie. After all, this is Ireland. This isn't Hollywood. I'd listen to Harvey Weinstein. I'd listen to Robert Evans. I'd listen to Darryl F. Zanuck.

Five movies produced by Darryl F. Zanuck:
1. "The Grapes of Wrath" 1940.
2. "How Green was my Valley" 1941.
3. "Gentleman's Agreement" 1947.
4. "All About Eve" 1950.
5. "Viva Zapata" 1952.

At least I'd respect their opinion. They've done things! They haven't just ponced around the Irish Film Centre drinking cappuccinos in a leather jacket. But you set aside all this bile and eventually acquiesce. Because Ben has the Development Cheque. And if we do get money from the Film Council, he'll be the one to decide how much I get. That's funny, because writers are the ones with the ideas, but the producers are the ones that get the money. We're the ones who pay for their nice fancy offices while we sit in our spotlessly clean, rent-free, semi-detached houses, trying to incorporate their suggestions. It makes me so angry. And where does all the money go? I have this theory. Film producers spend the development money paying for their medical bills. It is a well known documented fact that most film producers suffer from a medical condition called 'dried tongue syndrome'. This is caused by persistent licking of envelopes and stamps as they endlessly seek out bursaries for *your* work and this affliction demands constant medical attention and care.

April 16th 220 days to go

Sometimes I feel my life is one long Laurel and Hardy movie, where I'm both Laurel *and* Hardy. Take today for example. I am in deep, deep trouble. Orla, the next door neighbour, knocked on the door and asked to borrow the hoover. I forgot the 'Only give Orla the old hoover' rule and lent her our new hoover. She told me she'd drop it over later. Thinking about it subsequently as I tried to relax, I figured Kirsten would never know because Orla will have returned the hoover by the time Kirsten gets home. But whilst I was just coming out of the shower I heard a knock on the door. It must have been Orla. I went down to see who it was but just saw Orla's car drive off. She might not be back for hours. Or days. What happens if Kirsten wants to do some therapeutic hoovering when she gets home? What will I do? She'll kill me. To calm my nerves I took four drops of something called Bach's Rescue Remedy. Mother swears by it.

April 17th 219 days to go

Trouble in paradise. Orla dropped back the hoover when I was in town. Kirsten hit the roof when I got home. I hope she isn't serious about buying a third hoover.

April 23rd   213 days to go

I think I'm going to fall out with Kieran. Then again, I am a serial 'faller outer'. All my life I've always seemed to fall out with people. Then we patch things up and hang out with each other for a while. Then we fall out again. Although as I get older I realise that I know less and less people to fall out with. Memo to myself. Must start meeting new people soon, who at some future date I can fall out with.

But I am very annoyed with Kieran. He never rings me. I always have to try and organise our meetings and then most times, like tonight, at the last minute he cancels. Trouble is, I become quite needy with my male friends. I become emotionally dependant on them. Being a Creative Lower Being, I have a lot of spare time on my hands. I ring them up every second week, and ask, "Do you want to meet up for coffee or drinks?"

Then we end up hanging out for a few years and having the same conversations over and over again. Then they seem to start growing tired of me and every time I call them and they agree to meet up it's like they are doing me a favour. And then I start feeling unappreciated and I start wondering how come *they* never ring me? How come I always have to ring them. Why do I always have to make the effort?

Then I realise if I didn't ring them, I'd never see them, because they are men after all and ultimately they couldn't give a fuck. As long as there is some fuckin' bearded stranger on some fuckin' barstool in some fuckin' bar that they can talk complete shite to, they are completely happy. They don't need me. But I need them. I need my male friends.

I first felt this sense of neediness in college. I started College in Galway in 1981. I studied Commerce. I was very depressed there. I hated Commerce. My parents insisted that I stick with it as the world of business had plenty of employment possibilities. My subject list sounded like a Groucho Marx routine.

Margaret Dumont (1889-1965) "Stately, long suffering American comedy actress, a regular in many Marx Brothers movies."

'First you've got Macro-economics. Then Micro-economics. Coming up next is Development Economics followed by International Economics. We then have a subject called Economic Economics. After lunch we have Sales Management. Then there's Production Management. Then there's Business Management and Management Management. The following day we have Financial Accounting, Management Accounting, Accounting Management and Financial Management' — puts cigar back in mouth, wiggles grease-painted eyebrows and exits stage left.

Another reason for my abject unhappiness in college was my lack of progress with the distaff side. Since that night of my Inter Cert, I had only ventured to one or two other discos and was therefore a complete novice with the opposite sex and still very much *virginus intactus.* Unlike my brother, Colm. My hunch had been correct. He had a girlfriend. I spotted him one night walking hand in hand with a very attractive school girl when I was down Salthill with Austin and Michael walking towards Claude's pool hall.

"Is that Colm?" Austin said in disbelief.

"Yeh." I said. "Seems so."

Colm saw us, but pretended to ignore us. We started to laugh and slag him off, as we tried to cover up our own embarrassment that between the three of us we'd never gone out with a girl and were a complete disgrace to our gender. My parents were worried about me. Parents are strange like that. When you are growing up, during your adolescence, on the one hand they are always saying, "Don't go to bed with any woman. Don't get anyone pregnant. Don't you dare have sex outside of marriage." And this is drummed into you again and again and again.

So you end up being fucked-up about women and fucked-up about fucking, and you stay in most nights, but then suddenly you turn 18, and your parents look at you and despite all their warnings they start secretly thinking: He's 18-years-old. He never goes out. He still doesn't have a girlfriend. What's wrong? He has a penis, hasn't he? Last time we bathed him, 11 years ago, he seemed to have one. Why isn't he using it? Oh Christ, he's not *gay*, is he?

My confidence was so low I didn't know what I was. Maybe I was gay, I thought. Maybe those two nerds I hang around with, Austin and Michael were gay. Maybe even Gerry was gay. Gerry was my best friend. The person I felt most empathy with in the whole world. I met him while working on a college magazine during first year and we were very close. One could say unnaturally close. People thought all sorts of things about us. It didn't bother Gerry. It bothered me. But I wanted him all to myself. I didn't want to share him with anybody. He was the only true friend I had and we had a certain magic together, because we were on the same wavelength, and could tell what the other one was thinking, with a glance, a look, an inflection of the voice. I was very dependant on him.

Two years older than me, he was a sort of mentor. A

kind of shrink. An oracle in an anorak. I took on board everything he said. He was my fountain of wisdom. Then he met a girl. Lorraine. He stopped spending time with me. He'd hang out with his new girlfriend. I couldn't stand her. We both started vying for his affections. She was winning. I felt jilted. I started reacting like a wronged wife. He'd say he'd ring me at a certain time and he wouldn't ring. He'd be out with her. And the following day he'd ring to apologise.

"It's o.k., I was just sitting by the phone the whole night, that's all," I'd say snippily.

I'd get ratty and bitchy and feel cut-up inside. He could get laid all he wanted, it wasn't about that, it was the time factor. She was disrupting our quality time together. Then she started turning him against me. She'd say things like, "Why hasn't Manus got a girlfriend, why is he always hanging around with us?"

Under pressure he began to meet me less and less. We'd meet up for a clandestine coffee in the student canteen and start having an interesting conversation when she'd turn up. That would change the whole dynamic of the situation. At other times I'd meet him and he'd have bumped into another one of his friends, Albert. Now, I didn't mind Albert. I quite liked him as a person. But I didn't want him there. Then. I didn't want to have to listen to Albert talk to Gerry and Gerry talk to Albert. I wanted to talk to Gerry. I would visibly deflate. Albert would say "Hi" and I'd say "Hello," in wounded disappointment, hoping he'd get the picture and leave.

Then I'd half-heartedly join in the conversation, trying to get a grip on my irrationality but the longer Albert stayed the more I'd become consumed with an inner rage, and I'd think, "Cool it, cool it, don't blow it, Gerry won't like it," but then I'd think, "Fuck it, I want to talk to Gerry, quality time, Lorraine will be here in 40 minutes," then I'd go into a deep sulk, become catatonic, mumble replies, stare into space, hate myself, hate Albert, hate Lorraine, hate everything.

Eventually, Albert would have to go, and now I'd be pissed off with Gerry. He knew he was meant to meet me. Couldn't he have told Albert he'd see him tomorrow or later? He could have told Albert he was busy. Maybe Gerry's getting tired of me? Maybe he wanted Albert along because he can't abide my company anymore? I better watch my step. I better snap out of this sulk. I'd die without Gerry.

Lorraine started taking an interest in me. Maybe she was worried about my relationship with Gerry, maybe she too thought we were gay. She made it her business to get to know me. She figured what I needed was a girlfriend. To get laid. To divest my emotional energy elsewhere so she could have Gerry. She introduced me to a friend of hers, Mairead, a science student who she'd found out fancied me. Mairead always wore a blue denim jacket and black leggings, was built like a fridge and seemed to have no ankles. But then again I was no oil painting, just an acne-riddled midget in unfashionable cardigan, brown corduroys and a pair of worn-out Clark's shoes.

One evening, we went to a college choir recital together in the Aula Maxima. It was a very tense occasion. Afterwards she suggested we go to the Student Bar for a drink. Her tipple was Satzenbrau and, throwing caution and good sense to the wind, I started knocking back glasses of vodka and orange. After my third drink, Mairead had almost become quite attractive in a homely bovine sort of way.

Closing time arrived and as we left the bar, she grabbed hold of me and suddenly I was attacked by an enormous slobbering tongue. As I gasped for air, she suggested we go back to her flat in Corrib Park. I cooly said "O.k.". Being drunk for the first time, that walk to Corrib Park seemed to take no time at all. It was like my whole body was being carried by an alternate life force.

Suddenly I looked down and realised that alternate life force was Mairead, as she boisterously put me over her shoulders, demonstrating to me the best way to transport a kayak. We arrived in her flat. I sat down. She told me to get up, we were going to her bedroom. She started to undress. The drink started to wear off. The full enormity of the evening's proceedings were beginning to dawn on me as she pulled me under the sheets.

Getting Laid with Mairead (1984) 3m. ** D: Herbert Ross. Manus Mannion, Mairead O' Mara. Predictable tale of an older woman seducing a younger, insecure man. [R]

Further fumbling ensued as more items of clothing were removed. Full of expectant passion, she rolled onto me like a Sherman tank and started searching for Bob. He was playing hide and seek. But she knew a thing or two about finding him. And helping him reach his full potential. Despite having enormous difficulty breathing, I went with the flow and got into the rhythm.

Suddenly my parents were in the bed with me. "Don't you dare go to bed with anybody, don't get anyone pregnant!" they said. All this distraction and angst started to affect Bob. Mairead noticed this in the midst of her low pleasurable purring. "Don't worry, I'm on the pill," she said impatiently, yanking at a reinvigorated Bob again. I felt relieved. I laid back and awaited my destiny. Splat! It arrived sooner than expected. She looked at me disappointedly, her large mammaries hanging downwards inside her Stranglers T- shirt. She tried to reactivate an exhausted yet quietly exhilarated Bob, but it was no good. "I'll set the alarm for six," she said. "I want my orgasm!"

The following day I arrived home with a sickly grin on my face. Things are going to change now, I vowed. My life will be different. For I am man. I am strength. I am creation. And from my loins much seed has flown. I am man. I went to mother.

"I am 20 years old. I want to move my things into Number 3," I declared.

"That's out of the question," she replied. "Number 3 is for guests."

"But we never have any guests," I protested once again. "That room lies vacant 365 nights a year!"

"Well, in case. On the off chance. Your cousin Carol turned up there not so long ago," she said.

"That was the spring of 1975," I retorted.

"Was it?" she said surprised. "The time really does fly, doesn't it," she muttered as she left the room.

April 24th 212 days to go

You know when you think about somebody you haven't thought about for a long time and the following day you are going up an escalator holding a cauliflower and you look up and there that person is? Well it happened today. I saw Mairead. She's got old. But she's lost weight. It's hard to believe at one stage in my life I was so obsessed with her. But that term in college, I had become obsessed with her, and obsessed about the joys of getting laid.

Getting Laid with Mairead Again (1984) 48m. * D: Ken Finkleman. Manus Mannion, Mairead O' Mara. A young insecure man with sex on his mind, pursues a slightly older woman. Pointless and tedious sequel to "Getting Laid with Mairead". [PG-13]

One day I sought her out on the college concourse. She seemed in a hurry but agreed to meet up for a drink that evening in the Student Bar. I ordered a double vodka and orange, but she only had one bottle of Satzenbrau. She told me she had to get up early for a lecture the next morning. We kissed briefly outside the archway of the Aula Maxima before she headed up Newcastle Road. I looked forward to our next meeting as I jauntily walked home.

A few days later, I tracked her down again. This time, she agreed to meet up for a lunchtime coffee in Smoky Joe's, a small coffee shop next to the tennis courts at the front of the college grounds.

Afterwards, outside, we shook hands rather formally but before we parted I asked, "So when will we meet up again?" "Soon," she said, as she scampered off. I smiled happily as I headed to that Production Management lecture.

A week went by. She seemed to be keeping a very low profile. I waited for her outside her lecture theatre but couldn't find her. I called up to her house, but there was no answer. Finally, I left a note on one of the Faculty of Science noticeboards and as I waited for a reply, wondered whether I had misread the signals. I listed the facts logically as I saw them. First date: full-on penetrative sexual intercourse. Second date : a drink and a peck on the cheek. Third date : a coffee and a handshake.

After much analysis I realised there seemed to be a definite trend to the sequence of events. It was plainly obvious this was leading in a certain direction and there was only one conclusion to be drawn. Evidently, she was so in love with me, she needed some time and space to adjust to the reality of my existence in her life. The following Tuesday, I was re-reading my notes on Maslow's Hierarchy of Needs in the Arts and Commerce library when I looked up and there she was, standing over me. I smiled at her compassionately.

"We need to talk," she said, in a businesslike manner.

Finally, I mused, she can do without me no longer.

We went downstairs to the student canteen. "The place of our first meeting," I whispered romantically. She bought two coffees. Tar-like substance from an old silver grey machine in two styrofoam cups. She walked back to our table. She sat down and looked at me.

"Manus, I like you a lot, you're a nice fella," she said.

I was surprised. That's a little underwhelming for a statement of undying love.

"But, I've got exams coming up. Let's leave it for a while."

I was taken aback. "What do you mean?"

"Well, let's leave it for a while. Us. Let's leave us for a while."

"Well, we have left us for a while. I haven't seen you in ten days."

"Well, let's leave us for a longer while."

How long was I meant to wait for her? I was becoming slightly perplexed by her behaviour. But since I was dealing with such an emotionally delicate creature, I tried to be understanding.

"How long, a month?"

"No. Longer."

"Huh?"

"What I'm trying to say, is... let's leave it open-ended."

"Open ended?"

"Manus, o.k., I'll be blunt. Let's not see each other any more!"

I was shell-shocked. I started to hyperventilate as a slow panic grabbed hold of me.

"Is that alright?" Mairead asked, with a slight worry in her voice.

I sat there in a state of numbness.

"It was just a fling. You took it too seriously," she said smiling.

I nodded. She caressed my hand momentarily as she got up.

"You'll be alright, won't you Manus?" she asked. Not waiting for a reply, she then quickly continued," I have to go. Bye."

I cleared my throat but couldn't get any words out and started to fidget meaninglessly with a sugar sachet as she walked away into the distance.

April 30th 206 days to go

Kirsten noticed the numerous bottles out the back, in our empty bottle container this morning and asked me to dump them. I mumbled I would. But I'm not too sure if I will. The problem first arose about four weeks ago. That day, after much thigh pummelling in the morning, I had decided to do something useful and dump our bottles in the bottle bank close by, in the grounds of St. James's Street Hospital. I had never been much of an environmentalist before I met Kirsten, but she has gradually changed certain aspects of my behaviour. Dumping bottles was one such change. Before I met her I dismissed it as a waste of time, too much hassle, no one else does it, why should I? But eventually after eleven years I had gradually got used to doing it because I was, after all, a disciple of routine. A disciple of routine is the type of person, who once they get used to doing a certain thing in a certain way, do this certain thing in this certain way until they malfunction and die. It is considered a hereditary problem and is more common in men.

I went to the back of the house and placed the various bottles in a large loose bag. I set the alarm, left the house and walked towards St. James's Street Hospital. As I approached the bottle bank, I realised it wasn't there. Though loath to leave the bag of bottles where the bottle bank used to be, I was equally reluctant to lug them all the way into town as I had planned to meet Kieran in Mocha Madness later that afternoon. I figured the bottle bank would be back the following week, since there was no notice up announcing its actual demise, so I reluctantly placed my bag of bottles next to where it used to be and went on my way.

A few weeks later, after another non-productive day on 'The Shamrock Sumo Club', I walked to the hospital with a new bag of bottles. The bottle bank still wasn't there. But of course now there were about 60 bags of bottles left by other people, placed where it used to be. I walked over to the Pathology Department, the nearest building.

"Where's the bottle bank?" I asked.

The desk clerk looked up. "What?"

"It's gone," I said.

He seemed surprised. "Has it?"

"Yeh."

He then said, "Ah sure, I never liked it there anyways, it was a nuisance, should never have been there."

I wondered whether it was going to be put back. He didn't know. Another desk clerk appeared from behind a door.

"Billy, do you know what happened to the bottle bank?" desk clerk one asked. Billy, desk clerk two, thought about it for a moment and then said, "It should never have been there in the first place, I'd have moved it ages ago."

I asked Billy whether it was going to be put back or if they were going to move it to another part of the hospital. Billy pondered this for a moment and then said, "I don't know. Go to Administration, they'd know."

He pointed vaguely, somewhere to the right and I thanked them both and left.

I couldn't find Administration. So the next day I rang the hospital and asked who can I talk to about the disappearance of the bottle bank. I was put through to Technical Services. A woman answered the phone. I introduced myself and started my story.

"Hello, I used to dump my bottles in the bottle bank, it's been gone for the last three weeks. I was wondering..."

"Where used it be?" she inquired.

I made an important mental note. The person I have been told, could answer my query about the St. James's Street Hospital bottle bank did not know where, in the grounds of the hospital, the bottle bank was situated.

"It used to be beside the Pathology department, before that it was on the way out near the James's Street exit," I continued.

"And it's gone," she said in a matter-of-fact manner.

I made a second important mental note. The person I have been led to believe, could answer my query about the bottle bank did not know it had been removed.

"Yes it's been removed, and there are bags of bottles just piling up where it used to be. Will it be replaced? Maybe someone should put up a sign saying 'Don't dump your bottles here anymore!'" I said, a little exasperated.

"I'll try to find out," she said. "What's your extension?" she then queried.

"No I'm just a member of the public. I don't work in the hospital. I just dump my bottles there."

"Huh?" she grunted.

"Yes, there are actual members of the public in this area who actually make an effort to dump their bottles," I said with a slight, self-righteous tone creeping into my voice. She took my number and said she would find out what the story was and ring me. A fortnight went by. She hadn't called. I decided to ring her. I wearily reintroduced myself and reminded her of my query. The woman on the other line seemed a little confused and eventually said I must have been talking to Nuala, but she's on holidays at the minute. I sighed, and wondered could she help me. She said she'd look into the matter and asked for my extension. I told her I didn't work in the hospital, I was a mere member of the public who dumped his bottles there.

She took down my number and promised to ring back. That was last week. As stated earlier, this morning Kirsten noticed the mountain of bottles piling up at the back of the house. After she left for work, still not having being contacted by Technical Services I decided to ring once again. Nuala was back. With barely concealed contempt I reintroduced myself again, and wondered if she remembered the whole bottle bank saga.

She asked me to run it by her again. I did so. She said my best bet would be to ring the Recycling Division of Dublin Corporation. Why didn't she tell me this three weeks ago? I wondered to myself. I asked her if she had their number. She said it was in the phone book and briskly said goodbye. She had more pressing matters not to attend to. I eventually rang the Recycling Division of Dublin Corporation after spending twenty minutes trying to find the correct number in the phone book. A woman answered the phone. I explained my situation.

"Oh, the bottle bank in the hospital! We had to remove it for safety reasons," she said enigmatically.

"What do you mean?" I inquired.

"People weren't using it properly," she said, continuing in an opaque manner. "We had to take the decision."

I pressed her further. She seemed extremely reluctant to elaborate. Eventually she said, "Syringes. Drug users were dumping their syringes in it."

"Oh."

I immediately had this image of a civic minded junkie collecting all the used syringes from his friends, putting them in a bag and driving to the bottle bank on a Saturday morning.

Then I had a suggestion. "Well, you didn't necessarily have to remove the whole bottle bank. That just inconveniences people. Why not just install a separate syringe bank for the junkies?"

I could tell by her long pause that she wasn't impressed by my idea. She then told me that the nearest bottle bank was in the car park of the Shopping Centre in Crumlin. So I now face a dilemma. Because I don't want to have go to Crumlin. It's not on my way into town. It's a big detour. And it's dangerous. And I only have two hands. And holding two full bags of bottles, I'd be easy prey if some DLTswanted to mug me. No, I'll have to tell Kirsten that Crumlin is not on the agenda. I'll have to be assertive. We'll have to come to some other arrangement.

May 4th 202 days to go

Kirsten had a very bad sleep last night. She told me it was my fault. I have started to snore. She later looked up snoring on the internet and claimed that, according to studies by the Edinburgh Western General Hospital, men are eight times more likely to snore than women because men have more muscle and fat around their necks which relaxes at night and can partially restrict breathing. A number of factors can contribute to snoring. Being overweight. Drinking alcohol. Eating large meals close to bedtime. And sleeping on your back. She has suggested that I review my lifestyle.

May 5th 201 days to go

Another day. Another film producer. Had a meeting with Sarah Dunlop of Emerald City Films about 'Spud Zombie', my zombie idea set during the Irish Potato Famine. I had decided to go to another producer because I wanted to work with someone other than Ben. The meeting started off very well. She liked the very dark, offbeat, quality of the treatment and was impressed by the sample scenes I showed her. She told me she was definitely interested in trying to produce it. But gradually, to my horror, she started turning into Ben. She looked at me and told me she had some suggestions of her own.

"How about bringing in an English landlord, and his family, who live in the big house, and they have lots of food and supplies but they don't share their wealth. And maybe some of their tenants end up being Spud Zombies and end up terrorising this landlord and his family. This could give the movie a zeitgeist issue."

"A zeitgeist issue?" I repeated.

"Yes. The uneven distribution of resources in this world. The burgeoning anti-globalization movement. The poorer countries, symbolised by the Spud Zombies, demanding a fairer share of the cake."

She smiled at me.

"It's just an idea. Think about it."

Then her mobile rang. She checked who was calling.

"I have to take this."

I thought about her idea. Desperate to have another project in the system, after she finished her call, I told her it was an interesting perspective and I promised I'd email her the new amended submission later in the week.

May 7th 199 days to go

Hung around town in the afternoon. Bought Bob Dylan's 1970 album "New Morning" on C.D. in Tower Records. Dylan used to be *a tour de force*, now he just seems forced to tour. Later, waiting for my bus in the torrential rain, I vowed to pay only the minimum fare. Recently, I have started my own penalty point system for late buses. The longer I wait, the less I pay. If my fare is €1. 20 and I wait more than twenty minutes, I only pay the next lower fare which is 85 cents. I also recalled that extra money I'd paid a few months back and the thirty cents I was owed by Dublin Bus. This reinforced my determination to pay the lesser fare.

I waited for my bus. And waited. Buses did go by. But none to my destination. They all seemed to be heading to this mysterious place called 'Out Of Service'. Where is this place 'Out Of Service', I pondered. Anytime I'm waiting for a bus, so many buses that approach seem to be going there. Who lives there? Obviously it has a wealthy demographic because they have such a regular and efficient bus service. Unlike the poorer areas. Eventually, the bus approached and I organised my change.

"Why is this bus so late?" I asked as I got on.

"I'm early actually," the driver replied defensively behind his oversized sunglasses. "See, the last one didn't run."

I looked at him wearily. I hadn't heard that one before. "85 cents!" I announced as I put the money down the chute. I grabbed at my ticket and made my way upstairs. I looked at the ticket which was valid as far as Thomas Street. I stared out at the grey, grubby metropolis that is Dublin's fair city. Fast food debris blew across Dame Street, homeless people huddled beside A.T.M. machines, and motorcycle couriers drove madly at impatient pedestrians crossing at a red light. If we are living through a so called economic boom period, where is the glamour?

As the bus worked its way slowly towards Thomas Street I noticed the elbow of my jacket had gotten wet leaning against the window, an oasis of residual water from years of rain and condensation. Suddenly to my horror, I saw a bus inspector. We had just gone beyond Thomas Street and onto James's Street. I hadn't paid the correct fare. I could be fined €250. I contemplated getting off at the next stop but he was blocking my escape route as he clipped a ticket across from me. He turned towards me. I handed him the ticket. He examined it.

"This ticket is only valid to Thomas Street," he said.

I didn't know what to say. I could tell him I was sleeping and I missed my stop. I could apologise and say I didn't know the correct fare and promise it wouldn't happen again, but why, why should I let this nonentity intimidate me? I decided to throw caution to the wind and for once in my life play it cool. I was going to play Dublin Bus at their own game.

"What's the difference in the fare?" I asked.

"35 cents," he said.

"I don't have the correct change on me at the moment," I said apologising, "But I'll tell you what I'll do. If you give me a bit of paper, I can write you an I.O.U. for 35 cents, and I can write down my address, and if you've nothing better to do in the next few days, why don't you call round to my house in Rialto and I'll give you the money."

He didn't like my attitude.

"Do you know you could be fined €250 for this," he said.

"Oh," I replied without flinching.

"Right, what's your name?"

I thought for a moment. There was a long pause.

"Grady Sutton," I replied.

Grady Sutton – (1908-1995) "Slightly rotund, American comedy character actor, usually seen playing bashful country boys."

He scrutinised me for a minute. A very long minute.

"Address?"

I quickly made something up.

"14 Well... Park... Drive... Phibsborough, Dublin 7."

He looked confused. "You said Rialto earlier," he said.

Panicking, I tried to cover my slip up.

"Sorry, Rialto, Dublin 8. Eh 14 Well Drive Park..."

"You said Well Park Drive before..."

"Sorry, sorry, sorry...", I spluttered, trying to remember exactly what I had said.

"Well, is it Well Park Drive, or is it Well Drive Park?" he asked impatiently.

I summoned up as much clarity as I could, given the situation.

"It's 14 Well Park Drive, Rialto, Dublin 8," I eventually stated with conviction.

Suddenly, while struggling to write up the details, he seemed to lose interest. He turned to me and said: "I'll let you off this time Grady, but this better be a lesson for you!"

He walked to the back of the bus. I sighed with relief.

May 15th 191 days to go

I've had an exhausting day. I was up late last night working on the 'Spud Zombie' amendments for Sarah. I finally emailed them to her early this morning. Feeling a small sense of satisfaction for having finally done something, I had planned to have an easy day.

However it was not to be. Before Kirsten left for work, she put her foot down. She insisted I finally dump those bottles. It is after all, one of my few allotted chores, like putting out and taking in the bin, and uh... anyway I was forced to go to Crumlin in the afternoon. And then Kirsten figured since I was going to the shopping centre to dump the bottles, I might as well take care of the shopping as well.

As mentioned earlier, I have a visceral aversion towards Crumlin and I especially hate having to go to that shopping centre. I've had nightmares of being stuck there for eternity looking for crème fraîche. So I vowed that after I dumped the bottles I would try and get my shopping done as quickly as possible.

I eventually entered the shopping complex. Hard, yellow, weather-beaten faces puffed endlessly on cigarettes as I rushed through the corridor, trying to avoid stressed 15-year-old mothers arguing with gaunt 16-year-old D.L.T.s as they manically pushed buggies. Running by a myriad of putrid smelling butchers and 1970's style bakeries, I eventually got to the supermarket. I grabbed a blue basket and frantically consulted my shopping list.

I searched for eggs. Where are the eggs? Where are the eggs? I want to get out of here as soon as possible, where are the bleedin' eggs? They used to be on that shelf. They are not on that shelf anymore. And the recycled toilet rolls used to be over there and now that's the vegetable section. Oh Christ! They have changed the layout! They always change the layout. Why? I came up with a theory. Supermarkets repeatedly change the layout of their stores as an underhanded way to increase prices. Here is how it works: The customer is already tense with his/her large shopping list. They become even more tense trying to find the new location of various products. And when they eventually do find the actual product they are looking for, relieved, they will just hastily pick it off the shelf and will not check the exorbitant price increase.

I continued desperately searching for the new location of the eggs. I eventually found them in the corner, near the meat section. I examined the eggs. I realised I had a problem. A case of shopper's indecision. As a belated environmentalist, would I purchase the free range eggs in the plastic packaging, or the battery eggs in the recycled packaging? If I bought the free range eggs, Kirsten would ask later, "Why did you buy the ones in the plastic packaging?" But if I bought the battery eggs she wouldn't eat them because she only eats free range eggs. As I increasingly became demented debating this conundrum in my mind, Nat King Cole crooned on the sound system in the background. Keep the music tranquil is the policy. Keep the revolution at bay.

Then some third-rate karaoke sensation walked by pushing a trolley of Scrumpy Jack, singing along to 'Unforgettable', though not remembering any of the words. I eventually decided to buy two packets of eggs; one packet of free range eggs in plastic packaging, one packet of battery eggs in recycled packaging and then devised an ingenious plan. When I got home I removed the free range eggs from the plastic packaging, and set them aside. I then removed the six battery eggs from the recycled packaging, and placed them in the now empty plastic packaging. I then reversed the procedure and placed the free range eggs previously set aside into the now empty recycled packaging. I then disposed of the six newly positioned battery eggs in the plastic packaging. It was an expensive procedure but at least the problem had been solved.

May 21st 185 days to go.

Kirsten got back early from work yesterday and wanted to go the theatre 'on the spur of the moment'. I told her it was out of the question. For, as expressed previously, I am a disciple of routine. And the words 'on the spur of the moment' are not part of my vocabulary. I denounce spontaneity with every fibre of my being. Kirsten has never understood that for his routine to be broken, one must give the disciple of routine at least two weeks advance notice of one's intentions. This is because having to break one's routine is like having to face a mini death for the disciple of routine. There are five stages in facing a Break of Routine.

1. Denial: When a Disciple of Routine is first informed he will have to break his routine, his first reaction is one of numbing shock. His world has fallen apart. He really cannot believe he is going to have to break his routine.

2. Anger: Then the Disciple of Routine gets angry about having to break his routine. Why him? Why does he have to break his routine? Why can't it be somebody else?

3. Bargaining: Then his instinct is to bargain. He promises to break his routine at some other unspecified future date. Just not now. Please not now.

4. Depression: He then becomes very depressed about his approaching break with routine.

5. Acceptance: Reluctantly he accepts the inevitability of breaking his routine. I repeated these facts to her again. Kirsten then told me in quite a forceful manner, that in two weeks time, the play will have stopped running. We eventually came to a compromise and I agreed to go to it next Tuesday night.

Later, thinking about it, I realised I was gradually turning into father. Firstly, with my increasing ability as I age, to rant incoherently on unrelated topics, and now with this 'routine' gene which seems to be dominating my behaviour more and more. If someone says to father, "Tomorrow night you have to go out for dinner instead of sitting at home," he will react in shock, then explode, have a tantrum and say, "No, no, that's out of the question. You can't break my routine. I had planned to sit in tomorrow night and watch the same weather forecast four times. Please, I need the comfort of my routine. I cannot be separated from my routine!" As seen from the above proposed trip to the theatre I react in exactly the same way. However if given a few weeks notice, father too, will go through the five stages and eventually accept philosophically that he will have to miss the weather forecast at some future date.

May 26th 180 days to go

I'm still trying to find out if Sarah is happy with the 'Spud Zombie' adjustments. I've left countless messages with her. Once she answered the phone and told me briskly she was busy and would ring me back. She never did. As a rule of thumb film producers never ring you back. Because they are too busy. Laughing. Aloud. In their nice plush offices. Thinking of all those writers out there. And knowing that when those writers come up with ideas, they have to come to them. And if that idea gets any development money, they get to keep most of the money for the various envelope related fees and dried tongue related medical expenses. And if the project doesn't get any development money it doesn't matter that much, because the film producer already has seven projects on the go anyway with seven other desperate writers.

My snoring is still causing problems. We've started to eat earlier, I've cut down on alcohol and lost a bit of weight over the last few weeks but none of this seems to help.

Kirsten has come to the conclusion that the snoring must be caused by lying on my back, inadvertently, while sleeping. She says she'll look into ways of preventing this. Meanwhile tonight I shall try wearing nasal strips.

May 27th 179 days to go

Had a turgidly boring time at the theatre. It was an improvised multi-media piece, put on by a company called First @ct, exploring the confusing, frightening post 9/11 world we live in. It was called 'The Twin Towers of Babel', although with the amount of rubbish spouted on stage it should have been re-named 'The Twin Towers of Babble'.

Spent most of the first half resisting an overwhelming desire to fall into a deep slumber. Finding it didactic and pretentious in my more alert moments, I wanted to leave at the interval but Kirsten insisted we stay. Although also disappointed with the play, she felt we owed it to the performers to stick with it until the end.

On top of that, after spending €28 for an evening's entertainment, she didn't want to be home by nine thirty. After the interval, between bouts of restlessness and extreme irritation, I started to daydream and recalled my own youthful enthusiasm for meaningful, pitiable drama during my college years.

It was all Mairead's fault. After she dumped me, I immediately sought out Gerry's company again. And it would be an understatement to say that Lorraine was not pleased to see me back in Gerry's life. She then suggested to Gerry to advise me to join the student Drama Society, Dramsoc. U.C.G. I might meet other new people, like-minded people, in a creative atmosphere. I also had ambitions to be a performer and this would help me with my craft. Gerry convinced me. He told me Dramsoc. were trying to find actors for a version of Samuel Becket's 'Waiting For Godot', that for some strange reason, still hadn't been cast. Maybe it was because the production had a first-time director, he continued, but every one deserves a chance and has to start somewhere.

I agreed to his suggestion and after our coffee I immediately went over to the Dramsoc. noticeboard to find out when auditions would be held. Tuesday, two o'clock, Room A107. I was the first there. I knocked on the door. "Make that entrance!" a voice barked. I walked in.

"Hello, I'm Manus Mannion," I mumbled nervously, looking up at an imposing figure.

"Hello, I'm Ivor O' Doherty," the figure replied.

Ivor was lanky, had a mullet, wore a pair of gold John Lennon granny glasses, and was dressed in green combat fatigues. I sat down. He wanted me to read for the role of Lucky and handed me a photo copy of Lucky's speech. I stood up and manically sped through it, riddled with nerves.

Afterwards, I sat down, utterly dejected. He told me he'd let me know. "Next," he shouted, "Make that entrance!" There was no one outside.

After a few days, I checked the Dramsoc. noticeboard. I was exultant. I had got the part. The cast were meant to meet Ivor in room A209, Monday at seven o' clock. I wasn't that familiar with Becket's oeuvre at that stage, so was disappointed to realise at our first cast meeting, that it was an all male cast. An untried all male cast. None of us had been in a student production before. Ivor scrutinised us for a moment and said our final cast member was late. He then cracked a rather laboured joke about waiting for a cast member. We laughed nervously. Then Albert walked in. Gerry's other friend. I hadn't realised he was in the cast. Lorraine must have had Gerry suggest he join Dramsoc. as well. Albert apologised for being late, nodded at me and sat down. Suddenly, after a slight pause, Ivor leaped up from his chair.

"I am your director Ivor O' Doherty. Not many of the established members of Dramsoc. have been prepared to risk their so-called careers by working with me. But I don't care. We don't care. For we will show them. This 'H Block Godot' will be talked about for years to come."

"H-Block?" I queried.

Ivor nodded with a glint in his eye. He had decided to take Beckett's characters out of their post-apocalyptic landscape, and make them more vital and relevant to the Ireland of 1984, by transposing 'Waiting For Godot' to a slightly belated hunger strike setting.

"Yes. My Godot will be set in the H Blocks." We all looked a little apprehensive.

"Tramp costumes are out. Shit covered sheets are in," he declared.

"Oh no," I sighed to myself.

"Real shit?" somebody asked.

Ivor's eyes widened. "I suckle on the teat of Stanislavski. We are Method. We will all have to experience that shit. The audience will have to smell that shit. Of course, it'll be real shit."

"Whose shit?" Albert asked tentatively.

"My shit, the lighting guy's shit, the costume designer's shit, it doesn't matter as long as it is real shit," expanded Ivor.

Albert and myself looked at each other. Ivor continued.

"If my Godot is set in the H Blocks what are they waiting for?" he asked like a demented lecturer. There was a pause.

"Food?" someone piped up in confusion.

"No," Ivor said impatiently.

"The Cleaners?" someone else added.

"No, Think! Think!" Ivor shouted.

"Freedom. Irish Freedom," Albert said in an almost bored manner.

"Yes! Yes! Yes!" Ivor bellowed. "Irish Freedom."

As the rehearsals progressed I sensed the production was going to be an unmitigated disaster. I was so relieved my parents were completely uninterested in my recent absorption in drama. However, I was in for a shock. The day of the dress rehearsal they called me into the living room.

"Your mother and I have had a chat," father said.

"Yes," mother said.

"What do you want to say?" I asked.

Mother began tentatively, "We just want to tell you that if you don't want to..."

Father took over. "What your mother's trying to say is, if you don't like the old economics and what have you, and you want to do a bit of the old acting or comedy or what have you, we don't want to stand in your way. I mean you're a grown-up now, sort of... and eh, it's your life."

I was stunned by his new-found understanding. He looked at mother.

"Just finish your degree," she said. "It'll be something to fall back on."

Father continued. "Yeh, something to fall back on. But at the end of the day whatever you want to do after that is fine by us. We will be supportive of your decision. What we're trying to say is no matter what you decide to do, we'll always be here for you because... eh...". He tapered off. I decided to help him out.

"Because you've got that old coat of mine cleaned at the laundry?"

"Yeh. Exactly."

Buoyed by this rare emotional moment, father then said enthusiastically, "And the first thing myself and your mother are going to do, is to go to that college play you are in," then adding in a semi-jocular manner, "to see if you've any talent at all!"

I clammed up. "I'd rather if you didn't do that."

"Arey, will you go away out of that," he said. "And miss our son's debut on stage?"

"We're genuinely interested," mother said with surprising sincerity. "You can't stop parents wanting to encourage and support their children in what they want to do."

"You won't like it," I protested.

"That's for us to decide. Now when does it start?" father added briskly.

"Monday night, eight o'clock," I said weakly.

Tossing and turning that night in bed, I tried to come up with a plan to prevent mother and father from witnessing this turd-filled train wreck of a production. Then I had an idea.

"It's sold out. The whole run. No tickets available," I said sadly at lunchtime, the next day.

"It's too bad. It would have been nice if you could have come, but that's the way it goes," I continued.

"But can you not get tickets for family members?" mother asked disappointedly.

I shook my head.

"Don't worry," father said from the other side of the table. "I thought there might be a problem getting tickets. Any show with my son in it is bound to sell out."

I looked at him in a puzzled worried fashion, not knowing if he was joking or serious.

He continued, "So first thing this morning, I rang my friend Joe Hogan in College Administration."

He beamed as put his hand in his pocket and held up two orange tickets.

"Joe dropped them off in the office before noon," he proclaimed. "Two tickets for the opening night of 'Waiting for Godot'."

My heart plummeted.

Stage Debut (1984) 133m. * D: Michael Blakemore. Manus Mannion, Albert Henderson, Mark Clayton, Ivor O' Doherty, Sean Reynolds. A young man finds himself in an ill-concieved version of Samuel Beckett's 'Waiting For Godot'. A tedious and at times very off-putting experience, with shoddy production values and some very amateur performances. [PG-13]

Ivor O' Doherty's 'Waiting for Godot' proved to be the most calamitous production in the annals of U.C.G. Dramsoc's history. Needless to say, my parents were mortified. Not only did the production stink, literally, but it created such a scandal that members of Galway Corporation and the university authorities insisted it close after only three performances. Ivor never directed another play and, rumour had it, ended up in Tripoli teaching English to one of Colonel Gadafy's daughters.

June 2nd 173 days to go

Bank holiday Monday. Kirsten is out hiking in Howth with her German friend, Petra. After all these years Kirsten doesn't have that many Irish friends. On the whole, she finds the Irish superficially friendly. She maintains that in the pub — that eternal land of the over-hyped 'craic' — an Irish person is everybody's lifelong buddy, but in the cold light of day it doesn't amount to anything *real.*

Sat at home and sighed most of the morning. I don't usually feel that guilty on bank holiday Mondays because everybody else is doing nothing as well. But today I felt a nagging sense of slow panic. Only two more bank holiday Mondays to go before my 40th birthday. What have I achieved in my life? Have I done everything I set out to do? Why am I so passive? If they modelled a toy after me they'd name it "In-Action Man". I have come to the conclusion that there were two types of people in this world. 1. Those that are driven. These are people like doctors, lawyers, and company presidents. They've got goals, direction, they know what they want and they go out and get it. The kind of people who at the age of twelve say, "I'm going to be Prime Minister one day!" Or the sort who walk into a bar and see a beautiful woman and announce loudly and dramatically, "That's the woman I'm going to marry!"

2. Those that hitch. These people lurch aimlessly from one thing to another. They muddle through. They don't know what they are doing, where they are going, they just wait for things to happen, wait for something to come along. But most of the time nothing comes along so they sit at home and watch old black and white movies on the television. I'm one of those that hitch. And I watch black and white movies. A great one was on this afternoon.

Sunset Boulevard (1950) 110m. *** D: Billy Wilder. William Holden, Gloria Swanson, Nancy Olsen. A struggling screenwriter becomes the gigolo of a faded silent screen star. Timeless, classic dissection of Hollywood. [G]**

I always presumed it was written by Billy Wilder and his first screen collaborator, Charles Brackett. So imagine my amazement as the opening credits rolled to see a third screenwriter credited, one D.M. Marshman Jnr. Who was D.M. Marshman Jnr. I wondered. What else did he do? I'd never heard of him. I am aware that screenwriters have never had the highest profile in Hollywood, 'on a par with props', as someone once said, but over the years I had become aware of certain names cropping up in the credits of movies from the forties and fifties. D.M. Marshman Jnr. was not one of these names. So I looked him up on the internet. Like Orson Welles after 'Citizen Kane', there was only one way to go for D.M. after 'Sunset Boulevard'. A couple of years later he was one of four writers on a movie called 'Second Chance'.

Second Chance (1953) 81m. * D: Rudolf Mate. Robert Mitchum, Linda Darnell, Jack Palance. Melodramatic plot set in Mexico with Palance hired to kill Mitchum's travelling companion, Darnell. [G]**

Then later that year he was one of six writers credited on a film called 'Taxi'.

Taxi (1953) 77m. ** D Gregory Ratoff. Dan Dailey, Constance Smith, Neva Patterson. Forgettable bit of fluff about an Irish girl who is helped by a New York cabbie to find her husband. [G]

After that, nothing. D.M. Marshman Jnr. just disappeared off the face of the earth. Maybe like Joe Gillis, the William Holden character in 'Sunset Boulevard', D.M., disillusioned with trying to hack it as a screenwriter in Tinseltown, actually did make it back to his own version of Dayton, Ohio. Or maybe he drank himself to death being unable to accept the lot of a lowly screenwriter.

Afterwards though, I felt guilty about watching the movie. I don't have the time to waste, watching something I've already seen seven times. I must do something. Worthwhile. Original. I sat at the desk for ten minutes. Then got up and started to lecture myself in front of the bathroom mirror. I examined myself more closely. I'm getting old. I'm also fat, have mysterious intestinal pains, and erratic circulation in my left foot and arm. I feel tired. I am an inconsequential blob of inertia. Maybe I should go and see the doctor.

Maybe there is something wrong with me? Or maybe its all in the mind and its just psychosomatic. I remembered that ten years ago I had loads of nervous energy. Now all I feel is nervous lethargy. I then noticed some nasal hairs and started removing a tuft of those minuscule follicular elephant tusks with a pair of tweezers.

My day didn't get any better after that. When Kirsten arrived home she suggested we get some shopping done since it's a bank holiday and the supermarket would be empty. We then spent two hours in the near empty supermarket. This is because Kirsten is a very meticulous and very paranoid shopper. She always feels the big supermarkets are out to screw her. And she never enters one unless armed with a calculator and magnifying glass. But before we get to examine the receipt at the checkout we have to pick our items first. And every item that's picked from a shelf must be scrutinised. When is the 'best before date'? Has that can of kidney beans been damaged in transit? Did I select that packet of frozen peas from the bottom of the freezer where it is coldest, or at the top of the pile, where it might already be semi-defrosted?

All this is perfectly admirable. But it takes time. And lots of it. Eventually we got to the checkout. As Kirsten tried to keep an eye on the scanner, I hurriedly put away our goods into our environmentally friendly cloth bags. Then the fun began. The checkout girl had difficulty scanning in the bar code of the specially reduced organic chicken. After a moment she said she'd get one of the girls to get another chicken.

"But that's the chicken I want," Kirsten said. "It's best before next Saturday and it's €8.70! All the other chickens are between €11 and €14 and are best before Wednesday."

She tried to scan in the chicken again, but it still didn't work. A small queue of irritated people looked impatiently at us.

Then Kirsten asked me to go look at the organic chickens again. Maybe she had got her facts wrong. I ran to the chicken section. She hadn't got her facts wrong. All the others were between €11 and €14 and were best before next Wednesday. I ran back. We decided to forego the chicken. Anyway, we had some ciabetta bread, salami and cheese left over from yesterday. The checkout girl continued to scan in the other items. We paid the bill. And were ready to leave. Just one more thing to do. Behind the counter, Kirsten furtively removed her small magnifying glass and calculator and started to manically examine every item on the receipt. Half way down the bill, she encountered a problem.

"It said peppers were 70 cents each on the shelf. They have charged one euro each."

I looked at her dolefully.

"You want me to leave it, don't you," she said accusingly.

Yes. I did want her to leave it. I'm Irish. We don't complain or make a fuss. When we get truly appalling food in a restaurant, and the waiter collects the plates and asks,

"Was the meal to your satisfaction, sir?"— we nod and say "Yes, it was lovely, thank you."

"But it's the principle," she continued. "They are always trying to rip you off!"

I sighed and she went back to the checkout girl.

"Excuse me, the red peppers are priced at 70 cents on the shelf, but you've charged me one euro."

"Well, that's what came up when I scanned it," the checkout girl replied.

"Well, that's not good enough. I would like to see the manager," Kirsten proclaimed.

The checkout girl got up and walked over to a suited nonentity with a moustache. He approached us. Kirsten explained her position.

"Well, they have gone up in the last week, we just haven't got around to adjusting the price label," he explained weakly.

Kirsten adopted a haughty tone. "Well, that's not my problem. I would not have purchased these peppers here if I knew they were a euro each."

The manager nodded his head contritely.

"O.k., we'll give you the peppers for the old price," he said, backing down.

He conferred with the checkout girl and agreed to give Kirsten thirty cents off each pepper.

Kirsten was triumphant. Another tiny battle had been won.

June 14th 161 days to go

The snoring problem has been cleared up. For now. Kirsten read about a possible solution in a magazine. And I reluctantly agreed to embark on said course of action. Every night, to ensure I don't lie on my back, I sleep with a freshly cleaned rucksack on in bed.

June 16th 159 days to go

James Joyce is Ireland's Mickey Mouse and Bloomsday is a Disneyland for academics. Like Leopold Bloom, I too knew a girl called Molly. Molly Prendergast. She wasn't one for intense passion-filled monologues, but at the time I was crazy about her. She was in my year in college and studied Arts.

A Glimpse Of Molly (1984) 71m. * D: Ulu Grosbard. Manus Mannion, Molly Prendergast. A bored college student loves from afar. Slow yet truthful slice of life drama. A low-key hybrid of 'Paper Chase' and 'Death in Venice'. [G]**

And I would get up early in the morning to be outside the Arts and Commerce library in college, just to catch a glimpse of her. It would be exam time in June. And there would be 300 students standing outside that library, trying to get in, to do some last minute study, and I'd see her and I'd be overwhelmed, and I'd jump inside my skin, and she'd be standing there waiting for that door to open, folders clutched defensively over her ample bosom, and I'd follow her up the stairs, and once inside the library, I'd position myself strategically at a desk close to her, but not too close, and during the day I would observe her now and again, sneezing, diligently revising some lecture notes, or sharing a joke with a passing friend.

Then once in a while, I'd look over but she'd be gone. I'd immediately get up. Seek her out. Be a low-key stalker. Discreet. In the off-chance she might bump into me in the corridor. In the off-chance she might smile at me. A smile that would make my day. Make my life. A smile that would fill me with a sublime delirium, a walking-on-air feeling, a smile that would make every recreational drug known to man completely redundant.

Suddenly, I'd see her rushing down the stairs, with some recently photocopied materials from the upstairs library. Time would stand still as I'd gruffly say hello. She'd look at me, smile softly and say hello back.

Ready to collapse, I'd suffer a kind of heart attack, without the ensuing medical complications, as she'd pass me by. I'd be unable to work for the rest of the day. I would be too euphoric. I would sit in the student canteen and talk pretentious parochial prattle with my friends from Dramsoc., but in the back of my mind I would be thinking, she noticed me. She smiled at me. This would go on for months. Exams would come. Exams would go. Exams would be failed. Exams would be repeated. But I'd just keep getting up early to wait outside that Arts and Commerce library hoping to catch that glimpse of Molly. And then it would be time for the January semesters and there would still be 300 students standing outside the library, trying to get in, and the doors would open, and again I'd see her, and I'd be overwhelmed, jump inside my skin, and I'd follow her up the stairs but wouldn't be quick enough in the stampede, to position myself strategically close to her.

She'd end up over the other side of the library, by the window, the sun shining down on her, a Madonna in a purple beret, and I'd be stuck in one of those cramped booth-like seats next to the International Economics Section. The kind of seats you always had to mind, and every time you got up for a break, you had to leave an 'I'll be back in ten minutes' note, or some scruffy Philosophy student who'd slept in late, would set your books aside and take your place.

Molly was in the Mountaineering Society. Not being naturally athletic, I still decided to join the Society as a declaration of my undying love for her. I hassled father to help get me a discount on a pair of mountain boots from Logue's shoe shop, and mother reluctantly bought me some of the latest rainproof climbing gear. I was going to become a climber without peer, would conquer any challenging peak and make my Molly bloom.

It was a Saturday morning. We were all meant to meet outside the Aula Maxima in our gear at seven thirty and Jimmy in the van would pick us up to scale a mountain next to Maam Cross in Connemara. I was rigid with the cold and felt a nauseating fear coupled with a certain thrilling sense of expectation. I had arrived early. It was seven twenty and still almost dark. I looked around. Four people had turned up. There was no sign of Molly. My sense of worried excitement increased. She'll turn up any minute, I thought, I might get to sit next to her in the back of the van, we might get to talk, it might turn out that we have similar interests. Boogie Woogie Piano players of the

1940's, Shelly Berman, and the complete filmography of Dan Duryea.

Dan Duryea (1907-1968) – "Lanky, whiny voiced American tough guy character actor of the 1940's and 1950's."

The time crawled by. It was now seven thirty-three. Six people had turned up. No sign of Molly. My nerves were on a knife edge. Half of me desperately wanted her to turn up, yet the other half was secretly hoping she wouldn't turn up, for I was so tense and frazzled at this stage I would probably be incoherent should we happen to break into that conversation about the unique stride piano playing style of Meade Lux Lewis. It was seven forty-one. Jimmy in the van arrived. We trooped on. Still no sign of Molly.

"Where's Molly?" I inquired weakly.

"Oh, she's gone home for the weekend," Sporty Aengus replied.

I spent much of the ensuing journey cursing under my breath like some apprentice Tourette's syndrome sufferer. On our arrival in Connemara, we immediately began our ascent. The rain lashed down over Maam Cross. Out of my depth and in fear of my life, I clasped to greasy rocks and grassy hillocks and held on tightly to various ropes.

I also experienced the ignominy, in mid-afternoon, of Sporty Aengus having to catch me, to break a fall. I caught a severe cold that day. Near pneumonia. I was ordered to bed by the doctor. A week later the Mountaineering Society were going down to Dingle. I was told Molly was looking forward to it. They'd be staying overnight in a hotel. They'd probably have a few drinks, inhibitions would be lowered, mountain boots would be cast aside, and before you could say "Kilimanjaro", Sporty Aengus would be defiling my Molly. I could not let that happen.

Still recuperating, I would get out of my sickbed and go to Kerry.

"Where are you going?" mother asked as I got up early for breakfast that Saturday morning in my climbing gear.

"I'm going to Kerry to climb a mountain!" I announced.

"You are not, you are staying in bed," she insisted.

"I'll be fine," I said.

Mother turned to father.

"Eddie, say something," she said.

"Don't be looking at me, I stopped understanding that fella years ago," he said wearily.

I was outside the Aula Maxima. It was seven forty-one. Jimmy in the van turned up. As I stepped into the back I inquired weakly, "Where's Molly?"

"Oh, she was offered a lift late last night. She's gone home for the weekend," Sporty Aengus replied.

June 24th 151 days to go

Finally sent off the re-written draft of 'The Shamrock Sumo Club' to Ben. However I'm still trying to contact Sarah. Sometimes I think that being a freelance writer is 10% inspiration and 90% waiting for people to return your calls and give you feedback. This has been going on for weeks. I keep leaving messages and writing emails and she just never replies.

Then after lunch the phone rang. I thought, at last, it might be Sarah. It wasn't. It was Dinny Bruce of all people. A name from the past. My London past. My comedy past. We used to do gigs together. He's moved back to Dublin and wants to meet up and discuss an idea he has for a radio sit-com. I've reluctantly agreed to meet up at some stage.

For many, Dinny Bruce is considered 'the step uncle of Irish comedy'. During the 1970's, in dull, grey risk-free Ireland, he used to bill himself as Ireland's answer to Lenny Bruce. Dinny wasn't exactly funny ha-ha, he was more funny peculiar, or as some critics remarked unkindly, funny unfunny. He would come on stage dressed as a farmer wearing big wellington boots, smoke incessantly and go on for hours about the problems he was having with 'the pigs'. A minority would laugh. Most would scratch their heads. Some would heckle. Dinny hated being heckled. He took it personally. And during his years in London, if he'd been heckled, after a gig he'd go up to the heckler and pretend to be friendly and forgiving and try to gleam information from the heckler about their own life.

Then the week after the gig Dinny would secretly stalk the heckler and find out his place of work. He would acquire the proper work clothes to blend in with this environment, and picking his moment, would unleash a torrent of abuse at the heckler, in the heckler's work place. He was reported many times but a judge finally threw the book at him in 1996 after an incident in an operating theatre when Dinny started verbally abusing a brain surgeon during the middle of a delicate procedure. The judge sentenced Dinny to three months in Wandsworth prison. Dinny's phone call brought back my time in London vividly. I looked up some old journals to relive the experience of being a Comedy Nobody.

Diary of a Comedy Nobody:
Wednesday February 8th,1995.
The gig last night in The Tee Hee Club in Ilford started

off quite well. I seemed to lose them though after "Hello, my name is Manus Mannion." Silence filled the air. Except for those few people at the bar. They seemed to like it and made some noise, although I was told later they were just watching some football match on the television. Have started the alarming tendency to heckle myself in the middle of my act. Must desist from this as it confuses the audience. Afterwards the venue owner, Graham told me he didn't think much of my act and grudgingly handed over the £30.

Friday June 23rd, 1995.

Good news! The Derek Osborne Agency or as they have recently renamed themselves, D.O.A., have taken me on. I'm not too crazy about that new company name and his is not one of the A list agencies, but at least it is a start.

Thursday October 26th 1995.

Had a dreadful gig last night in the Bound & Gagged Club. A strange looking guy mumbled something near the front of the stage during the middle of my routine and, after some deliberation, I looked at him and replied, "Isn't it awful when cousins marry." There was a small laugh from the audience, followed by an awkward pause. He then replied lowly, "Yes it is." A hushed silence descended the club as he went on to explain that he was in fact the product of continued consanguinity within his family over many generations, and that it wasn't his fault he looked deformed. He then started to whimper in a sensitive manner and was comforted by his friends.

Monday November 20th 1995.

Last night was rather disappointing. When Derek mentioned he was going to take me to dinner and "introduce me to a few people", I thought he was talking about people in the industry, script editors, or television executives for example. Not his sister and brother-in-law. Although they are very pleasant people. His brother-in-law manufactures garden gnomes.

Tuesday March 12th 1996.

A very poor gig last night, this time in Balham. Another Irish comedian was on before me, Dinny Bruce. That is a killer for any Irish act on the London circuit. Because he is going to cover much the same areas as you are going to cover. Afterwards, feeling sorry for me, Dinny bought me a drink and we got chatting. He's been on the circuit here for 8 years. He started off back in Ireland in the late seventies as 'Ireland's answer to Lenny Bruce'. He subsequently changed that persona and in the early eighties became 'Dinny Bruce — Ireland's only home based anti-Irish comedian'. But he still didn't get that many gigs in Ireland, and the gigs he did get would end in pandemonium and him being often physically assaulted. Eventually, figuring there was a bigger demand for anti-Irish stuff in the U.K., Dinny moved here in 1987. But by that stage anti-Irish stuff had become politically incorrect, so he had to re-invent himself again. He became highly politicised and wrote a very tight fifteen minute routine on the evils of Margaret Thatcher. A week after storming the Comedy Store with his new persona, Thatcher resigned, and within six months, hard-hitting political stand-up comedy was out of fashion. Five years later, he's still trying to find a new angle, and a persona he's happy with. At the moment, bizarrely, he's experimenting with wearing a black eye patch on stage. After our chat together he invited a few hecklers to our table, told them there were no hard feelings and offered to buy them a round of drinks. He then asked them what they did for a living.

June 26th 149 days to go

Sarah eventually called back to say she likes the new version of 'Spud Zombie' and will submit it to the Film Council. She apologised for not getting back sooner and said something like 'Oh, we kept missing each other'. Afterwards I thought to myself, no, we didn't keep missing each other. I kept leaving messages and you never returned my calls. That's not 'missing each other'. That's 'you not returning my calls'. Missing each other is I ringing you and leaving a message and then you ringing me back and leaving a message and then I ringing you again and leaving a message. The gall of these producers. Parasites in plush offices. I hate every one of them.

June 27th 148 days to go

At four thirty last night, Kirsten woke up and feeling very amorous suggested we make love. Though feeling groggy, I was quite partial to the idea. Afterwards, in a post-coital haze, I realised it was the first time I'd ever had sex with a rucksack on my back.

July 3rd 142 days to go

I am in Liechtenstein — a very big word for a very small place — with Kirsten. Visiting her parents, Otto and Babsie in its largest city, Schaan. Liechtenstein is a principality — another big word, located in the Alps, somewhere between Switzerland and Austria.

I sometimes joke with Kirsten that if Ireland ever became a coloniser, and with our new-found economic confidence and wealth, maybe it is time we started invading other places, Liechtenstein would be an ideal place to start.

The whole military campaign wouldn't demand too much preparation and planning, and even if things did go wrong, we would still occupy it in an afternoon before moving onto the Faroe Islands, Andorra and San Marino. Then we would have our own little empire. Granted, huge swathes of the world map would remain completely unchanged by our conquering exploits, but it would be a start and something to build on. Liechtenstein's terrain is mountainous, and is peppered with small farms and cultivated fields. Its cuisine is very *mittel* European and being originally part of the German confederation until 1866, their inhabitants still speak German.

Therefore, my communication with Kirsten's parents is, in its own way, as fraught as communication with my own parents. But at least there is a tangible reason for this. We do not speak each other's language. This is a problem. Otto, particularly, is very disappointed I still don't speak any German after eleven years living with his daughter. If truth be told, I have picked up the odd word of German, over the years. 1. 'Computer' —computer. 2. 'Elefant' — elephant. 3. 'Die Müllabfuhr kommt Dienstag Morgen' — The bin-men come Tuesday morning. But I know, in my heart and soul, it's just not good enough. How many conversations, realistically, am I going to have with Otto about elephants who have mastered the internet putting out the rubbish, over the course of the next ten days?

My favourite German word though is Geschlechtsverkehr - the German word for sexual intercourse which when directly translated becomes - wait for it - 'traffic jam of the genitals'. Needless to say the German language has never been renowned for its erotic literature.

Babsie, Kirsten's mother, is a hygienic fiend. One can't enter their apartment without having to take off one's shoes and having to put on one's 'Hausschuhe'. 'Hausschuhe' is the German word for slippers and during some earlier visits there, I sometimes neglected to take off my shoes immediately whilst entering their apartment. This was frowned upon. I tried explaining to Kirsten later, that in Ireland, the wearing of slippers in the house was always considered an optional afterthought. She quickly explained to me that in Liechtenstein the wearing of 'Hausschuhe' is most definitely mandatory. I replied that I still couldn't understand the seriousness with which this edict is implemented. She told me cultures are different. Countries are different. People are different. It is what makes the world interesting.

She then went on to tell me that there is a lot she still can't fathom about the Irish. For example, she still doesn't understand Irish people who, on a sunny day, drive to the beach, stay in their car, stare out at the sea and then just fall asleep. Or why the Irish never rinse off the suds when washing the dishes. Or how can they eat these things called 'cream crackers'? Point taken, I silently conceded.

Babsie has an inbuilt radar system to detect 'Hundescheiße', the German word for dogshit, when walking down the street. Almost like Auntie Philomena's awareness of churches on the bus. Sometimes when we are all ensconced in a rivetting conversation, well, when *they* are all ensconced in a rivetting conversation, I am just nodding enthusiastically whilst not having a clue what is being said, Babsie suddenly shouts 'Hundescheiße', and in the nick of time prevents Otto from stepping on some.

The first time I went into Otto and Babsie's bathroom, I had a complete panic attack. I was washing my hands, thoroughly, after making sure I had put the toilet seat down, having become convinced Babsie was outside the bathroom door, monitoring me, when I spotted a hairdryer connected to one of two electrical sockets in the corner of the wall, a few feet from the sink. Electrical sockets in a bath-room! Water and electricity, together! Coming from my part of the world that meant just one thing: Sudden electrocution and instant death. Hyperventilating madly, I manically turned off the taps.

As I tried to re-compose myself, I gradually realised, I was still alive and hundreds of volts of electricity hadn't actually pumped through me. I then noticed the small semi-removable lids attached to the front of the electrical sockets. This meant, if you wanted to use an appliance, all you had to do was pull up the lid slightly, and insert your plug. When you removed the plug of your appliance, the lid would naturally cover the plug holes again. So this is an example of a certain European practicality, that is absent in the Republic of Ireland, I mused.

I have experienced other cases of this practicality over time. By way of illustration, let us examine the different ways a person from Liechtenstein and a person from

Ireland peel an orange. When analysing this, one must seriously question, whether the Irish, as a race, have reached the Liechtensteiner level on the evolutionary scale. Liechtensteiner Methodology: The Liechtensteiner looks at the orange. He or she then takes a sharp knife, runs it down the exterior of the orange, making eight quick incisions. Then, the peel is quickly and easily removed in sections. The complete operation takes twenty seconds. Irish Methodology: The Irish person looks at the orange. He or she then looks at their thumbs. These thumbs are suddenly plunged into the exterior of the orange and some frenzied thumb burrowing proceeds. Small bits of peel are discarded willy-nilly, unwanted orange juice spurts upwards and the complete operation can take anything up to three minutes.

There are other differences between Liechtenstein and Ireland. For example dealing with inclement weather. In Liechtenstein when it rains, the Liechtensteiner looks up, calmly accepts it is raining, and removes his umbrella from his garishly coloured rucksack. In Ireland when it rains, the Irish person looks up and curses at the skies. He then sighs, shakes his head and continues to curse. He eventually hunches his shoulders, yanks at the back of his collar and hurriedly walks down the street in a quasi-Quasimodo like manner.

Or the situation at traffic lights. In Ireland, at a pedestrian crossing, if there is a 'red man' signalled to the pedestrian, but there is no traffic on the road, the pedestrian will cross anyway. In Liechtenstein, at a pedestrian crossing, and believe it or not there are one or two, if there is a 'red man' signalled to the pedestrian and there is no traffic on the road the pedestrian will wait. And wait. Under no circumstances does he or she motion in a forward manner until the 'green man' is signalled.

The above are just a few of the differences I have noticed over the years in my silent study of Inter-cultural Hiberno-Liechtensteiner relations. It is the type of topic I could discuss with Otto, if my German was, in any way, functional. Sadly it isn't. And as the time passes, I have felt Otto's increasing desperation in wanting to communicate with me, his prospective son-in-law. I particularly dread when Kirsten has to leave me alone in the living room with her father, when for example, she has to help her mother in the kitchen.

It happened again this morning after breakfast. The moments crawled by as we attempted basic conversation. Otto pointed out the window. "Schönes Wetter," he said referring to the nice day. "Ja," I barked, unintentionally mimicking the villains in one of those post-war P.O.W. movies. There was a pause. We both sighed. I hid behind my atlas. I only ever resurrect the atlas in emergency situations. And this was an emergency situation. I contemplated roaring out Kirsten's name but noticed she was still busy in the kitchen with Babsie meticulously re-washing those eggs.

Tonight was worse. We were in a bar having a few drinks. Throughout the evening, Otto, who can knock back his drink, was becoming more animated and desperately trying to connect with me. After my third Pils, though, I badly needed to go to the toilet. I got up quickly. After eventually finding the Gents, I hurriedly entered. Both cubicles were occupied, so reluctantly I went over to the urinal, unzipped my fly and started to pee.

Suddenly, the door opened behind me. Of all the males out there, in that crowded bar, who was the only one who had to relieve himself? Otto. I had another sphincter tightening moment. Of all the sphincter tightening moments in my life this was the most sphincter tightening. He walked towards me. I thought, Otto, it's quite a spacious urinal, you don't have to come this close.

He stopped, standing right next to me. Maybe he was trying to bond with me in some primal way, the way men, when peeing together sometimes bond. Allegedly. Or maybe he was trying to humiliate me. All six foot four inches of him. He unzipped his fly. He took out Wilhelm. Wilhelm, who helped create my girlfriend, was peeing next to Bob, who makes love to my girlfriend. Wilhelm and Bob. Wilhelm, from proud Prussian stock, standing erect, surveying all around him. Bob becoming intimidated, and unable to take the pressure, contracting to the size of a chick pea.

Otto started to urinate. He was a 'look ma, no hands' man. ('A look ma, no hands' man is a gentleman who unzips his fly, removes his member, places both his hands on his hips and urinates confidently.) Otto again tried to start a conversation. "Schöne Fliesen," he said. He pointed to the tiling. I nodded in embarrassment. There is one thing worse than two guys who speak the same language having a strained conversation whilst urinating, and that is two guys who don't speak the same language having a strained conversation whilst urinating.

July 5th 140 days to go

Still in Liechtenstein. We went for a drive this morning. We were home within half an hour. That got me thinking that Liechtenstein would not be a great place to film a road movie because the protagonists would arrive at their destination too soon. If they filmed 'Easy Rider' in

Lichtenstein, it would have been an eight-minute movie. Later on I was walking around town with Kirsten, when we bumped into an old boyfriend of hers, Udo. They went out together for a few years in the late 1980's. During a tense chat they cracked some joke about 'Vorspiel' and he went on his way.

Afterwards, I asked her what 'Vorspiel' was. She told me it was 'Foreplay'. And said it was the reason they broke up. Over a Weißbier she elaborated further. Like a substantial amount of men and women, herself and Udo, disagreed on the time they should spend on foreplay. She liked twenty minutes. Udo, was more inclined towards twenty seconds. As a man, I could understand this difference in perspective. But I kept this observation to myself. According to Kirsten, Udo had this theory. Sex was a train journey between Vienna and Paris. The trouble is, when the actual act begins, the man is already in Strasbourg whilst the woman is still queuing for her train ticket in Vienna. It is nature's big joke. Men and women are completely unsuited for each other, sexually. A woman needs time. A man needs relief. But most couples try to come to some arrangement. Udo was different. He kept a 'Vorspiel Akte'. A Foreplay File. Udo's Foreplay File was a source of deep disharmony between them. An Anglophile, he one day consulted the Oxford Concise Dictionary, where it stated — Foreplay is sexual activity that precedes intercourse. Udo thought, but define sexual activity? Is holding hands sexual activity? If you are lovers, I believe, it is. In fact every time lovers touch, I firmly believe that to be sexual activity. So each time period between sexual encounters, with his stop watch in tow, Udo with a certain Liechtensteiner Teutonic precision recorded each instance that himself and Kirsten happened to touch, in any way. He then made a note of it in his Foreplay File.

Then when they were about to make love, he produced his Foreplay File from the side of the bed, and read out the foreplay that, in his opinion, had occurred over the previous interlude. I imagined what the list might include. Possible things like, 'Held Kirsten's hand whilst walking through town on Saturday — 3 minutes, 10 seconds' or 'My knee leant against Kirsten's during that repeat episode of 'Heimat' on T.V, while sitting on the couch on Sunday night — 4 minutes, seven seconds', or 'Touched her elbow while handing her the shopping bag containing the bottled water, ciabetta bread, cheese and salami on Wednesday evening — 3 seconds.' Udo would then calculate the overall time of these exchanges, maybe 7 minutes 20 seconds, and then ask it to be deducted from the requested 20 minutes time slot allotted for foreplay. Naturally Kirsten would complain vociferously and contest each of Udo's Foreplay File entries.

This caused enormous strain in their relationship. In fact, one could almost say if it wasn't for that Foreplay File, I might never have met Kirsten because, in early 1991, she jumped at the opportunity of that job offer from Siemens in Dublin and, less than six months later, she met me on that fateful day in Eason's. And as they say, the rest is history.

July 9th 136 days to go

Had an idle morning. Felt an inner turbulence. I seem to have entered a cul-de-sac of creative pointlessness. Both of the film scripts are now with the Film Council, so I am 'between projects' as I await their verdict. Got myself into quite a state examining the permutations of the situation. Everything is so random. Which Film Council reader will I get? Say if the Film Council reader has a bad hangover the day he reads either of my proposals. And who are these readers anyway?

Frustrated screen-writers themselves, who have ended up 'teaching film' on substandard 'film courses', or writing self-indulgent precious articles for the odd Film Quarterly. In other words, embittered Creative Lower Beings like myself. Maybe one of the readers had a film script idea himself years ago, which never got produced. So he is loath to recommend any project of mine for development money because when he was young and he had dreams nobody ever gave him development money for his ideas!

Somebody like *this* decides if I have an income for the next year? Or maybe there is a similar idea already in the system. So many imponderables. I felt manic. I took my allowed four drops of Bach's Rescue Remedy. To take my mind off things further, I decided to do something I hadn't done in years. I decided I was going to put the stereo on very loudly and sing along to music.

Firstly, I checked if the next door neighbours' cars were there. They weren't. I picked out an Otis Redding C.D., pressed 'Play', and started moaning and shrieking at full volume to that sweet soul music. Then the door bell rang. I quickly shut up and hid. It rang again. The music continued to blare.

Then a note was dropped in the letter box. The neighbour across the road was informing us about a Residents' Association Meeting. I peered out the window. Was she smirking as she walked away. Did she hear my singing? Did she query how many other 39-year-olds in the Dublin 8 region sing along to 1960's soul tracks in the middle of the day? I felt acutely embarrassed. I turned down the music. The spell had been broken. I thought back on all those other times people have spoiled my crazed musical renditions. It happened regularly in the mid-80's, the year after I left college.

I got my Bachelor's of Commerce degree in 1984. For a few months afterwards, not knowing what to do, and being scared of the future, I just hung around the house. I felt completely isolated. Gerry and Lorraine had gone to the States. I'd no money. No girlfriend. No dress-sense. No idea. I spent my time hiding in the garage rereading old Beano comics or watching black and white movies in the living room, early afternoon, with the Venetian blinds drawn.

These movies always seemed to be from 1938 and starring Alice Faye.

Alice Faye (1912-1998) "Born Ann Leppert. Perky, Blonde American singing star of countless musicals from the 1930's and early 1940's. Retired early."

While watching the movies I always had my 'Halliwell's Filmgoer's Companion' at the ready as the credits rolled, so I could look up some of the more obscure actors in the cast list and see if they were still alive or what year they had died. Some actress born in 1918, who played the pert secretary would have died in 1949. A male cast member, who played the hero's loudmouth sidekick, born in 1898 would still be alive. This would seriously trouble me. What determines all this, I'd wonder? Why did she die at 31 and he's still alive at 87. Who decides? God? Or is just a case of anything can happen anyone at any time.

I was withdrawing from life. This concerned mother. Most days, she'd try motivating me into getting my life in order through the delicate Art of Incessant Nagging. She'd start comparing my situation with that of my next-door neighbour and contemporary, Noel Flynn.

"Look at Noel Flynn. Was in the same class as you in school, same year in college. I pick up 'The Connacht Sentinel' last week, and there he is in it, having won a scholarship to the Harvard Business School! And what do you do? Sit on your arse all day, doing nothing!"

I'd turn the tables on her.

"O.k., but what about Noel Flynn's mother? She runs her own highly successful suntan studio in town. And what do you do? Sit on your arse all day, nagging me!"

"How dare you use that kind of language with me," she'd say deeply offended. And then, in a tone of exasperated disappointment, would always finish with, "I don't know where we got you from at all!"

I'd leave the house in a huff. Think things over. After all, she and father had said as long as I got my degree I could do anything I wanted. And I was doing what I wanted. Nothing. These days were always the same. Dark, wet, and windy. I'd walk around the shops, aimlessly, pointlessly, killing days, killing time. I'd head home by four. That's when mother would be out shopping. Then for half an hour each day, before either parent returned, and before Colm got back from first year in college, I could put a record on in the dining room and loudly incorporate additional vocals.

Manus Boy (1985) 43m. ** D: Les Blank. Manus Mannion, Cora Mannion. A Galwegian nerd annoys his parents by continually singing along loudly to his favourite blues man, Muddy Waters [G].**

By this time, I'd developed a passion for the blues, which I believed perfectly complemented my love of humour because Comedy and the Blues, like Sinn Fein and the I.R.A., are two sides of the same coin.

Each week I'd listen avidly to 'The House of R n'B', presented by County Clare's answer to Dewey Philips, P.J. Curtis. I learned that the blues is an emptiness you can never lose. You have a hole in your soul if you can't feel those blues. There's a rawness to those blues, there's a purity to those blues, there's a clarity to those blues but there ain't no charity to those blues. Because there ain't nothing leaner, there ain't nothing cleaner, and there ain't nothing meaner than those low-down dirty blues. With the music blaring, I would suddenly try to become Muddy Waters. I'd try and achieve complete abandon as I'd growl along to Muddy's 'Hoochie Coochie Man'.

'Gypsy woman told my mother, before I was born'... But I could never relax. What happens if mother comes home early? That gypsy woman would have told my mother! So I'd position myself in the living room at the front of the house. 'Got a boy child coming, gonna be a son of a gun', screaming along to that driving blues beat, 'Gonna make pretty women, jump and shout, then the world gonna know, what this is all about'... but all the time looking out the window, keeping an eye out for returning cars or unwelcome visitors, 'Cos, I'm here, everybody knows I'm here', sometimes mother's car would pull up. By the time she got out she would be able to hear the 'racket' coming from the house. 'Cos I'm the Hoochie Coochie Man', I'd stop in mid-song and swiftly run back into the dining room and turn down the stereo. But if I got carried away, there could be a problem. I wouldn't hear people returning and father would come in and roar "Turn that flippin' thing down, jays, you've us all driven daft!"

All this added to the tension at home. Mother's nagging continued. She got on to father to get on to me. His attitude was "Arey, sure, we've brought him up the best we can. If he wants to mess up his life, that's his decision." Then he'd retire to his car in the garage, turn on BBC Radio 3, light his pipe and read his newspaper. Getting little support from her husband, sometimes mother would change tack in her approach and do that particular Irish thing of comparing one's own children with their first cousins.

"I see your cousin Alex has got that new job in Canada with IBM."

"Yeh?" I'd say in an uninterested fashion, eating my Shredded Wheat.

"Your cousin Patricia's doing very well in Melbourne with AIB."

"Really?"

"Look at Niall in Munich with Ciba Geigy."

"Yeh, but what about Eamonn? You never mention him, do you?" I would say starting to laugh demonically. She would just stare at me icily.

I loved cousin Eamonn. Compared to him I was a fully formed, mature young member of society. His mere existence got me off the hook so many times, I'll be forever grateful to him. Cousin Eamonn. He was that little bit odd. Different. Strange. Members of our extended family always referred to him in hushed, slightly anxious, compassionate tones. I remember him vividly in earlier years. He had horn-rimmed glasses, hair that always seemed to be greasy and he tended to blush a lot out of context. At one stage I felt a certain empathy with his outsider status but ultimately he was even too idiosyncratic for me. As he grew older he started to develop some obsessive compulsive behavioural abnormalities.

For example, he hated having to shake the hands of people. Our family only found out about this one week at mass. It was a sunny Sunday in May 1977. Father and mother were both dressed up and felt that perplexing adrenalin rush they both seemed to experience at that time from going to mass.

Myself and Colm just tagged along. The church was full. People coughed, babies cried, and a misguided spiritual expectation hung in the air. To our surprise we spotted cousin Eamonn sitting nervously in the seat in front of us. Growing up, cousin Eamonn hated that bit in the mass where the priest said, "You may offer each other the Sign of Peace." Like myself. But whereas each week I closed my eyes, scrunched up my face, stuck out my hand and endured it, Eamonn, throughout his adolescence, got up very early most weeks and went to seven o'clock mass. This way he could have a pew to himself and no one would bother him with their self-conscious entreaties.

Not this particular Sunday, however. He had slept in. The service began. Eamonn waited anxiously. Fr. Toher droned on and on. Arrived at the first reading. One of St. Paul's letters to the Corinthians. I started to daydream. I wondered did any of the Corinthians ever write back to Paul? And if not, why not. One never hears about the Corinthians' letter to Paul. It's always Paul's letter to the Corinthians. You think just once one of them would have written back. I mean it's not very polite never to respond. Maybe they considered Paul a bit of a crank. He spent all his time writing to them, yet they never replied. Maybe they were hoping that he might just stop writing one day. And go away. And leave them alone. Forever. Yet he kept badgering them with more of his lofty missives. I then figured Paul must have had dreadful writers' cramp with all those letters to the Corinthians because when he wasn't writing to the Corinthians he was scribbling off stuff to the Galatians, and the Ephesians and the Thessalonians too.

As Fr. Toher reached the sermon, I noticed Eamonn nervously removing his jumper. Ten minutes later Fr. Toher had arrived at the consecration. As 'take this all of you and eat it' was monotonously delivered, Eamonn wiped his brow and took a tense breath. I wondered what was wrong. For non-experts of the liturgy, the Sign of Peace bit comes very shortly after the 'Our Father'. Fr. Toher swiftly passed that benchmark.

Eamonn was aware we were now approaching the critical section as Fr. Toher rambled on monotonously. "Lord Jesus you said to your apostles, I leave you peace, my peace I give you. Look not on our sins but on the faith of your church and grant us the peace and unity of our kingdom where you live forever and ever. Amen." There was a beat. Then, Fr. Toher finally announced. "You may offer each other the Sign Of Peace." There was that initial pause, some of the parishioners shuffling and staring at the ground, others slightly embarrassed and smiling awkwardly as they tentatively offered each other their hand in friendship.

Eamonn didn't react and avoided all eye contact. The moment seemed to have passed. He felt relieved. He'd escaped potential torment. But unfortunately he hadn't noticed his uncle Eddie was behind him. Father was unlike most parishioners, and strangely for a man of his character, became particularly expansive and enthusiastic during the Sign of Peace bit, and shook as many hands as possible during the time allotted. He caught Eamonn in his sights, tapped him on the back, and as Eamonn turned round in horror, father smiled in recognition. Eamonn blushed. Father then stuck his hand out firmly under Eamonn's nose and said with loud conviction, "Peace be with you!" Eamonn started to sweat. As he raised his hand, involuntary spasms ran through his body. Father moved his hands towards Eamonn's. Overcome with panic, Eamonn suddenly punched father in the face. Father fell backwards, his nose starting to bleed profusely. Some of the other parishioners stared at Eamonn and shrieked in bafflement. Eamonn just took his seat, stared on ahead and started to sway gently. From that day on, cousin Eamonn was a touchy subject in our household.

July 17th 128 days to go

This day 18 years ago I left home and moved to Dublin. It was six months after I got my degree. I had applied for an AnCO Course. Well, mother had applied, on my behalf. It was a course in Executive Development. I would learn how to develop as a potential business executive. Filled with a sense of inevitability and fatalism, I went on a day trip to Dublin for the interview in Middle Abbey Street.

With much prodding from my parents, I had laboured to turn a new leaf and become a new me. Mother had even bought me a manual on how to succeed in interviews. The 165-page book could be summed up as follows: Be articulate. Be confident. Be assertive at all times. Deport yourself properly and dress well. If you look good, you'll feel good. Listen intently and appear interested. Do not avoid eye contact when asked a question and turn up on time. I was grateful for the book because I figured if I did the exact opposite of what I was advised to do, I wouldn't be selected.

However, it didn't work out like that. Despite slouching in late, mumbling all my replies and staring at my shoes for the whole interview, I got the placement. That meant

I would be moving out. Mother could hardly contain her tears. Of joy.

The Executive Development course was slated to start in mid-July. I finally would be leaving home. Maybe that would be a good thing. Firstly, I'd have some money in my pocket as I would be getting paid for this course. Secondly, I'd see some of the world. Okay — not the world — just the grimy capital city of a small insignificant koala bear-shaped island off the coast of mainland Europe. But at least it would be a start. My parents drove me up to my auntie Ellie and uncle Clem's house in Glasnevin. I planned to stay with them for my first few weeks in Dublin while I settled in and tried to find a flat of my own.

The Executive Development course was based in Leeson Street. Each morning for six weeks Fergus and Brian from a company called Dynamic Synergy Incorporated taught fourteen of us how to draw graphs, discuss investment, devise strategies, be competitive, impose benchmarks, and achieve our goals. It was an invigoratingly pointless experience. Apart from meeting Caroline. At this stage I was still incapable of reading signals from women. I was never sure if they liked me or not.

But with Caroline, all this changed. She had blue eyes, blonde hair and always wore little brown booties and a leopard-skin coat and had the most divine sensuous, husky voice. We were instantly attracted to each other. And this time, I knew it was for real.

What caused this attraction? The explanation was very simple. I'd read it in some book. Pheromones. Pheromones are subtle odours that are emitted by us, which influence our choice in partners. And over the years results from various scientific tests indicate that we can identify which people have more robust genes to our own, simply by smell. And when we identify these partners we subconsciously are attracted to them, for bonding with someone who has stronger genes than us makes our potential offspring sturdier. So, at the end of the day, it is all down to pheromones.

The first time I met Caroline, that first day of our course, she was instantly drawn to me. I was drawn to her. And I could see how she could make my offspring sturdier. She was ambitious, confident, and knew where she was going. She also had a car. An old blue Morris Minor. We'd make love in it, up the Dublin mountains. It was a whirlwind romance. She wanted to move out of home. I wanted to move out of auntie Ellie and uncle Clem's. We decided to move in together without telling either set of parents. We paid a deposit on a cosy flat on Beechwood Avenue in Ranelagh. We were all set to move our stuff in. It was perfect. The course would finish, I'd have saved a bit of money, I'd have a tenacious girlfriend, a flat, I'd be set up, could go on the dole, decide what I really wanted to do with my life. Then one night, a few weeks later, we were in her car up near Rockmount and she told me she wasn't attracted to me anymore. I was shocked.

"What's wrong?" I asked.

She told me she had realised this on the same day that her hay fever had cleared up.

"Hay fever?" I queried.

"Yes," she said. "I got it later than usual this year."

I had noticed her voice had gradually become less husky, but I hadn't paid much attention to that. Now, the potential gravity of the situation began to dawn on me. In a clinical scientific way it all began to make total sense. Her sense of smell had been all askew on the day we'd met. We should never have got together. From her perspective. And when I thought about it more, I wondered, realistically, what genes did I have to offer her, that could have made our offspring sturdier. An inability to go out for a meal 'on the spur of the moment'?

She said it had been a terrible mistake. She told me bluntly, as she inhaled some nasal spray, that she was now secretly repulsed by my pheromones. She then announced that one of her friends would move in with her to the new flat, for the time being. She paid me back my half of the deposit. Heartbroken, I now had to find alternative accommodation.

I scoured the 'to let' pages of the Evening Press and the Evening Herald. Loose change frantically in hand, I'd anxiously make endless phone calls in grubby phone boxes, ticking off the dwellings that were still on offer with a pencil, and crossing out the ones that were already taken. I'd make appointments to view certain places at certain times. I'd head to a place, stand in line with seven other rain-soaked suckers and wait for some fat, sleazy, red-faced landlord to pull up twenty minutes late, in his big Audi, keys dangling from his pocket. He'd amble to the door, try to find the right key and show the person at the top of the queue the accommodation. This usually consisted of a poky, dark, dungeon of despair, with a long light bulb flex hanging from the ceiling almost entreating you to use it as a speedy noose to end your interminable misery. The smell of stale cigarette smoke and old frying fat was a constant feature. For this rancid putrid hovel the landlord would be looking for an astronomical rent. I realised after a few weeks of this that I couldn't afford a hovel of my own and might have to hovel share.

I was not keen on the idea of sharing living space with a complete stranger. Obviously I'd had some experience with the concept, living with my family for all those years, but at least I knew mother, father and Colm didn't sleep with axes under their pillows. Well, mother and Colm, at least. Father had succumbed to that brief unhinged paranoid phase in the mid-70's when he began suffering from 'The Capgras Syndrome'. This is an affliction where a person becomes convinced that his nearest and dearest have been replaced by doubles. He snapped out of it though one evening when he saw me trying to fix my bike. He realised then that only his firstborn son could make such a complete mess of replacing a broken chain.

I eventually went to look at a place on Leinster Road in Rathmines. Two bed-sits on two different storeys, but with a shared kitchen, bathroom and toilet. This set-up wasn't too bad I figured because at least I would have some privacy. Also the place smelt fresh and looked clean. I met the landlady, Mrs. Mooney.

She seemed to like me. She then told me the place had been recently renovated and myself and the other tenant, Maurice, were the first tenants in a while. She asked me what I did?

Biting my tongue, I told her I worked for a company called Dynamic Synergy Incorporated. She said that was good, because she preferred letting to people who worked. She told me the deposit was two weeks rent in advance, £44 and she would collect the rent every Friday after she hoovered the place. I told her I was very interested in moving in, and took £75 from my pocket, the final pay packet from my Executive Development course and confidently counted out the money, handing her £50.

She smiled and told me she'd get me the change. My course finished. I received my certificate in Executive Development. According to the government, I was now a fully developed executive. I immediately signed on the dole. The initial plan was to sign on for a few weeks. Weeks became months. Months became years.

Hatch 22 (1986) 58m. * D: Philip Saville. Manus Mannion, Gippo Brady, Redser Norton. Multilayered ensemble piece, set in a dole office, charting the lives of a group of unemployed people in Ireland of the mid-1980's. [PG]**

I'd arrive at the dole office on Victoria Street at half past two, each Wednesday, greeted by four queues coming out the door. There would be much bustling and barging, and unhappy mutterings at the slowness of it all. "Jays, that new girl at the hatch is very slow, it's a bleedin' disgrace."

Sometimes a scuffle would break out and amidst the pandemonium someone would turn up behind you and, ignoring the mayhem, would tap you on the shoulder and ask politely in his Dublin 4 accent, "Is this the queue to Hatch 22?" I'd shrug my shoulders as the solitary guard on duty would try to restore order.

Eventually, I'd get to the top of the queue. As I was about to sign the form, I would notice the phantom biro thief had struck again. In Dublin in the mid-80's, all the dole offices attached an old bit of string to all the biros positioned at the hatches, so no one could steal them. This wouldn't stop the phantom biro thief, who would bring in a pair of scissors every few weeks and just snip them off. The dole officer would then give me her biro. Because of the impatient queue behind, I'd sign my name very quickly. Almost like a busy star signing his autograph. Almost. Then she'd say coldly, "Pay Hatch B," and I'd move on to a second queue.

Being a disciple of habit, I got into a certain routine on dole days. Then one day the dole officer told me, that my signing-on time had changed. I'd have to collect it Tuesday morning at half past eleven. This was a very worrying development. Too many variables. Who'd be in the new queue with me? Or the queue opposite me? Imagine it is somebody I know, who I don't really like, and they want to know my business, and I'll be stuck with them, having to chat to them every Tuesday morning for the next year or two.

My worst fears were realised. That next week Gerry's friend, Albert, was in the queue across from me. He'd moved up to Dublin too. Was trying to make it as an actor. His only role so far was also in that ill-fated college production of 'Waiting for Godot'.

I contemplated turning up a little early or a little late on the Tuesday morning to avoid Albert, but dole officers were always real sticklers for timekeeping. Then one week, Albert told me with a big grin on his face that he'd actually got an acting job with Curious Lemon Theatre Company, on full pay. He wouldn't be signing on for eight weeks as the play he was in, a radical all-male nude version of Lorca's 'The House of Bernarda Alba', was doing a nationwide tour.

Though relieved at not having to see him for two months, I was also filled with a slight envy and vowed to try and sort myself out and finally decide what I wanted to do.

July 29th 116 days to go

Something awful has happened. This morning, I received an official looking letter in the post. I opened it and realised I had being summoned to appear at Court No.32 next Tuesday morning, to be part of a jury pool. Sitting on the couch in a state of shock, I went through the five stages of Breaking your Routine. 1. Denial: No, they can't have picked me. Not me. What about all those other fuckers out there? 2. Aggression: There's no way I'm turning up for that jury pool. End of story! 3. Bargaining: How can I get out of this? I'll get a doctor's note or get someone to write to the judge telling him that I'm busy, that I have relaunched my acting career and am in a play, or I have resumed my comedy career and have comedy gigs. In a different jurisdiction! 4. Depression: This is going to be such a drag. What happens if it's a murder trial and I'm picked? I could be stuck there for months. 5. Acceptance: Ah, what's the point, I suppose I'll just have to turn up and do my civic duty.

July 30th 115 days to go

When I was about eight years old I was sitting in the living room with father and an old movie came on the television. He looked at it for a moment and he said to me "I think I've seen this movie before, but I'm not sure." And I thought to myself, how can you not remember if you saw a particular movie or not?

Fast forward thirty years. I was sitting in one my favourite licensed premises, Mulligan's of Poolbeg Street, with Kieran last night. We were drinking and I was telling him about my jury service dilemma but during the whole evening he kept staring at this woman at the other end of the bar. And he turns to me at one stage and he says, "You know, I think I've slept with that woman, but I'm not sure." And I thought to myself, how can you not remember if you slept with somebody or not? Later he told me he thinks he met her during that time we were in a blues band together. TojoMojo. It was the first time I met Kieran.

This is TojoMojo (1988) 67m. * D: Declan Lowney. Manus Mannion, Kieran Finn, Nagisa Yamada, Ed Ryan. A fly-on-the-wall music documentary chronicling the fall and steeper fall of a Dublin blues band. [PG]**

The band had been set up by Dublin-based Japanese drummer and blues enthusiast, Nagisa Yamada. We played on this novelty aspect of our line-up by calling ourselves TojoMojo. I was lead singer. A guy called Ed Ryan was lead guitarist and Kieran was bass guitarist. I don't know why we hired Kieran because he knew nothing about the blues. He thought Howlin' Wolf was a shipyard in Belfast. Since Nagisa considered himself the star attraction, he insisted on positioning his drum kit at the front of the stage.

Obviously, being lead singer, this annoyed me. I liked to jump around whilst singing but with that drum kit in the way I had no room to manouevre. After one very sparsely attended gig in the U.C.D. Student Bar, Nagisa sat us down. He had spotted what was going wrong. It was the lead guitarist, Ed's fault. Ed lacked emotion. Not in his guitar playing. But in his face. Nagisa had this theory. To be a great blues guitarist, not only do you have to have nimble fingers for all that fret work but you also have to have flexible facial muscles, to contort your face in just the right pained way as you hit the proper chords.

However, Ed, through no fault of his own, was completely granite faced and incapable of changing his facial expression. Nagisa then bizarrely decided that during our next gig, since I had more flexible facial muscles I should stand next to Ed during Ed's sinus clearing guitar solos and react to the chords by contorting *my* face. I told him we'd just be laughed at. But Nagisa insisted. We were laughed at, but strangely, started to develop a cult following. Unfortunately that doesn't sound as good as it seems. It's a question of proportion.

For example, in America if you develop a cult following, it means you have a basic fan base of maybe fifty thousand people who have latched on to your particular sensibility. In Ireland, though a cult following means a fan base of four or five, and this usually comprises of a slightly unbalanced woman from Leitrim and her three-legged dog. After two months I left TojoMojo citing artistic differences, an aversion to travel and chronic cramped cheek fatigue.

In retrospect, I was always too much of a purist to persist as a blues singer. In other words, if it ain't black, it ain't blue. I figured a white Irish guy singing the blues is as lacking in authenticity as an Afro-American man playing the spoons in a céilí band. I never regretted for a single minute quitting my career in music especially when, after my departure, two German brothers joined TojoMojo, and the band subsequently reinvented themselves as a heavy rock covers outfit called Doppelgänger Headbanger.

August 5th 109 days to go

Nerve-wracking morning in Court No. 32. First we were led into a big hall and had to confirm we had turned up. Then we went downstairs and waited. And waited. Eventually a televison monitor came on in the corner and the trial judge listed the case and started to choose our allotted numbers randomly. When someone was picked, they'd smile sheepishly or curse under their breath and be led away to the court room.

Then they would be asked by the judge if they had any reasons or possible conflicts of interest to prevent them being a member of the jury for this particular case. If they said no, the judge asked the council for the prosecution and the council for defence, if they had any problems with the proposed jury member. Sometimes a jury member would be rejected. I noticed when they were rejected, it was usually because the prospective jury member resembled a D.L.T. At ten to twelve after the judge had selected juries for six cases, he thanked us for coming and asked us to turn up again tomorrow morning at nine thirty for more jury selection. Whilst walking home I started to think. Given the type of juror that was continually rejected, I decided to check if I had any shiny tracksuits and oversized trainers when I got back to the house. I hadn't.

August 6th 108 days to go

Second day in Court No. 32. Still haven't been picked. Can't take much more of this. The number closest to mine was selected. Once again the only jurors rejected were D.L.T.s. This time, after being discharged by the judge, only to be told to turn up again tomorrow, I went to an Oxfam shop on George's Street and bought a second-hand shiny tracksuit. Kirsten has given me some old trainers. Tomorrow morning I will muss my hair with excessive gel and for a day will become a D.L.T.

August 7th 107 days to go

I am in the casualty unit of St. James's Street hospital. I was set upon by some other D.L.T.s as I was walking down Thomas Street dressed as a D.L.T. heading towards the courts. In attempting to escape I twisted my ankle and fell heavily onto the road. After waiting for six hours, I was eventually seen to. The nurse says I'll just have to take it easy for a few days and pack the swelling with ice. Kirsten got her to write a note for the judge.

August 13th 101 days to go

It has been lovely weather for the last four days. But I can't believe the stuff I'm hearing on the radio. What is it with this country? It rains two hundred and fifty days of the year but after four days of sunshine, they start talking about a drought!

With my bruised ankle I have been housebound — which doesn't make a huge difference because even during non-bruised ankle times I remain mainly housebound. I have realised though that I have been remarkably lucky with my health up to now. T

he last time I was laid low was after that bout of concussion I got during my time with Curious Lemon Theatre Company.

The Artist and the Pain (1986) 124m. * D: Peter Yates. Manus Mannion, June Cleary, Bernard O' Brien, Richard Carr. A story of two people. The Artist and the Pain. The Artist, a promising actor, has his career constantly stalled by the Pain, an overweening, pretentious and unpredictable theatre director. Slightly camp yet quietly satisfying backstage romp. (PG-13)**

I got the acting job with Curious Lemon through Albert, Gerry's old friend. We'd met up in Bewley's Café on Grafton Street. I was shocked to see Albert's condition. His arm was in a sling and his neck was in traction. He told me he'd had a mishap and could not play the role of Sir Andrew Aguecheek in Curious Lemon's up and coming version of Shakespeare's 'Twelfth Night'. The company were badly looking for an immediate replacement. He had recommended me. He told me I had to meet the director, Nigel, but there was a 99% chance I'd get the role. I asked him about the money situation. He said the money would be very good because the director is very well connected.

"He's taboo rich," Albert said, enigmatically.

"What's taboo rich?" I asked.

"He's rich, but he doesn't like talking about it," Albert replied.

I thanked Albert and took down the details. The meeting with Nigel, the director, took place in an old garage off Baggot Street that had been converted into a theatre space. Nigel, who was English, was instantly impressed by my grasp of the iambic pentameter and hired me on the spot. I mused on the fact that many theatre companies and Arts organisation in this country seem to be run by Englishmen. Yes, why do so many Englishmen hold powerful positions in the Arts in this country?

But thinking about it further, the answer is very simple:

We Irish, are still very impressed by the posh, perfectly clipped R.A.D.A Oxbridge accent. Because not too long ago, we were all peasants. Even the forefathers of self-important interviewers. And when the self-important interviewer on the interviewing panel hears those refined south of England tones, he goes into a trance and feels he must agree with what this voice tells him or he'll be evicted, or worse still, shot. Then he comes out of the trance and recommends that the perfectly delightful Englishman gets the job.

The day of my first rehearsal arrived. I walked in the door and was slightly unnerved. I noticed one cast member had a crutch. Later, an actress' nose bled profusely throughout the blocking of a scene.

Eventually, the rehearsal had to be curtailed early as the sound box caught fire. During lunch, I asked the actor playing Sir Toby Belch, who would work with me the most, to tell me more about Curious Lemon Theatre Company. This melancholic older actor, Bernard, whose face had come out in an awful rash, began to relate the tale. Curious Lemon Theatre Company was set up by Trinity graduate Nigel MacBeth in early 1985.

After converting that old garage off Baggot Street, he and a few like-minded theatre enthusiasts had begun to stage plays. Bernard then told me sarcastically that Nigel had been the domineering visionary of Players T.C.D. in the early 1980's, a would-be genius, a legend in his own rehearsals, a director who wanted to make 'relevant' and 'artistic' statements by re-examining classic texts and making them his own. Sounds a bit like Ivor O' Doherty, I thought, only with breeding. Sadly though, Bernard continued, Nigel had absolutely no talent. More disturbingly, he insisted on being called Mr. MacBeth, during each rehearsal period, which of course broke the timeworn theatrical taboo of uttering the word 'Macbeth' in a theatre. Bernard informed me that for hundreds of years that play has always been referred to, by the superstitious thespian community, as 'The Scottish play'. Nigel, a theatre obsessive, dismissed this as a childish old wives' tale. His actors though weren't so sure. I shifted nervously in my seat. Bernard listed examples of Curious Lemon productions that had been continually plagued by mysterious illnesses, falling scenery and random fires.

He asked me had I noticed the physical state of the cast this morning? I told him I had. He told me, June, the actress playing Viola, had never had a nose bleed in her life, before working with Nigel. The actor with the crutches, Richard, had fallen off the stage from the same spot twice in three weeks.

He then told me to look at his own face. He got that rash six months ago, from make-up he used in the theatre's dressing room. He then informed me what had happened Albert. A lighting operator had fallen on him. The lighting operator was in a coma but hopefully he'd pull through. Then there were the continuous bad reviews. Although, Bernard stated, the general consensus was that this was completely unrelated to Nigel's patronymic.

His what?" I asked.

"His surname. His patronymic," Bernard said, deriving a certain relish from repeating the word. I nodded.

"So why stay in the company? Why not claim incapacitation like Albert, and leave?" I queried.

"We're actors, dear boy, we act," he said, and then announced rather dramatically, "And anyway, the show must go on!" He then started to cough violently and nearly choked on his chicken sandwich.

The following day I had my accident. All because of Nigel's great enthusiasm for 'trust exercises'. This is where, during the rehearsal process, one actor stands on a table and allows himself to fall, happy in the knowledge, that the other cast members, standing next to the table, will catch him.

The logic being that the actor has to completely let himself go whilst falling, and trust his fellow cast members implicitly. This creates a bond between actor and fellow cast members which will stand them in good stead when they are on stage, playing to eleven people, in a freezing theatre in Athlone.

As I reluctantly got on the table, I assured Nigel that I already trusted my fellow cast members implicitly. He wanted proof.

"Theatre is a war, actors are the foot soldiers, and the performance is the battle," he said. "And once that battle starts, you have to be able to depend on your fellow soldier. Now jump!"

I stood on the table. It was a very tall table. I looked down on five of my fellow cast members. 'Cast' being the operative word. Richard's foot was still in a cast. June's nose bleeds had subsided, but she'd sprained her wrist doing a cartwheel during a warm up exercise. It was in a cast. Our Malvolio, Derek, had his left arm in a cast. He'd become so worried about injuring himself during the production that he'd got drunk at home one night and accidentally fallen down his stairs. Bernard was wearing a bandage over his left eye, as his facial rash had spread and his left eye had become infected.

To cap it all, Shane, our Feste, was in a wheelchair, temporarily immobilised as a result of being given the wrong injection for a knee injury. On the point of jumping, I came to the conclusion that this motley crew of wounded tragedians were not the ideal bunch of people to catch a falling star. My assumption proved correct.

Aug 21st 93 days to go

I am in Galway. My Auntie Maisie died. Having arrived at the funeral home with Colm and my parents, I was led in to see her body. Lying peacefully she looked slightly similar to her old self. Yet different. It was as if someone had let her air out. The skin on her forefinger reminded me of the decaying outer layer of a leek. On the way down on the bus, I had looked up the death notices at the back of the paper.

And there it was, Maisie's life reduced to a tiny paragraph. All the conversations she had and people she met and things she did, and the dreams she had, and the films on the telly she prevented her nephews from seeing due to her incessant visiting, all forgotten and replaced by just one short passage announcing her demise, how much she'll be missed by her loved ones, and where and when her removal and funeral will take place.

At the end of the day that tiny paragraph is all anyone is left with before departing. I don't believe in an afterlife. Only afterbirth. And after afterbirth, is death. I view life itself as a busy medium-priced hotel. At some stage you check in. And during your stay in that hotel, you try and keep things tidy, not make too much noise, conduct yourself the best way you can, and eventually it's time for you to check out. And the guy behind the desk seems genuinely sorry to see you leave, but is he really going to remember you five minutes after you've left? I don't think so. Someone else will have checked in. And afterbirth will go on.

Sometimes though, I wish I believed in some greater scheme of things. It might help allay my fears. Because as you approach middle age, one dominant thought preoccupies your mind. It is that thought I had all those years ago, when consulting my movie reference book while some old black and white movie credits rolled. Anything. Can happen anyone. At any time.

However a lot of people can't cope with that truly terrifying thought. So they seek security. Peace of mind. And they believe in this mythical fantastical figure. God. A kind of Santa Claus for slow learners. And then the above sentence changes and becomes, anything, can happen anyone *else*, at any time. But not me. Because I've got this omnipresent bearded entity looking out for me. And watching over me. And protecting me. And as long as I say my prayers every night and collect those mass-going brownie points each week, I'll be o.k. Nothing bad will happen me. Ever.

Before I left Dublin this morning, I stared at the blank condolence card Kirsten had bought for Auntie Maisie. Ever practical, sensing that we might need more and more of them as time went by, and always on the lookout for a good bargain, she had bought a batch of ten specially reduced condolence cards last year. I had used one of the cards in the interim period for another funeral in Galway, when Austin McLynn's younger brother had died in a motor cycle accident.

I tried with much difficulty to write what I wanted to convey to Uncle Dan and the family. I test wrote a few drafts on a bit of paper. 'Dear Uncle Dan, Catriona, Eoin, Dan Óg, Bridget, Terry and Anne, at times like this words probably seem so inadequate to sum up your loss. Just to let you know our thoughts are with you, Love from Manus and Kirsten'. No 'love from' is too strong, I thought, I hadn't seen Uncle Dan and his family for years. How about an 'All the Best'? But that's more like something you write on a holiday post card, I figured. 'Regards' seemed a bit flippant in the circumstances. I fretted some more and just couldn't make up my mind. Maybe I should just write, 'From Manus and Kirsten'. Keep it simple, formal and to the point. I sought Kirsten's advice. But she had some other doubts.

"Thinking about it, you can't use that card, it's the same condolence card as the last one we signed," she said.

"What do you mean?" I inquired.

"That last funeral in Galway you went to, last October," she elaborated.

"Yeh, but Austin's family doesn't know Maisie's family," I protested.

"You never know. Galway is such a small place. They might bump into each other," she continued.

"They won't," I said, looking at my watch and realising I had to leave soon to catch that intercity bus.

"You never know. They both know us. And then they might start to chat," she continued, not backing down. "If the funeral was in some other part of the country, or abroad, I'd have no problem, but as it is you'll have to get another card."

I tried reasoning with her."Even if they did start talking to each other on the street, would they immediately start comparing the different condolence cards they received from us"? I said.

"It's too risky. It could happen. You'll have to get another card on the way to the bus," she said with finality. Then she left for work. Later, I set the alarm, left the index-linked burglary money on the table which has recently been increased to €40, given the exorbitant rise in the cost of living, grabbed my bag and left the house. After making quite a detour, I finally bought another card which looked very similar to the first card but wasn't identical, and signed it 'Best Wishes from Manus and Kirsten'.

Aug 22nd 92 days to go

I'm not a big fan of funerals. Firstly, I hate having to say "Sorry for your loss," to the grieving relatives. It is not that I am overcome with sorrow when saying this. It's the exact opposite. I get an uncontrollable urge to start giggling. In other words, reacting in a completely contrary manner to what's expected. Auntie Maisie's funeral proceeded like any other funeral. Every one of her good points was highlighted.

If Hitler had had an Irish funeral the priest would probably have spent the eulogy talking about the early promise he showed as a painter. In their own way, all church services are a bit like a fascist rally - with everyone on Prozac. Ponder the brainwashed addicted way the congregation answer prayers in 'Seig Heil' unison. Or the way everyone stands when they are being told to stand. Or sit when they are being told to sit. Or kneel when they are being told to kneel. Although on a positive note with all this standing, sitting and kneeling, mass can also be considered a kind of aerobics for old people.

I started imagining my own funeral service. I probably wouldn't get Auntie Maisie's numbers. And it's no more than I deserve. I've spent my whole life circumventing humanity. How can I then expect people to turn up at my funeral? I would restrict the service to the crematorium.

Thinking like a comedian, I figured it's a smaller room, and therefore easier to fill.

And as my coffin would be heading towards its final flame-ridden ending, I pondered on what song I'd like to go out on.

1. 'Another One Bites the Dust' by Queen. This would be humourous, but people might think I was a Queen fan. Or gay. Not that there is anything wrong with being a Queen fan or being gay. But one wouldn't want to confuse the mourners as they muffled silently and hysterically into their handkerchiefs.

2. 'Don't Get Round Much Any More', by The Ink Spots. This Duke Ellington penned number is quite profound, because once you die, you really don't get round much anymore.

3. 'I Just Wasn't Made For These Times', by The Beach Boys. If ever a song summed my whole life up, it is this song. As I get older, increasingly I feel I am now just a walk-on in somebody else's century.

August 23rd 91 days to go

After the funeral yesterday, as we all gathered outside the church, I saw cousin Eamonn. Unhinged cousin Eamonn. I made a mental note. Never offer him condolences when either of his parents, Auntie Ethel and Uncle Willie die.

I had heard he still suffered from handshake phobia. I hadn't seen him for a long time, since we ended up inadvertently sharing accommodation with each other on Leinster Road in 1987.

The Hermit (1987) 267m. * D: Andrei Tarkovsky. Manus Mannion, Miriam Walsh, Eamonn Collins. In a flat in Rathmines, a directionless young man vegetates, and becomes lost in his own world. Ponderous, and painfully slow dissection of a disintegrating mind. [PG-13]

My acting career never took off. Instead I settled into a life of long term unemployment. My routine was one of deadening regularity. After leaving the dole office in Victoria Street on my one morning out, Tuesday, I would head to Kelly's Café and Grill on Camden Street and have a high cholesterol stodgy fry up. I would then head home to Leinster Road and hide under the bed for another week, cut off from the world, doing nothing but watching old movies on that small second hand portable black and white television in that little room with my one bar heater and my slippers.

To paraphrase Rodgers and Hammerstein again, I was 23 going on 80. A trainee nursing home resident, surviving on dodgy orange frankfurters and tins of yellow-pack beans. And I wondered why I was so passive and inert. Why wasn't I out there engaging with life? Why wasn't I like my cousins or the guys I went to school with? Focussed, together, active!

Mother had been right, when she said I had no "get up and go", only "sit down and stay". She also had that other wonderful phrase, "The only place success comes before work, is in the dictionary." Once again, Alice Faye was a constant in my life. Every time I turned on the television it was always an Alice Faye movie. And every time I saw an Alice Faye movie I asked myself what was I doing the last time I saw this Alice Faye movie? And the answer was always the same. Nothing. Alice Faye symbolised my inability to actively participate in life. My life had become an endless season of Alice Faye movies. I loathed myself for wasting time watching these movies, especially when I'd seen most of them before, yet I was addicted to them.

There is a certain exhilaration in watching a very old movie. Especially late at night. With the lights off. And every thing is tranquil and every one is in bed. Asleep. Except you. And the only sound is the low cackle of that rapid-fire 1930's dialogue. Time seems to stand still as you are transported to a different era and lost in sepia-tinted escapism. You wish you were back in that time. You wish you were in that movie at that time. You wish you were a Jack Carson, or a Franklin Pangborn, or a Granville Bates, or any one of those great old Hollywood character actors who kept re-appearing in countless movies during that period.

Eric Blore (1887-1959) "British comedy actor who specialised in playing put upon butlers and idiosyncratic types."

And each time you see these characters in a movie, it is like seeing an old friend, and for ninety minutes they keep you company as you become sublimely withdrawn.

I'd hate leaving my rented room. Timing a quick sortie to the bathroom or the kitchen became traumatic. But I had to wash, urinate and eat. Sharing that kitchen was the worst. It was not that bad when you were sharing a kitchen with someone who worked, like Maurice, for at least then you had the whole day to time your meals around avoiding him. He could have an early breakfast, you could have a late breakfast. You could have an early dinner, he could have a late dinner. It was perfect. You never saw him. Never had to socialise with him. But it was the people who didn't work that caused a problem, and it being the 1980's, this was a big problem.

After eleven months on Leinster Road, Maurice left and Miriam moved in. I don't know what Miriam did, maybe like me, she was involved, vaguely, in the Arts , but I couldn't stand sharing with her. Especially those first few weeks. I'd never know if she was in. If she had eaten, if she was going to eat, if she wanted to make a cup of tea, if she was going to have her friends in, if she was going to start strumming that guitar, or turn on that stereo, I just never knew. I just could not relax for one moment. I was always on my toes, always on the lookout.

Breakfasts were particularly problematic. Let's say it wasn't Tuesday, and I woke up at my normal time. Eleven o'clock. I'd lie awake and think, has Miriam had breakfast? I'd wait ten minutes and listen. Not a sound. I'd hurriedly put on my clothes. Sneak out to the kitchen. Feel the kettle. It would be lukewarm. That would be a good sign. She'd have used it. I mean, it was quite late. She's probably had her breakfast and left, I'd think. It was a sunny day, she's probably gone out with Liam to the beach or the mountains.

Great! I could relax. Listen to some music. I'd sneak back into my room and would pick up my tape recorder, and would scurry back towards the kitchen. The coast would be clear. I'd re-enter the kitchen. I'd close the door. That would be an excellent idea, for if she was still here she'd have to knock apologetically, and it would be slightly awkward and embarrassing for her to have to come into the kitchen. So I'd start to prepare my breakfast and start listening to my cassette. 'Great Crooners of the 1930's'. One can only listen to so much blues, and given my obsession with old movies, it seemed perfectly logical that I would also develop a liking for that sweet and sentimental dance band music of the inter-war period.

Classics to croon along to while eating your breakfast:

1. "Wrap your troubles in dreams" 1931 — Bing Crosby with Gus Arnheim and his Orchestra.
2. "Time on my hands" 1931 — Al Bowlly with the New Mayfair Dance Orchestra.
3. "Anytime, Any day, Anywhere" 1933 — Chick Bullock and his Levee Loungers.
4. "Stars Fell on Alabama"1934 — Jack Teagarden with Benny Goodman and his Orchestra.
5. "Beloved" 1934 — Harlan Lattimore with Victor Young and his Orchestra.
6. "You're driving me crazy" 1930 — Guy Lombardo and his Royal Canadians.
7. "I only have eyes for you" 1934 – Dick Powell with Victor Young and his Orchestra.
8. "Say it isn't so" 1932 — Rudy Vallee and His Connecticut Yankees.
9. "Prisoner of Love" 1931 — Russ Columbo with Nat Skilkret and his Orchestra.
10. "Bye Bye Blues" 1930 — Bert Lown and his Hotel Biltmore Orchestra.

One thing would be missing though. The newspaper. Damn! I'll have to sneak down three flights of stairs and, by the time I get back, she'll be in the kitchen having forgotten to pack the sandwiches for Liam and herself. I'd leave the music on loudly and jam the door tightly, then she'd think I'd still be in there and when I don't answer she'll think, maybe, I've hung myself or something. You know, 'slightly peculiar unemployed black and white movie addict kills himself in kitchen of flat'. I'd rush down to the shop to buy the paper. The chatty old dears in the queue ahead of me would always keep me waiting, rabbiting on about some nice man on their street who's just had a stroke. I'd eventually make my purchase and rush back upstairs. I'd be on page 6. World News. Trouble brewing in Azerbaijan. George Metaxa and The New Mayfair Orchestra would be playing in the background, my egg would be medium, and everything would be perfect.

Then, all of a sudden, I'd hear a door bang. Or I'd think I'd hear a door bang. I'd jump up. Turn down the music. Stick my ear against the closed door. And listen. Is it her? Is she back? Maybe it's the guy downstairs, maybe it's someone in the bathroom. I'd re-compose myself and try to relax. I'd turn Nick Lucas and his Crooning Troubadours back up. I'd have some toast. Another cup of tea. Page 8, I'd read a profile on Oliver North, then once more, I would think I'd heard something. A door open. I'd turn down the music, again. Cock my ear against the door.

Then I'd hear that sound that spelt death to the morning. The faintest of knocks. But gradually a knock that would become more assertive. I'd reluctantly push the fridge away from the door, which would slowly open, as Miriam would walk in. Gaunt and perpetually in brown leather she'd say, almost inaudibly, in her sing song Cork accent:"Sorry for disturbing you."

"It's o.k." I'd say, as I'd nearly choke on my last piece of toast, "I'm nearly finished here."

"No, no, it's o.k," she'd protest, "I only want to put on the kettle for a cup of tea."

She'd put some water in the kettle and turn it on. Initial politeness would turn to strained silence.

"I wish I'd got up earlier. It's a lovely day," she'd say. "I won't be in the flat that much anyway, I'll be out a lot."

I'd nod. And I'd know. Once I heard that sentence I'd know that she would always be around. But it would be the not knowing when that would get to me. The thinking that maybe just once she might not be around. But she'd always be there. Every minute of every hour of every day.

I'd be in my bedsit watching an Alice Faye movie on Channel Four.

King of Burlesque (1935) 83 m. ** D: Sidney Lanfield. Alice Faye, Warner Baxter, Jack Oakie, Mona Barrie. Run-of-the-mill backstage musical in which a burlesque producer dreams of staging a classy Broadway Show.

There would be a hesitant knock on the door. "Sorry for disturbing you, it's me again. That gas cooker. I'm still having trouble getting it to light." It would be another day. Another Alice Faye movie.

That Night in Rio (1941) 90m. * D: Irving Cummings. Alice Faye, Don Ameche, Carmen Miranda, S.Z. Sakall. Carman Miranda shines in frothy Twentieth Century Fox mistaken identity musical.**

I would hear another knock on the door. "You're probably tired of me at this stage, listen I won't disturb you again. Just one thing. Where's the best laundry around here?" It would be a week later. Oh look. An Alice Faye movie at quarter past two.

Tin Pan Alley (1940) 94m. * D:Walter Lang. Alice Faye, John Payne, Betty Grable, Jack Oakie. Enjoyable musical with Oscar winning score set before World War One, chronicling the ups and downs of show-biz hopefuls.**

I would hear yet another tentative knock. "I'm expecting a registered letter from my mother. I wonder would you sign it for me, because I'll be going out for a few hours."

This went on for months. I was going insane. Little did I know that there would be a time when I would come to miss Miriam. One morning, a week after Miriam had moved out, I scurried into the kitchen and saw a frighteningly familiar visage in horn rimmed glasses. He reacted in a similarly panicked manner. It was cousin Eamonn. He was to be my new next door neighbour.

"We share a kitchen?" I inquired incredulously.

"Guess so," he said. Unsmiling. And blushing. I tried to compose myself.

"How are you?" I said. In a totally forgetful state of mind, I put my hand out for him to shake. He looked down at it momentarily, and then started to sweat and hyperventilate. His right hook to my jaw was powerful and immediate. It wasn't the best of beginnings. Still we settled into a pattern. In the middle of the night when we least expected the other to make tea, we'd nervously bump into each other with our empty mugs on the darkened stairs.

I'd make some light comment on his no longer greasy, but very long, prematurely greying, flowing hair. He'd tell me he always let his hair grow very long because he wanted to avoid small talk with barbers. That's the kind of thing, I'd come up with, I would acknowledge to myself later.

The weeks went by. I realised I was sharing a kitchen with a slightly bizarre grotesque version of myself. If he got into the kitchen first at breakfast, he'd push the fridge against the door. He, too, loved listening to old music while eating, except his choice was mawkish American country songs from the 1940's. And the music of 10cc. He loved 10cc. As he would say in one of his rare, lighter moments, "Cleanliness is next to Godley and Creme." He, also, used to stay in his room all day watching old black and white movies. He was even a member of 'The Sons Of the Desert', the Laurel and Hardy fan club and each month he'd get 'The Sons of the Desert' literature in the post updating him on the latest Stan and Ollie news. Stuff like, I'm only guessing here... that they were still dead?

Cousin Eamonn and myself both hated being in the same living space as each other. He felt I was spying on him, I felt he was spying on me. He felt I was always around. I felt he was always around. But he *was* always around. Or seemed to be always around. His mother, my Auntie Ethel, used to ring him every second night. Sometimes I was unlucky enough to answer the communal phone in the hallway. His family all thought it was wonderful that we had ended up sharing together.

My parents, though, weren't as pleased. Still fuming over The Sign Of Peace incident. To my utter amazement though, Eamonn had a girlfriend. Some nights she'd ring him up and ask him to meet her in town for a pint. Like most male members of my extended family, his dependancy on his routine would kick in, and unprepared to do something 'on the spur of the moment', he would feign tiredness and say he was already in his pyjamas. That wouldn't deter her and she'd arrive in the flat later, at about eleven o'clock, and they'd eventually make love to the sound of Bob Wills and his Texan Playboys. Rhythmic mattress noises, interspersed with random grunts and groaning, would emanate from the room next door. I'd hear his girlfriend gradually becoming more stimulated until she would reach a climax and let out a howl, like a banshee in heat, that would literally shake the walls of the house. I realised I needed some big changes in my life. I had to move out of Rathmines. I had to find myself. I had to fulfill my destiny.

September 1st 82 days to go

I got a letter this morning from a government sponsored training body called Screen Scene Initiative. They notified me about an intensive course they are running to help budding screenwriters over three weekends in October, tutored by New Yorker, Diane Schwartz, who according to her resumé seems to be a bona fide Creative Lower Being. She has worked extensively in the television and film industry in both the U.S. and Britain and runs the Film Studies Department at the University of Huddersfield. For the pleasure of listening to Diane guide us through story analysis and development, structure and plotting, and an examination of genre and marketing, Screen Scene Initiative want €600.

They want ME to pay THEM to do a government training scheme? When did they start pulling that one? In my day, THEY paid YOU to do a government training scheme. Are they bonkers? Do they honestly think I'm going to dish out €600 to hear some Tinseltown second rater who did some script editing on four episodes of 'Thirtysomething' in 1990, and has ended up lecturing in the North of England, bore me for three consecutive weekends on protagonists, plot points and quarter act climaxes? No way.

September 2nd   81 days to go

With all this economic success the country has become like a 'mini me' America. However, the smallest gestures reflect an underlying malaise. Today, as I was queuing at an A.T.M. machine on Dame Street, I noticed a young businessman in a suit about to walk into the bank with a freshly lit cigarette.

As he entered the bank, he stepped over a young homeless man begging. He then realised he couldn't go into the bank as it was a smoke free zone. He came out, took a deep drag of his cigarette, and offered the rest of the cigarette to the young homeless man. He smiled at the homeless man, and felt ever so smug. He genuinely believed he was doing a 'good deed'. "Take it," he said, filled with charitable goodwill. The young homeless man looked up, shrugged his shoulders and accepted the gift. The businessman darted inside, feeling like Mother Teresa of Calcutta.

September 3rd   80 days to go

Ben rang me this morning. He said the Film Council liked the latest draft of 'The Shamrock Sumo Club' but had some suggestions and have given him some development money. We then arranged to meet up and discuss these. They want to get rid of the Japanese company and Ben agrees after all. The inclusion of the company makes the script too 'busy'. It should be about these wonderful characters in Mountbellew, their wants, their needs and the obstacles that prevent them from attaining those wants and needs. Because this creates conflict. And conflict is drama. And drama is good. He would like another draft by the end of the month.

Kirsten got back late today. She told me, while in town, on her way home from work, she decided to drop into Marks&Spencers to buy a few things. Though being surprisingly empty, she got delayed by an extreme case of shopper's indecision. Over what bananas to buy. Organic or Fair Trade. What is more important, she wondered, our diet and health or the rights and well being of third world banana growers? A time consuming dilemma. After twelve minutes standing and staring at that small hill of bananas, she ended up purchasing both options. Like me and the eggs a few months back. Luckily we have that banana cake recipe lying around somewhere. And that food mixer. Why has shopping become so complicated?

September 6th 77 days to go

Have started snoring again. It all started about a week ago. Frankly, I had got tired wearing that rucksack in bed. It is because I spend so much of my non-sleeping hours lugging around that rucksack. I am sick of that rucksack. For I am the epitome of that early twenty-first century phenomenon — Rucksack Man. Rucksack Man is prevalent in all the major population centres of the western world. He is observed mainly in record shops and book shops. He doesn't own a car.

As with the Creative Lower Being, Rucksack Man can also be split up into two main categories.

1. Cool Rucksack Man: Cool Rucksack Man has always got the latest rucksack, usually dark grey, and this rucksack always compliments his jacket and his fashionable pitch-black, secondhand bicycle. He is confident with his place in the world and has a very strong self-assured image.

2. Sad Fuck Rucksack Man. Sad Fuck Rucksack Man always carries an orange rucksack which never goes with anything he wears. He usually has too many things in his rucksack, and sometimes looks like he's carrying around the chopped up body parts of a close relative. When it rains and he is lugging his load down Exchequer Street, Sad Fuck Rucksack Man resembles a slightly demented and overgrown member of Santa's little helpers. Rucksack Man rarely looks like he is overburdened with a healthy bank balance. And, always seems to have a lot of spare time on his hands. This can lead to 'rucksack skirmishes'.

Rucksack Skirmish Case Study A: You are in a record shop, flicking meaninglessly through the reduced C.D. section and you try to turn when from behind, a Rucksack Man is trying to turn simultaneously and both your rucksacks become entangled. You both delicately try to manoeuvre out of your trapped positions. This can take some time, amidst much intermittent cursing under one's breath.

Rucksack Skirmish Case Study B: You are turning into the aisle of a bookshop when you suddenly see another Rucksack Man approaching. You swerve trying to avoid him, he swerves trying to avoid you, but it is too late. Rucksacks have collided. Again much grumbling and lowly cursing ensues as you try manfully to by-pass each other between the book shelves. Rucksack Skirmish Case

Study C: You are entering an internet café. A Rucksack Man is leaving at the same time. The door way is not designed to withstand the girths of two rucksack-carrying men. Rucksacks collide and both Rucksack Men become stuck.

I never had any of these problems in the old days when all year round I was a mere Bulky Anorak Man. Bulky Anorak Man was common in Ireland from 1955 to 1990. Stuffed all sorts of things in his many pockets like newspapers, bottles of Fanta and bicycle lamps. One or two of this near-extinct breed can still be spotted in the odd bookie's office.

When did anoraks start getting such a bad name? I mean if you wear an anorak nowadays, you are a suspected child molester who likes exposing himself in train stations. But I come from a place where it rained 52 weeks of the year. I come from anorak country. And when I was growing up nobody looked cool. We didn't know any better. We were simple but we were dry. We were the anorak people.

Then, all of a sudden, anoraks became unfashionable. Years of tradition went out the window. You had to leave that anorak at home and just wear a jacket. But jackets have much smaller pockets. Thus you brought along the rucksack.

But the anorak people were used to their anoraks. And anytime they went out, they'd catch heavy colds, influenza, sometimes even pneumonia. In order to survive they stayed indoors, their social lives became non-existent, and they would read about all sorts of things: The name of the bravery medal awarded to messenger pigeons during the Second World War, the fact that Andy Warhol only ever wore green underpants, the name of the personnel on that Tampa Red recording from 1946 or the amazing titbit that Sigmund Freud suffered from pteridophobia, a fear of ferns.

And then, on the few occasions they did venture out, they would bore their friends with this newly found knowledge. Hence their friends started referring to them as 'Anoraks'. And, in an instant, the anorak wearing 'Anorak' became a kind of social leper in the lollo rosso infested Ireland of the 21st century. This infuriates me and I think it is time we bring back the bulky anorak in all its glory as an antidote to this image conscious, celebrity-obsessed age.

September 8th 75 days to go

As I was still struggling to complete the new draft of 'The Shamrock Sumo Club', my producer Ben came up with a plan of action and decided to send me for a week to an artistic retreat in County Sligo, The Montague Keeble Centre. I have just arrived. The welcoming note on the lovely wooden writers' table in my room stresses to respect the other artists' privacy, yet there are no locks to any of the doors. Montague Keeble was a famous actor manager who left his stately home in County Sligo to the nation, to be a place where artists from all disciplines could go and create.

In other words, this place is overrun with Creative Lower Beings. I am amongst my breed. I am surrounded by writers, poets, musicians, and visual artists, who have all come to this secluded spot because they feel they have something to offer. Something to say. Artistically. But have they really anything to say? I am not so sure. Because every song has been sung. Every joke has been told. Every thing has been done. And we're all just getting old. This is the realization I have made as I slave over another 100 page draft about an overweight man who spends much of his time in a nappy.

Have just had dinner. I am forced to so daily with the other residents because Montague Keeble stipulated in his will that the residents have to make an appearance every day at seven for dinner and engage in 'thought-provoking, stimulating conversation'.

One of them complained about some snoring in an adjoining room. I stared down at my coq au vin. The food is very retro up here. There are all types of Creative Lower Beings present. A slightly hysterical middle-aged lady was sitting next to me. I always seem to attract the odd ones.

They always latch on to me like a leech and divulge their inner most secrets after five minutes. Her name is Bernice and she is a poet. She has very thick glasses, a bizarre twitch and the opinions of a six-year-old. She announced to me that her favourite artists were Brendan Behan and Shane McGowan and then ordered a bottle of white wine for herself. No surprises there. During dessert she tried plying me with some drink but I declined. I just hurriedly finished my melon balls, made my excuses and left.

September 9th 74 days to go

I met Andrew, a rather intense writer over breakfast this morning. He is trying to write a best-seller but he claims he has a big problem. For it is now the accepted wisdom that a miserable Irish childhood is the passport to literary fame.

But Andrew told me his Foxrock childhood was not particularly miserable. So he blames his elderly parents for his lack of literary success. If only they had mistreated him in some way, deprived him of footwear for example, or banned Vitamin D from his diet and caused him to get rickets, or if at night they had sneaked into his bedroom and secretly placed lice in his hair, he would have suffered more and he would have overcome that suffering, and he would be a glowing example of triumph in the face of adversity, and would have a great tale to tell that would be bound to sell.

He told me he badly needs a best seller after his former agent sold the worldwide rights of his previous novel, 'The Bingo Operator's Revenge', for an undisclosed two figure sum. Although he claims when it was published, the review in The Irish Times described it as 'unputdownable'.

However, I was later told by another writer, Sam Duffy, that the review referred to the adhesive mess that was the book's cover as opposed to the quality of the work. Sam has grievances of his own.

The main focus of his scorn is chick-lit. He claims that 95 % of the people in publishing today are flashy ladies in pointy boots. The agents, the editors and the readers. And whose work do they recommend? Work by other flashy ladies in pointy boots. It's that whole 'flashy ladies in pointy boots' conspiracy, Sam maintains. He told me, in previous centuries, women writers such as Mary Ann Evans, had to change their name to a more masculine sounding one like George Eliot in order to get published, but nowadays it is the complete reverse.

He is seriously thinking of submitting his next novel as Samantha Duffy. Talking some more to Sam, or Samantha, I later found out that mine is the only room in the Montague Keeble Centre without en suite facilities. This annoys me. I don't mind having to get up at two o'clock in the night and risk my life going down those stairs if everyone else has to do it too, but not if I'm the only one! Now Old Man Negativity has raised his ugly head. Why is it always just me? All the others can urinate, defecate, and wash at any time of the day or night, yet I have to contemplate whether I really need to have that leak and have to plan my showers like a military operation.

September 10th 73 days to go

I had a good morning's work although I was distracted now and again by Yolanda. The eternally smiling Yolanda is from Melbourne and I am convinced that she does not have a musical note in her head.

She gave a recital last night for the other guests in the Music Room. People smiled glassily, and sat on their hands, resisting the temptation to cover their ears as she went through the first ever performance of 'The Afterlife Concerto'. Some rich industrialist's wife had died of cancer and he had written poems to commemorate her spirit and commissioned Yolanda to put this verse to music. It was the musical equivalent of a steel claw scraped down a blackboard.

But afterwards, we all said we enjoyed it enormously, as we sipped on some passable Chilean wine and nibbled on some vol-au-vents. It's good to be a writer up here, though. Better than being a musician. Because you can be completely talentless as a writer but none of the other guests will ever know. For the musicians, it's different. They rehearse out loud each day in the Music Room and you can hear their every bum note. And you do.

September 12th   71 days to go

Last night I was caught in the middle of a World War Two air force picture. Messerschmidts flew by at a great speed. Suddenly I awoke. The Messerschmidts had shrunk to the size of midges. Spent an hour from five to six trying to kill one with an old newspaper. Of course, I didn't kill it, I just thought I killed it, and went back to sleep. Ten minutes later the whirring noise in quadrophonic sound started up again.

I'll spend my last three nights in a much nicer room. I've been moved. Bernice left a few days early. My new room is a beautiful place. Full of lovely book shelves and antique furniture. I can't help ruminating on the fact though, that they stuck me up in that poky stuffy suicide trap for four days, yet they let Bernice the Poetess stay in this beautiful room. This room is so much more spacious, brighter and bigger. And taller. Much taller. And that could cause one small problem. I've already spotted four midges nestling in the beautiful Edwardian ceiling, just biding their time, waiting for dark.

Met another damaged soul over dinner. Same salad bowl, different planet. She has that perpetual 1980's dress sense, wears outlandish make-up and told me she has been in and out of an insane asylum. She's American. She told me in the States artistic retreats are called colonies and the residents are called colonists. I also found out why Bernice was in the very nice room. Because Bernice is the very successful poetess, Bernice Quinlivan. And the more successful a Creative Lower Being you are, the nicer room you get. Later when I got back to my room and was flicking through some of the books from the bookshelf, I spotted four of Bernice's Anthologies. Not so much slim volumes as anorexic ones. I could not make head nor tail of it. It seemed complete doggerel to me. In fact, I feel poets have it easy creatively. If they come up with five words, two commas, and a full stop, they can consider it a productive morning's work.

September 13th 70 days to go

I had a fitful sleep in my new room. And it wasn't caused by the midges. Woke up at four and went to the loo. This was a cause for much celebration. I can utilize my en suite facilities! I don't have to furtively scurry down a dark flight of stairs! Celebration was short-lived however, when I realized that the cistern takes an age to refill and flows like a brook for three quarters of an hour. Ended up picking out a book from the bookshelf and reading the truly amazing story about the obscure Irish Revolutionary, Old Ira Members.

Old Ira Members was an old I.R.A. member, the most prominent Jewish member of the I.R.A. in 1916. He was born in Poland in 1887, and at the age of 29, in March 1916, living alone and in some squalor just outside Cracow, he got a telegram from his uncle Manfred Members, who had gone to Hollywood, and become a big motion picture producer.

The telegram read, "Ira, come over to Hollywood, I'll put you in the new D. W. Griffith movie 'The Birth of a

Nation.' I'll make you a star! Your Uncle Manny." But Ira was uneducated and he didn't know where exactly Hollywood was. So he went to a bookshop and looked up an atlas. He noticed there were two Hollywoods on this earth. 1. Hollywood, California. 2. Holywood, Co. Down. Ira was confused. He returned home and looked at the telegram. Sadly for Ira, and until the day he died, he always claimed this was the turning point in his life, the telegram girl dictating the telegram was a poor speller and had spelt the Hollywood with one 'L'.

Though slightly puzzled, Ira came to the conclusion that his destiny lay in a small town in Co. Down. In mid-April 1916 Ira booked himself on a ferry from Hamburg to Larne. It was a very bumpy and dangerous ride, through those U-boat infiltrated seas, but he eventually reached his destination on Monday April 24th 1916. The day of the Easter Rising.

He then got on a train to Holywood . He disembarked at the train station, but no one was there to greet him. No studio heads. No photographers. No starlets. He was crest-fallen. He walked down the platform and suddenly was approached by a short man in a long overcoat. The man turned to him and said in a West Belfast accent, "Are you here for the shooting?" Ira perked up. "Yes, 'The Birth of a Nation'!" "Absolutely! Up the Republic! Follow me!" the man replied. Ira followed the man and his life as an unlikely revolutionary began.

September 17th 66 days to go

Have been home a few days. Sent off the reworked version of 'The Shamrock Sumo Club' to Ben. I have also started working on a new idea. For televison. I have complete contempt for it myself but as I approach my 40th birthday I must make compromises. It is not a scripted idea, but an idea for a reality television programme format. Because actual programme formats, that you can sell worldwide, is where all the money is nowadays. Who needs actors spouting arduously crafted lines when there are enough idiots out there who are prepared to make unscripted fools of themselves. This is what I came up with this morning.

'Te$t of Character' is a six-part reality television series. It is about people who have overcome a former addiction/vice but are now faced with their biggest challenge yet. Surrounded by a film crew and strategically positioned secret cameras filming their every move, each week two different contestants fight their impulses over a seven-day period, in the hope of winning the €100,000 cash prize.

1. Two ex-alcoholics are asked to work in a fully stocked bar for a week.

2. Two reformed thieves are asked to work in a bank, or jeweller's for a week.

3. Two formerly obese weight watchers are asked to work in the kitchen of a first class restaurant for a week.

4. Two reformed gamblers are asked to work in a casino for a week.

5. Two ex-smokers are asked to work in a cigarette factory for a week.

6. Two former compulsive masturbators are asked to work in a newly opened sex shop for a week.

September 23rd 60 days to go

There are three types of people. Those that are inside the tent. Those that are outside the tent. And those that don't even know where the tent is. Naturally, I belong to that third category. I have always felt that sense of disconnection. The worrying thing is though that the older you get you start to feel even more disconnected. Your semicircle of friends dwindles until one day you look across the table and realise how lucky you are to have at least found a soul mate. Kirsten. My long suffering significant other. Without her, I'd be lost. I'd be the cup without the saucer. The rose without the petal. The Bishop of Down without Conor.

Over the years, there have been a few insignificant others in my life. Probably the most significant of those insignificant others was Natalie.

Natalie Wooden (1988) 106m. * D: Robert Benton. Manus Mannion, Natalie Fleming. An unstable actress and a struggling comedian form a tempestuous dependency. An intriguing tale about two fractious, desperate characters. A sort of 'Withnail and I' meets 'Who's Afraid of Virginia Woolf'? [PG-13]**

I'm not too sure if I could class Natalie as a girlfriend. Natalie saw me more as a friend. I hoped the relationship would move on from friendship because Natalie was so beautiful and I badly wanted to engage in mate selecting practices with her. But it was not meant to be. I'd met her after a comedy gig in 1988. Though still living in Rathmines, I had initiated some changes in my life, and had quit acting for good. In retrospect, I was never very serious about my acting career. As the famed English actor of stage and screen, Sir Ralph Richardson, once said, "Acting is merely the art of keeping a large group of people from coughing."

And after my brief sojourn into blues singing with TojoMojo, I had eventually decided to bite the bullet and start performing stand-up comedy. At last.

However, stand-up comedy proved more difficult than I had envisaged. Writing new material was a constant problem. Rock bands have it easy, I thought. Rock bands can be performing a gig and in the middle of the set they can throw in someone else's song. No one in the audience thinks, "Oh, I heard that before. They didn't write that one. Of course the question is now, how much of the other stuff did they write?" No, they get away with it. They just call it a cover version.

I sometimes fantasised, as I slaved over an unfinished one-liner, about doing cover versions of other peoples' comedy routines. But it wasn't allowed because in the comedy world that's called stealing. I can categorically state that I never stole anyone's material. Except once. In my very first stand-up gig in Dublin I did steal a Bob Newhart line.

But in hindsight, "That's all from me. Good Night," was not one of his funnier ones. In desperation to come up with new material I even put an ad in the paper looking for a collaborator. I got one reply, from a 93-year-old French man called Jean Luc Charensol. He'd been a top official in the Vichy Government during the second World War and after his release from prison had moved to County Wicklow in the early 1950's.

I tried explaining to him, when he turned up on the door step of my flat on Leinster Road, that I was looking for a comedy writing collaborator. He was disappointed. He then suggested that since he'd travelled all the way from Blessington, and he was out for the day anyway, he might as well give comedy writing a try. I reluctantly agreed. We sat in my room for the whole afternoon and came up with the slightly surreal, yet sadly flawed, 'Maurice Chevalier goes into a hardware shop in Tipperary' routine.

The night I tried out this routine for the only time, Natalie was in the audience with a group of people I knew. Afterwards I gravitated towards their table and waited, in that way comedians do, to be told how much they liked my act. I then could feign modesty, and say, "It was a slow night, you should see me when I'm really on song."

But no one said anything. Except after a long pause. Natalie looked up at me and stated, "Making people laugh must be the hardest job in the world."

I pondered on this. I then replied, "It isn't actually. It's the second hardest. Tracking hurricanes is harder."

I then sat down next to her. I seemed to connect with Natalie. She told me she wanted to be an actress. I told her I'd been an actor but now had found my true vocation.

"Oh, and what's that?" she queried. I stared back at her blankly.

As we left the pub, she invited me back to her flat for coffee. On the way there I remembered thinking, "This is it, of all the guys in the venue tonight, she struck up a rapport with me, this incredibly beautiful woman has struck up a rapport with me and invited me back for coffee."

So we sat and talked and after a half an hour I thought to myself, "This woman is slightly maladjusted, could be trouble."

After an hour I amended my initial prognosis, "This woman is a lunatic, steer clear, do not get involved."

But I did get involved. In a non-involved way. I was her non-sexually intimate constant companion. A glorified chaperone that everyone thought was doing some bladder bumping with her. It was so depressing. We had a sort of a drinking coffee relationship. Always drinking coffee and discussing why we can't go to bed with each other, and that we can both cope with this situation. Well she could cope with this situation. In fact, she was quite happy with this situation, whereas I wasn't so amenable to the idea. And she would always be late for these coffee appointments.

We'd arrange to meet at two thirty. I'd leave my flat in plenty of time. I would savour that journey into town, because it was always nice to go into town for a reason, rather than just hanging out there killing days, killing time. So I'd be there at two twenty-five. I'd always be early.

People with nothing to do, apart from one comedy gig every fortnight, are always early for coffee appointments. They time their lives around coffee appointments. And I would stand outside the coffee shop. Bewley's on Grafton Street. I always waited outside. Never went in. Because if I went in I'd have to order a coffee immediately, and keep an eye out for her constantly, and keep telling people, "Yes, I'm keeping this seat for somebody," and I would usually end up just becoming a ball of nerves.

So I'd be standing outside Bewley's in reasonably good

form, watching the pedestrians go by, and looking forward to seeing Natalie. But Natalie wouldn't show up. The minutes would go by. It would be now two forty five, I would be getting worried. "Maybe she said, three-thirty," I'd think, "maybe she said Wednesday, maybe she said the Coffee Inn."

My mind would start to play these tricks, and I'd fantasise about some time in the future when people might have portable telephone receptacles and it would be possible to contact them to clarify arrangements. But I would dismiss this as too fantastic. I'd contemplate going to the Coffee Inn on South Anne Street but it would be too late because if I did so and she arrived in Bewley's and didn't see me she'd think I'd left and then she'd leave, so I'd have to stay put. It would be three fifteen. A few passing drunks would start to bother me.

I'd get agitated. "Maybe she's met someone else, someone she's been intimate with, sexually, maybe they went home last night, together, maybe he's with her right now, maybe they're just getting up after twelve hours of unbridled passion."

I'd decide, right, that's it, I'm leaving. So I'd walk. Up Camden Street. And I'd make promises to myself. Never again. This happens all the time. I'm sick of her. That's it. Finished. She can keep some other sucker waiting from now on. So I'd get back to my flat, walk through the door, it would be twenty past four, and the phone would ring. It would be Natalie.

"Where are you?" she'd ask.

"I'm here in my hallway," I'd respond in a bored yet wounded way.

"Why aren't you at Bewley's?" she'd wonder plaintively.

"Because I was there until three thirty," I'd bark back.

"But I got held up, I had such a frightful morning," she'd

say sadly. Then there would be a pause. "Are you coming in?" she'd ask coyly. I'd sigh and think of all those promises I had made to myself. And all those edicts and declarations on the way home. Then I'd think of the long empty evening that awaited me. "O.k., see you in half an hour."

Being a black and white movie obsessive, I saw Natalie as a cross between Mae West and Greta Garbo. She'd ring up and say in quite a suggestive voice, "Come on up and see me." Half an hour later I'd turn up at her place and her mood would have changed.

She'd tell me, "Go away, I want to be alone."

She was always depressed about her acting career going nowhere. Now, I personally, never rated Natalie as an actress. I felt that, off stage, she had presence, but on stage, she had absence. In fact, during that whole time I knew her, she only ever got one role. Playing Ophelia in a Longford town production of 'Hamlet' for the To Be Or Not To Be Theatre Company founded by *enfant terrible* Bosco Waldron. Less enfant, more terrible, Bosco Waldron strode the Fringe theatre scene of 1980's Ireland like a figurine. He'd been born on Denmark Street and from an early age, his life bore an uncanny resemblance to that of Hamlet.

As a teenager, his father had died mysteriously in the back garden of his house and subsequently his Uncle Claude had moved in with his mother Gertie. Unable to confront his uncle about the suspicious circumstances of his father's death and the subsequent domestic arrangement with his mother, Bosco rashly decided, on turning 21, to become an actor and cooked up a bizarre plan. He would spend his inheritance money putting on productions of 'Hamlet' in towns and villages all over Ireland. Hence the To Be Or Not To Be Theatre Company was born.

The plan also entailed Bosco, playing the part of the Prince of Denmark himself in every production and inviting his mother and uncle to the performances. Whilst on stage or standing in the wings Bosco would then gauge their reaction. They would invariably leave just after the play within the play scene, 'The Murder of Gonzago', not because they were feeling guilt-ridden and uncomfortable but because the productions were usually so appallingly bad.

As of now, nearly 15 years later, one can safely say the plan has not worked. Bosco's inheritance money has long run out, and for the tenth year running, a grant application for The To Be Or Not To Be Theatre Company has been turned down by the Arts Council. But Bosco still persists in putting on increasingly desperate and more slimmed down productions of 'Hamlet' around the country. Rumour has it, he has even reworked it as a one man show and last year performed all the parts himself in Clonakilty. His long suffering mother and uncle still come to his productions but still haven't fathomed his obsession with Elsinore.

The day Natalie got the role of Ophelia we decided to celebrate. And that was the night she turned to me in O' Neill's pub on Suffolk Street and said, "This is the moment, I want us to make love." I gulped twice as I placed my pint glass of Guinness with that twist of black currant on the table. If only she got cast more often, I thought. "In your place. A bath. A warm bath. Just the two of us. Let's go," she whispered. We left the pub. I hailed a taxi. I was determined for us to get back to my flat before her amorous mood deserted her, as it had so often in the past. In the back of the taxi she kissed me passionately for the first time. But I was suddenly pre-occupied. What about the immersion? I thought. We'll get back, I'll have to turn on the immersion, it will take at least forty minutes to warm up, what will we do in those forty minutes? A kettle! I can keep filling up the kettle and boiling it and pouring it in the bath. No, that will take too long. She nibbled friskily on my ear.

"Do we have to take a bath, why not go straight to bed?" I asked.

"It has to be a bath. In warm water, our two bodies will mesh and become one," she replied kissing my neck. The taxi arrived at my flat. I handed over the fare and we speedily alighted. We walked hurriedly to the door and I fumbled for my keys. We got inside. She removed her coat and hugged me.

"Lets go to the bathroom and start running the water," she said taking me by the hand, "for my water is already running."

At the top of the stairs I turned to her and said in a deflated fashion: "I have to turn on the immersion first though."

Disappointment was etched on her face. "Oh," she said, "how long will it take?"

"Five or ten minutes, at most," I said, gritting my teeth and leaving her standing there.

Half an hour passed. Natalie was bored, smoking one of her long, brown More cigarettes, in the kitchen, flicking through a magazine and listening to a tinny tape of 'The Gay Caballero', Frank Crumit, on my battered cassette recorder. Looking up she asked, "Has it warmed up yet?"

"We're almost there," I said. "I'll just check one more time."

I scurried to the bathroom. Turning on the tap, I detected a slight increase in temperature from the arctic deluge. Cold to tepid, I thought. I cursed my fate. Here was my one chance with this woman, this woman who had occupied my sordid little universe for the last eight months, this woman that I was obsessed with, hated, idolised, stalked and now I knew in my heart and soul that the moment was passing. I looked at myself in the mirror.

Suddenly, Old Man Negativity started inhabiting my thoughts. He'd been a frequent visitor since the age of 14. Say if she does agree to go into the bedroom, how will Bob fare? What happens if Bob isn't up to it? Can Bob take that kind of pressure? After all this time waiting to be with this woman? I wouldn't like to be in Bob's shoes. She'll probably ask you to wear a rubber. That'll smother Bob. Bob has never liked rubbers. He feels hemmed in, they cramp his style, he'll be like a flesh-coloured miniature frog-man in a frog suit gasping for oxygen, he'll become all flaccid and detumescent. I slapped myself on the face. "Stop it!" I whispered. "Be positive. Just seize the moment!" I purposefully walked back into the kitchen. Suddenly, I looked up and was horrified. Cousin Eamonn had made one of his infrequent nightly tea-making sojourns, and was just staring at Natalie. As she stretched out her hand to introduce herself, I hurriedly intervened. I was a nanosecond too late. Whilst shepherding Natalie out of the way I received the full blast of Eamonn's sweet crisp right hook. That put paid to our evening of passion.

September 26th 57 days to go

Out of synch with humanity. Example 389. I was on a crowded bus going into town this afternoon, when an old woman got on. Feeling a strange sense of chivalry, I immediately stood up and offered her my seat. She looked at me.

"Are you saying I look old?" she asked.

"I'm just offering you a seat..." I stuttered.

"What age do you think I am?" she continued.

"I don't know, I mean..."

"Well you must think I'm old. What age do you think I am?" she persisted.

"Ehm... seventy something?... eh late sixties?" I mumbled.

"I'm forty fuckin' eight years old, ya stupid fuckin' eejit. Keep your seat. I can stand. I've a few years left in me yet. Cheek of some people!"

I had headed into town to finally meet 'the step uncle of Irish comedy' Dinny Bruce, in a greasy café off O'Connell Street. Dinny insisted on meeting there, because he used to frequent it in the late 1970's. It was quite an unsavoury place. He was just about to dig into his large plate of sausage, egg, beans and chips when a junkie walked in and sat down opposite us.

The junkie then took out his syringe and proceeded to sterilise and clean it by inserting it into the spout of a vinegar dispenser which lay on the table. He then just got up and went out the door. Probably was going to dump his syringe later in some bottle bank. Or maybe he was going to hang onto it until next weekend, until he'd used up a few more, and save himself making too many unnecessary journeys.

Dinny looked at me and mentioned that he'd suddenly lost his appetite and wasn't that hungry after all. We left the café and went to one of those new coffee shops with the word 'Mocha' over its door, on North Earl Street. In our anoraks, and resembling refugees from some bygone era, we looked around and realised we were surrounded by 'cool' people. Cool young people. With their mobile phones, strong self-images and thought-revoking conversations. Myself and Dinny were never cool. In fact that was one of the few things I always liked about him. He was so uncool. Yet looking at him I realised that there is a certain longevity to un-coolness. Cool dates. Uncool is timeless.

Drinking from that overpriced mug of cappuccino, and shouting over that over-loud Chet Baker C.D. that played in the background, Dinny told me he had finally quit performing as a stand-up comedian. There are too many comedians today in Ireland, he claimed. It is a ridiculous problem. He wondered what can be done about it? How can we, as a nation, ensure that in twenty years' time their number hasn't multiplied even further?

Dinny wants to stamp out this scourge right now. He has obviously given the situation a lot of thought because he has even formulated a plan. Firstly, primary and secondary school teachers must play their part. All over the country at the start of the school year, members of the teaching community must be vigilant and root out the class clown in each of their classes. Once the class clowns have been identified in the individual schools, their names must be forwarded to the Department of Health.

The Department of Health will send these class clowns to a team of child psychologists. The psychologist will sit each individual child down and try to find the core reason for his or her need to create laughter, his or her need for approval and their craving to be the centre of attention. *All of the time.* After an intensive six-week course of therapy the child will be returned to class a perfectly normal, inoffensive, young person. The tab will be paid by the tax payer.

But in the long run these psychotherapy sessions will enormously benefit Ireland as a society because, Dinny insists, we as a community will be spared future generations of Irish stand-up comedians on some digital channel spewing forth their predictable, puerile, unoriginal, comic observations. I nodded silently. Or those same comedians, he continued, appearing on one of those interchangeable panel shows, at some future date, and engaging in 'the Dubious Art of Disposable Sneering', as they labour to come up with something 'witty' and 'amusing' about the week's events.

I tried to change the topic but Dinny was on a roll. He continued on his theme. Why wait twenty years? Why not just firebomb the bar of the Gilded Balloon one night during the Edinburgh Fringe Festival? That would eradicate a whole generation of Irish comedians. Taken aback, I looked at him worriedly. He smiled and muttered sheepishly that he was only joking.

Dinny then told me how glad he was to be finished with performing and started jabbering on about how wonderful it is to write for the radio, and how it was always something he wanted to do. Sure Dinny. Keep talking. I'll try not to laugh. He asked me had I ever thought about giving it a try. No I hadn't, I said. He wondered why not. I kept quiet. Didn't want to dampen his misguided enthusiasm by sharing with him my theory on writing for the radio. The fact that it is a 'down the list' thing to do. It is something one does, for negligible money, while trying to do other things. More important things. It is never a priority. I have never heard somebody at sixteen announce, "My greatest ambition in life is to be a radio writer!" It is something unfulfilled, lonely accountants, or mothers of five from Laois do, to cater for their 'artistic' side.

Still enthused, Dinny began to tell me his radio sit-com idea. Dinny maintains that all great sit-com's have characters trapped in enclosed areas, and that the comedy comes out of how these characters relate to each other in that confined environment. Dinny wants to set his radio sitcom in a nose. You cannot get more enclosed than that is his logic. The two main characters will be nostrils, side by side. He is also thinking of bringing in a cantankerous next door neighbour character called Mr. Phlegm who is always causing trouble. It will be ideal for radio, he claims, because the listeners will be able to create the images in their own minds.

He is toying with either calling it 'Nose World' or 'On the Nose'. I told him I preferred the former because the latter was too, well, on the nose. He then asked me was I interested in working on it. I declined and told him I was much too busy with my T.V. idea and assorted other projects. After finishing his cappuccino, he told me we should hook up again sometime, we should 'keep in touch', and talk about the old days in London. I said I'd like that very much and told him I'd give him a call. I was lying. Anyway, I don't like being reminded of that time in London.

September 28th 55 days to go

The Comedy Nobody (1996) 106 m. * D: John Duignan. Manus Mannion, Dinny Bruce, Derek Osborne. A comedian spends three years on the comedy circuit in London attempting to hit the big time. Another show biz hard-luck story with nothing special to elevate it out of the ordinary. [PG]

The Comedy Nobody was worried. The gig was only

seven hours away. At some stage that night, he would have to walk out on stage and face that sea of tattoos, that alcoholically induced boorishness, that raucous Saturday night crowd. He'd never felt comfortable performing in front of a big crowd. He'd never had that easy rapport with them and they had always intimidated him. If truth be told, the stage was never really his home. It was more like a B&B in Waterford. During off-peak season. His perfect room to play was one that would be nearly empty. A small room, that would hold 50, and maybe 16 would turn up.

Career-wise this wasn't a very clever preference, for if he played to small groups of people, very few audience members would ultimately catch his act and he would never become a success.

The tension before gigs was becoming unbearable. The Comedy Nobody would have a whole afternoon to spare, so firstly he'd go to the cinema, but always in the back of his mind would be that date with comedy destiny at nine o'clock. Will they laugh tonight? God, please make them laugh tonight! In the cinema he'd stare at the exit sign. He would be already planning the quickest way out and his underground travel route to the comedy venue before the opening credits. He'd watch the movie anxiously.

Heat: (1996) 172 m. ** D: Michael Mann. Al Pacino, Robert De Niro, Val Kilmer, Ashley Judd, Jon Voight. Overlong, over-rated action thriller with obsessive cop Pacino trying to nab clever crook De Niro and his gang. [R]

The film would end. He'd need to urinate. He'd run to the cubicle. He'd worry about how embarrassing it would be if a really tall man came in to urinate in the cubicle next to him and looked down over the partition. As he'd unzip his trousers and try to find his tense member he'd ponder on how difficult it is to find somewhere just to pee in London without having to pay. He'd then half remember a security code for the gent's toilet in the Charing Cross Hotel, where he'd been drinking once with another comedian and every time he had to go for a leak, he'd forget the code and have to run back up the stairs and ask the concierge to repeat the number.

On leaving the cinema he'd reluctantly accept the fact that he had to eat something. He would always end up in one of those budget Chinese restaurants off Leicester Square where he'd half finish an oversized portion of beef, green pepper and black bean sauce. He always ate too quickly and afterwards, still having hours to kill before the evening's gig, he'd end up doing the same things over and over again. He couldn't escape. This was his life. Like oyster sauce, it kept repeating. There was a safety in things repeating. There was a safety in failure. The cosiness of failure.

With constant pain in his neck and back, he'd trudge around with a long face, peeping into trendy shops off Piccadilly Circus. Who are these people? These beautiful cool people. Leading jet set lives. As opposed to his own Fokker one-set life. Legs weary he'd walk around Oxford Street meaninglessly, pointlessly. He'd make his way to a second-hand record shop. He'd see a record album in some corner, coffee stains on its cover, reduced to £1, that he owned in Galway all those years ago, and he'd remember vividly the time it was first released. The poster, the hype, giving the girl behind the counter a down payment in the shop so she'd set it aside for him, eventually buying it, running home, and unpacking it. Removing it from its sleeve, the smell of the vinyl, the loud chunk of the needle, and that first anxious play, nervous with worry about potential vinyl scratches.

Overcome with an unexpected sense of acute nostalgia, and a yearning for more cosseted times, he'd leave the second hand record shop and wander around some more. He'd then enter a bookshop and go over to the same section, that he always went to, the movie section, and feel that same feeling. Again. Things still repeating. Like oyster sauce. Then he'd spot a book he'd bought as a teenager. He'd pick it up and touch it. His finger tips would be charged with memories. He'd feel the hold of the old. The pull of the past. He'd cling on to the book, and wouldn't want to let it go. But he'd have to let it go. Because it's gone. It's true what that writer guy Hartley said. The past is Sri Lanka. Or a different country. Or whatever.

Finally, it would be time to head out to the gig. On his way to the underground station he'd run through the comedy routine he would do that night in The Banana Cabaret Club in Acton Town. It was much the same routine that he did every night. After all, he was a disciple of routine and one of his routines was doing his routine the same way over and over again.

He'd moved to London in late 1993, after five years of struggling with his career in Dublin, to try and become a star. But London was less a case of a star is born as a star is miscarried. It was now 1996 and he was on a treadmill of terminal oblivion. He was getting work but he was going nowhere.

Everybody wanted to be a comedian. There were thousands on the circuit. Guys out with their mates having a few drinks would get up and tell a few jokes during an 'open spot'. They'd get a positive response and would think, "I can do that!" They'd go back the next week and get another positive response and before you could say "Perrier Nomination", they'd be on the circuit and would be further up the bill than the Comedy Nobody.

But the Comedy Nobody still had that comedy bug. Because when a gig went well and people laughed at his jokes, it was the greatest feeling in the world. They looked at him. They loved him. They wanted him. And all those thoughts of inadequacy and insignificance that had hounded him from an early age passed momentarily. But lately, nights like this were becoming more rare.

Waiting for the tube, he'd breathe in that subterranean smell of humanity. Junk and rats on the tracks. Pissed people arguing. Hassled people trying to get home. Japanese people with expensive, fashionable clothing, carrying expensive fashionable bags. His stomach taut and tense. The contents of his stomach churning in rhythm as the tube rattled into view. Sitting on that crowded tube train the tedium would be livened by a busker who would step on at Hyde Park Corner. The unhappy, trapped commuters, already fixing their gaze to their newspapers, would now practically glue their daily read to their noses as the musical entertainment would walk up and down the aisle, rendering tunelessly a version of The Beatles 'You Never Give Me Your Money'. The busker would then sheepishly ask for a contribution at the end of the song, smiling smugly at his ironic cleverness in picking that particular song title. Trouble is, they would never give him their money, and he would be completely ignored as the commuters' newspapers would become substitute shrouds. The busker would alight at Baron's Court.

Up until that very last minute before the Comedy Nobody walked into the venue he could turn around and leave. But he was a professional. His currency was laughter. Lately though, he'd been suffering on the foreign exchange markets. Most times he'd be the last act of the first half. That meant he still wasn't established and successful enough to go on in the second half and close the show. After some strained chat with the other performers, suddenly the audience would be seated and it would be time to start.

The M.C. would come on and try to rouse the audience with his bargain basement banter. After about eight minutes of half-hearted audience participation, the M.C. would give up and announce the first act. It was usually a young hungry guy invariably called Lee. The Comedy Nobody would secretly hope for Lee to fall flat on his face for he knew that if a comedian died before him, he would instinctively feel it wouldn't be his night to die. Conversely, the better the comedian before him did, the more pressure he would feel. Lee would be doing well, he'd have no material, mind you, he'd be just a knob comic, a gag and bone man, but he'd be killing them, they'd be lapping him up. He'd be whipping them into a frenzy. Suddenly the Comedy Nobody would be overcome with panic as the laughter of the audience would build to a deafening crescendo. I've got to follow him?

The audience will be exhausted! Then all those negative doubts would re-enter his mind. Doubts that would always re-surface two minutes before going on stage. Am I actually that funny? I'm just another statistic on the circuit, why should the audience bother? Maybe my stuff won't work? He'd eventually be announced on stage and would be facing twenty minutes of Russian roulette. If they laughed he'd be top of the world, if not, he'd have no escape. He'll be a dead man. He'll start to squint, scared to look at those un-smiling faces behind those lit candles, a jaded metaphor for a comic's funeral. His lines will start lacking the fluidity and fluency they sometimes have, his heart will start beating fast, his throat will go dry, the audience will start to murmur, and no one will be listening. And he'll wonder, how can he turn this round? And then he'll realise that he can't. This is his material. This is his life. This is all he has and they're not interested.

Thankfully most times, he wouldn't die. The gig would go o.k. They always went o.k. He'd never get big laughs. He'd get genuine smiles. He'd never 'storm', as they say in the business, he'd sort of 'light rain-shower'. A nagging anti-climactic feeling and emptiness would silently gnaw at him as he would analyse the gig on the tube journey home. If he'd put that bit in there, or if he'd left that bit out, maybe it would have been better. He vowed to improve. But he didn't. Success kept eluding him. He'd had such big dreams concerning his career. He had wanted to be Woody Allen. Now he'd settle for being Foster&Allen.

October 4th 49 days to go

In addition to not having that easy rapport with barmen, or that ability to talk complete shite with strangers, an aptitude for haggling is another Irish trait that seems to have bypassed me completely. I was forcibly reminded of this yesterday when myself and Kirsten got some wallpapering done. When we purchased the wallpaper two weeks ago, the wallpapering shop had recommended a handyman and said they'd never had any complaints about him yet. Thinking about this on the way home that day, Kirsten dismissed this seal of approval by rightfully claiming that the Irish never complain about anything anyway.

Sadly, her instincts about the handyman proved correct. Since she was at work it was my job to let him in and oversee things. He arrived two hours late. Handymen think you have nothing better to do than sit around all day waiting for them to turn up. It's beside the point that you *have* nothing better to do than sit around all day waiting for them to turn up. Once pleasantries had been exchanged and a cup of tea offered, he started to get down to work.

As he put up the wallpaper slowly, I monitored proceedings from afar. Hovered discreetly. Kept an eye on what he was doing without being too intrusive. Because they hate being watched. I also had to secretly record his visits to our bathroom. And what he did in there. This is one of Kirsten's primary concerns when we have a handyman in the house and she is detained elsewhere. Do they visit the bathroom and what do they do in there?

Kirsten arrived home early around five. She wanted to have a look at the work done. She was not happy. Although her mood lightened somewhat when I told her lowly that the handyman had been to the loo twice, but thankfully both times it was just a number one. It was getting late. He started putting his things away in his van and finally approached us for his payment.

We asked him to wait a minute as we self-consciously huddled in a corner and tried to come up with a strategy. After much manic whispering and frenzied calculations we eventually devised a course of action. Although he was looking for €500 we would be assertive and insist we weren't paying him a cent more than €350. We showed him the wallpapering areas we were unimpressed with. The glue stains. The sloppy workmanship in some of the corners. The blotches. He nodded. We told him we felt he shouldn't be paid the whole fee. He asked how much we felt he should be paid. We looked at each other and said "€350." To our amazement, he didn't contest the amount and just said, "O.k., I'll take the €350. No problem."

Relieved we said "O.k." We paid him and then he left. We joked about it a bit and prepared to make dinner. Then Kirsten started to think. She always starts to think after a situation like this occurs.

"We should have only offered him €300," she said. Then she used the 'H' word. "We should have haggled."

I tried placating her unsuccessfully. "But we agreed if we got him down to €350 we'd be happy!"

"We could have got him down to €300. We're so stupid!" she said. "Why are we so stupid?" she repeated shaking her head, as she started manically chopping a locally sourced onion.

October 10th 43 days to go

Another day at Setback Central. 'Spud Zombie' was turned down by the Film Council. I'm still in shock after reading that reader's report that Sarah sent me.

REF: 2O6DF3 READER: HW
READER'S REPORT DATE: 15. 09. 03.
TITLE: Spud Zombie
DIRECTOR-APPLICANT'S NAME: Sarah Dunlop.
PRODUCER: Sarah Dunlop.
COMPANY: Emerald City Films.
FORMAT: Screenplay.
GENRE: Zombie Movie.

SYNOPSIS: In Ireland, during the potato famine, the population is terrorised by zombies whose heads are in the shape of giant potatoes.

COMMENTS: The premise of 'Spud Zombie' is utterly

predictable. It seems to draw on such films as George Romero's 'Night of the Living Dead' and its deadpan sick humour is heavily influenced by some early Sam Raimi. It is also quite similar, but far inferior to another project,'Potato Fright' which has recently received development funding. Unlike 'Potato Fright', 'Spud Zombie' lacks any sort of originality and there seems to be little passion driving this project. The writer fails to put a personal mark on the material and the whole script seems to exist in a vacuum inhabited only by other movies. The sample scenes are prosaic and do little to elevate the present submission.

RECOMMENDATION: Pass.

October 13th 40 days to go

Still reeling after the 'Spud Zombie' debacle. My worst fears were realised. There *was* a similar idea in the system. Then again, as has been repeated over and over again, there are only seven stories out there. Trouble is, most of them seem to include zombies this weather. Maybe it's just as well it was rejected. If they had given Sarah and Emerald City Films funding, I'd have spent four years writing and reworking the script.

It might eventually have got made with a specially written role for some has-been available American actor. Like Judge Reinhold for example. To give the movie a profile. Over here. On release, it would have got a dismissive two-line review in the Irish Times, no one would have gone to see it, because no one goes to 'indigenous' movies, and it might have run for a week. Sometime in 2009 it might have been shown on the television at half one in the morning. Then in fifteen years time it might have turned up on some retrospective of Irish made movies running in the Irish Film Centre, where it would be shown once to an empty cinema at two o'clock in the afternoon. I have come to the conclusion that all endeavour is futile.

October 17th 36 days to go.

Kirsten wanted us to go to a Homeware shop this afternoon. She wanted to get a new work top for the kitchen. I was fine with the one we have. O.k., it looks a bit faded and grimy, but I can live with that. It doesn't bother me. But it bothers her.

I said to her, "You go to the Homeware shop."

"No. I want to involve you in the decision."

"But I don't care, it's just a kitchen work top," I replied. "I trust your judgement."

She stared at me. We had suddenly switched gears from conversation mode to stand-off mode. This lasted all of ninety seconds. Eventually we came to a compromise: I agreed to go to the Homeware shop. Once we arrived, we looked around for a shop assistant. A friendly, young black South African man approached us wondering did we need any help. We asked him about the various types of kitchen work tops on display. He gave us a detailed breakdown of each type, its make, and the colours available. He went off to help another customer.

We discussed what he'd just told us. Or what we thought he'd told us. You see we only understood 40% of what he had said. He knew his brief, and he was a very nice young man but because of his accent we were completely baffled by the details he had imparted. So we needed further clarification. But then we faced a dilemma. If we go to another shop assistant, a white shop assistant, how will that look? Our South African friend might notice and he might think we are racist. And we are not racist. So we eventually went back to him to ask for some further elucidation on things. He gave us a further spiel. This time we understood even less as we nodded in an engaged and interested manner. We took home some brochures and told him we'd think about things.

October 22nd 31 days to go

A month to go until I'm forty. I have hit a wall. Waiting for things to take off but things never doing so. Proposals being turned down. Ideas that are accepted spending years in development. Time is finite. I don't even enjoy watching old movies anymore, realising life is too short to waste watching an hour and a half of this dated junk. I saw one today. With Alice Faye.

Wake Up and Live (1937) 91m. ** D: Sidney Lanfield. Alice Faye, Jack Haley, Patsy Kelly, Walter Winchell. Breezy, yet formulaic musical about competing radio personalities.

I sent off that telly idea to a few production companies but I don't hold out much hope for it. Everything is random. In the lap of the gods. Kirsten is getting tired of my listless despair. It is just that I am devoid of hope. Fifteen years ago I would be depressed about my lot as a Creative Lower Being, but I would always go to sleep at night imagining a better future. But now I've realised, this is that future and that future is no future at all.

October 24th 29 days to go

Having become increasingly exasperated with Crumlin shopping centre over the last few months, I've started doing my grocery shopping at the Marks&Spencer food hall on Grafton Street recently.

However, I've encountered a different set of problems there. It is all because of my new dark blue fleece jacket. Kirsten bought it for me about three weeks ago. As a surprise. She was tired of looking at my bulky anorak. It was a good bargain too. So I tried it on. And I really liked it. It really suits me. I love wearing that dark blue fleece jacket. It is so comfortable. And so loose fitting. I guess, to borrow a phrase used in the fashion world, it is so me.

But every time I put it on and go to the supermarket, members of the public think I'm one of the staff there. I am constantly being accosted by complete strangers wondering where certain items are. It has happened at least ten times in the last fortnight:

"Ground almond?"

"Don't know."

"Capers?"

"I don't work here."

"Hair gel?"

"Do I look like the kind of guy who still stacks shelves?"

"Diet free Coke?" "

You need more than Diet free Coke to lose some of that weight, Muffin Boy."

"Cullen's big grey, recycled disposable bin liner bags, the packet of 20, for €7.80?"

"Could you be just a bit more specific?"

"Pro-biotic yoghurt?"

"Leave me alone, can't you see I'm holding a blue basket — I'm a flippin' customer!"

Today was the same. While attempting to find some organic avocados I was approached at least four times. I suppose I'll just have to stop wearing my dark blue fleece jacket.

Once I completed my shopping, my day didn't get any better because at the express checkout queue I got into an argument. I was just standing there, waiting in line, holding my two organic avocados when I noticed the woman in front of me had more than five items in her basket. Maybe I was suffering from post 'complications in-wearing dark blue fleece jacket' syndrome but I was in no mood to be tolerant. I decided to say something.

"Hi, eh, excuse me, but you have more than five items in your basket. The express checkout says five items or less."

"I'm in such a dreadful hurry." She batted her eyelids.

I think she was trying to flirt with me. I was going to tell her it was no use because I was born without that flirting and picking-up-signals gene. I continued to stare at her coldly.

"Sorry. It says five items or less." For a moment she was puzzled as she noticed my dark blue fleece jacket.

"Do you work here?"

"No. I don't work here!"

I then pointed at the notice above us.

"It says five items or less!"

She was surprised at my persistence. She was a middle-aged lady, probably from some salubrious Rathgar neighbourhood, who was used to getting her own way.

"You're not going to make a scene are you?" she asked incredulously, arching an eyebrow.

"Actually I am," I replied. "Somebody has to. I don't even have a basket. I'm just holding two organic avocados. Why should the guy holding two organic avocados be delayed in the queue because a well-heeled housewife from Dublin 6 has more than five items in her basket. What's the point in having an express checkout system if people like you abuse it?"

She nodded at the bored checkout girl. "Well, *she* won't mind."

"She will if I have anything to do with it," I piped up.

The lady from Rathgar eventually got to the top of the queue. She chattily apologised as the checkout girl scanned her items. All eleven of them. I counted. The checkout girl just blushed and told her not to worry. After a bit more small talk, the lady from Rathgar put her items in the bag, paid with her credit card and left. As she turned to ascend the escalator she smiled at me triumphantly. Livid, I stood at the top of the queue waiting to approach and reproach the checkout girl. But with perfect timing, just at that moment, she finished up her shift and was replaced by a slightly cross-eyed guy with an over enthusiastic manner and an unresolved comb over problem.

October 25th 28 days to go

Angst in adagio. That inner cauldron of tension continues to brew within. My depression can't lift. Especially now that the evenings will be getting longer. I have always been prone to S.A.D., seasonally adjusted despair, although sometimes I feel I suffer from a particular virulent form of it, P.A.D. Permanently adjusted despair.

This morning I felt so low I went into the kitchen and contemplated overdosing on Bach's Rescue Remedy and knocking back that whole small container. But common sense and economic prudence prevailed. Later, I picked up the paper and read that my state of physical and mental lethargy could be down to the early onset of the Andropause, the male menopause. Oh Christ! I was such a late developer and now I'm hitting the Andropause!

Ironically in the same paper, there was another article on some simple devices to achieve happiness. It told depressives to smile at people! With my teeth? It would freak them out. It suggested I buy a plant. Nurture it. Watching it grow will bring you joy. Yeh. Knowing my luck, I'd be allergic to it and I'd come out in a rash. The article went on to mention physical exercise. Exertion releases endorphins into your system which make you feel naturally good. Join a gym? Not me, given my unresolved 'nakedness in public' issues. The piece then proposed meditation. I've tried meditation. Once.

In the middle of it, while approaching a state of tranquil well being, the neighbour's burglary alarm went off and I nearly got a heart attack. The article finally suggested that a downbeat person should simply try and make other people feel good. To do special things for your friends. Surprise them. If you feel you have brought joy to people, you will feel joy.

But that wouldn't work either. If I started surprising my friends with acts of kindness they would think there is something wrong. Even Kirsten would be suspicious. She'd wonder what was I up to. So, I'm afraid there are no solutions from that article. But I know I need to change. Everything. My mental approach. My attitude to life. My career. And all this was re-enforced this afternoon by a very clear signal. I was walking over the Halfpenny Bridge when I saw a young homeless guy hold up a sign with the prophetic words 'Change Please' written on it.

October 31st 22 days to go

I read this morning that River Phoenix died ten years ago today. I wonder if River Phoenix had lived and he'd had a son, and the son had grown up, what would the son have called him? The Old Man, River? Tonight I was flicking the channels and I came across a profile of my old friend from the Montague Keeble Centre, Bernice Quinlivan.

And it got me thinking. In a way, I wish I was Bernice Quinlivan. I never thought I'd say that, but if I died and came back in another life, I'd like to come back as Bernice Quinlivan. At this stage in my life I'd be happy being Bernice Quinlivan. Despite those glasses and that bizarre twitch. Because as a writer she knows her world. She knows her people. She's happy with her place. Slice-of-life, small town poetess. She writes a poem, then another poem, before she knows it she has an anthology, it gets published, it doesn't sell very well but at least she's a minor somebody. She's Bernice Quinlivan. And she gets invited to poetry readings. And she gets to go to some nice hotel in Listowel, with some other poets, and the organisers buy her a few drinks and a few more drinks and put her up in nice accommodation, and then she comes home to her Bernice Quinlivan world, and her husband of 28 years, Oliver, is waiting for her. And he is very supportive of her and after all these years still looks like a roadie at a wedding.

And a few months later, she comes up with some more of her little ideas, and she writes them down in a little coffee shop on that little note book she always carries around, and before she knows it she has a couplet, and then lo and behold, a poem and then two poems, and before you can say Bernice Quinlivan she has completed another anthology. And it gets published and it doesn't sell very well but at least she's Bernice Quinlivan. And then they make her a member of that select club for artists, Aosdána. And she's given a fez and learns a secret handshake. And each year she receives a Bursary – the slightly unsavoury sounding cnuas – and now, she's made for life.

I should be a poet. Not a screenwriter. In this country poets are revered. When Bernice writes a poem, nay when she comes up with the idea for a poem, does she have to run it by a producer first? Or a script editor?

"Eh, Bernice, I think you should move that comma, on line four."

No, she just trusts herself and writes it. And she knows it will be published. Whereas as a screenwriter you can't just go ahead and write. Well you can, but then you have to give it to somebody, an 'expert' in the industry, usually a producer, and they decide if they want to take on board your project, while they sit in their offices all day helplessly laughing out loud. And then they say they'll think about it as they give you their enlightened, perceptive input and you go home and wish life was simpler.

And you wish you were Bernice Quinlivan. And you contemplate killing yourself and coming back as Bernice

Quinlivan, but then you remember there is already one Bernice Quinlivan, and maybe the world isn't big enough for two Bernice Quinlivans.

November 5th   17 days to go

My life is a bad sit-com waiting to be cancelled. I've got sinus problems. I have ever increasing breasts. I have a beer belly. I suffer from palpitations. I have cluster headaches. A touch of reflux oesophagitis with the possible existence of *helicobacter pylori* in my gut. I suffer from dysthymia. I think I suffer from irritable bowel syndrome. My neck is stiff and every morning my back aches. Decrepitude beckons, mortality waves hello. Time passes, bus passes, old age, death.

With all these on-again, off-again ailments, Kirsten finally persuaded me to go see the doctor. Reluctantly, I agreed to do so. Today. On my way there, I rationalised about things. And for once in my life I utilised the Power of Positive Thinking. I don't look pale. I haven't lost my appetite. I'm still quite young. Why am I worried? By the time I arrived in his office, I was feeling at peace with myself and admonishing myself for being such a self-obsessed hypochondriac.

Then I made a fatal mistake. Fatal being the operative word. Waiting in the surgery I picked up a couple of health leaflets to kill the time. Kill being another operative word. The first one said heartburn can give you throat cancer. So I put that down. The next one said a paunch, and weight around the abdomen, can lead to bowel cancer. I put that one down. The next one said the heart is the engine and if an engine is acting erratically it needs a complete examination, including stress tests, E.C.G.'s, and the wearing of a heartbeat monitor or the consequences could be grave. Grave being yet another operative word. I immediately put that one down.

After perusing over those three pamphlets, I had cramps in my stomach, felt acidic in my chest, and had a racing palpitation. I was contemplating going to the loo and making a swift premature exit when I was told the doctor was ready to see me. I'll get the results of my blood test on Friday week.

November 10th 12 days to go

I'm a bit worried about the blood test results. Visited the parents over the weekend. I decided to treat myself and take the train. There is one thing I have learned from train travel over the years. If you are on a train and there is a low-key lunatic sitting opposite you, rummaging in his Dunnes Stores bag and staring sadly into the distance and muttering to himself, he will not get off at an early stop. He will remain on the train as long as you do. Or, if he does get off at an early stop, your sense of relief will be short-lived as his place will be taken — by *two* low-key lunatics sitting opposite you. Rummaging in their Dunnes Stores bags and staring sadly into the distance. For once I was grateful when we arrived in Athlone and were told, due to unforseen circumstances, we had to leave the train and take the remainder of the journey by bus. Once on the bus, to sweeten the pill they treated us to a movie. Starring Ben Affleck. Again.

When visiting Galway nowadays it seems things have remained exactly the same, yet have completely changed. Colm is happily married with a young family, and is rolling in the money with his estate agency in Tuam. Obviously my parents have got older. On Saturday I was briskly walking down Shop Street ahead of them, when I looked behind and for a moment thought, who are these two old people following me?

Father's latest bone of contention is the problem of roaming dogs. Plastic bottles filled with water randomly lie in both the front and the back garden.

"What is the point of that?" I asked on Sunday morning.

"To deter roaming dogs," he explained.

"In what way?"

"They just get panicked by a plastic bottle with water in it. They think it's a bomb waiting to go off or something," he said enthusiastically.

"In all my years in this house, I have never seen a pack of roaming dogs in the back garden," I said.

"Oh, they're out there," he said with conviction. Then there was a pause and he looked at me. "Ready to pounce." He then looked around furtively and winked at me. I was going to point out that randomly placing half-filled plastic bottles around a garden defeats the whole purpose, from a visual perspective, of maintaining that garden in a tidy and orderly manner. But he was too engrossed in waiting for the canine invasion.

November 11th 11 days to go

Kirsten had this morning off. After breakfast as I was leaving the house to do some gratuitous grocery accumulation in town, she noticed something.

"How come you don't wear that new dark blue fleece jacket anymore? I thought you liked it."

"I do. It's just, it's a complicated situation."

She looked at me sceptically.

"I'll put it on. It's fine," I said.

"You don't have to if you don't want to," she replied.

"No. No. I will. I like it. I'd forgotten about it, that's all."

Wearing the dark blue fleece jacket, I eventually arrived in town and ambled into the Marks&Spencer food hall. As usual it didn't take long for me to be accosted. This time she was middle-aged. Gruff. A country woman. Wearing a slightly dirty grey mackintosh, thick beige tights and trainers. Looked like a nun on holidays. "Do you know where the auld Thousand Island Dressing is?" she inquired.

I looked at her for a moment. And paused. And then it hit me. Why not have a little payback time? With my first victim. This woman in the grey mackintosh. Yes. This brusque rural type will suffer the consequences of six weeks of perpetual harassment. It won't be pretty but I have no choice. Sometimes a man has to take a stand. Has to change his situation. And has to strike back. And she, this countrywoman, Sr. Bernadette on vacation, is going to be my quarry.

I looked at her. I smiled my warmest customer friendly smile.

"Thousand Island Dressing?" I repeated.

"Yeh!"

Then I nodded in an informed manner. I paused again. A long pause. A relishing pause. A Thousand Island Dressing pause.

"Yes, I think I do. I know exactly where it is," I said. "You hang on there, I'll get it for you." "Kraft! Get me the Kraft one!" she said stridently.

"No problem," I shouted back.

I briskly took a left and walked towards aisle number three. Reaching the top of the aisle, I bypassed the check-out counter and took another left. Spotting Sr. Bernadette between the aisles, still awaiting my imminent return, I stooped suddenly behind another checkout counter before quickly and furtively stepping on that escalator going up. I felt invigorated. Life doesn't get much better than this. I threw my head back and started to laugh. Loudly and demonically. For today at least, there would be no more customer queries. I had shown them. I had shown them all. This was one man not to be messed with.

November 12th 10 days to go

As well as my fortieth birthday coming up, it is also the fortieth anniversary of the assassination of John. F. Kennedy. And last night I saw this incredible documentary that shed new light onto this ongoing mystery. The centre piece of the documentary was a recently discovered, alleged statement made by Lee Harvey Oswald's mother, Marguerite, on her death bed in 1981.

Marguerite Oswald's Alleged Death Bed Statement:

'Kennedy's assassination was a terrible mistake. It was all the fault of one man, Dr. Eugene Pallette.

Dr. Eugene Pallette was the Lothario of Dallas. He wasn't really a doctor, in fact no one really knew what he did, but wherever he ended up, he had this ability to ingratiate himself with important people and women especially found his seasoned sexual charisma irresistible. Marina, the wife of my boy Lee Harvey, began having an affair with Pallette in October of 1963. Lee Harvey found out about it. He always had a mean and violent streak and was consumed by jealousy.

He then read in the paper that President John F. Kennedy was coming to town on November 22nd. Since Pallette was well connected with local dignitaries, Lee Harvey knew that he, Pallette, would automatically get a place at the front of the crowd at Dealey Plaza, to cheer on the passing president. Always handy with a rifle, Lee Harvey devised a plan. He would shoot Pallette from the sixth floor of his place of work, The Book Depository, as the president's motorcade drove by.

In other words President Kennedy's visit would be the perfect distraction for my boy's murder of his wife's lover. At the last minute though, on the morning of November 22nd, Marina found out about Lee Harvey's plan. She rushed to the corner of Dealey Plaza to warn Pallette. As the president's motorcade approached, Lee Harvey pointed his gun and aimed at Pallette.

As he was about to pull the trigger he saw Marina run into view. This distracted him slightly and he certainly didn't want to kill Marina because he loved her dearly, so he jerked to the left as the gun went off. Mayhem ensued as my boy slowly realised he had accidentally shot the president. Meanwhile another irate husband, a man called Billy Bob Cropper, was stooping behind the grassy knoll, nearby. He too had Pallette in his sights because Pallette had been carrying on with his wife, Mary Beth also. As Billy Bob was about to shoot, a worried Mary Beth had run to the other side of Pallette to warn him of her husband's plans. Billy Bob saw Mary Beth at the last moment and he also adjusted his gun slightly to try and miss her, but in doing so, let it off accidentally, again shooting the unfortunate president. However, being a determined fella, Billy Bob persisted in trying to shoot Pallette, only this time hitting Governor John Connally. I heard belatedly that there might have been one or two other irate husbands in the vicinity with loaded shotguns also out to get Pallette on that morning but I cannot confirm this. All I can say is that one man, and one man alone, was responsible for the death of our president, and that man was Dr. Eugene Pallette. My boy, Lee Harvey, was just an unfortunate victim of circumstance.'

November 14th 8 days to go

I went to the doctor's office this morning. I was completely tense. It took ages for him to see me. In that time, I went through all the permutations. Say if something is wrong with me. Imagine all the time I've wasted, I thought. I swore if it was just general, all round fatigue, I would change. No more self pity. No more, my life's not going the way I wanted it to go, why can't I be successful? No more, that guy's earning a €100,000 a year. Why can't I? No more, why is his John Thomas bigger than Bob? No more, why is this guy getting the greater laughs? I swore I'd visit my parents more often. I swore I'd even go and support Galway at G.A.A. matches. At that moment I became convinced I had a brain tumour and was experiencing complete personality change. I swore I wouldn't take Kirsten for granted so much anymore. I swore I'd greet people warmly and openly on the street. I swore from this day on I would approach things positively and would defeat Old Man Negativity. I would banish those blues and start paying my dues. I would not be embittered and would be effusive in my praise of others. I would see the bigger picture and realise that the problems of one Creative Lower Being don't amount to a hill of flageolets in this crazy world.

The doctor then called me in. He gave me the results. Everything was fine. Okay, my liver reading is a bit up, but that's to be expected. This whole experience has been a real jolt to my system. I am so relieved. This is my epiphany. My road to Damascus. I have been given a second chance. And I will grasp it with both hands. It is up to me and me alone to make the best of my future, to maximise my potential and to achieve an inner fulfilment. My choices are clear. No more messing around. No more wasting time. This is it. This is the show. This is not the dress rehearsal. I must enjoy it. 25 years of navel gazing and self-loathing will be consigned to history. This is the beginning of a change and I will embrace it fully.

November 17th 5 days to go

So much for the change. BBC Radio 4 have just commissioned Dinny Bruce's nasal sit-com. I can't believe it. That talentless oddity has somehow convinced the powers that be in Broadcasting House that it is a worthwhile project. I bumped into him today on South William Street. He was on the other side of the road. I tried to instigate that 'tacit synchronicity of avoidance' but it was pointless. Beaming and energised, he bounded over to me and told me his news.

November 21st 1 day to go

The days of minimal means might be over! Dara from Jupiter Television rang today and told me they loved the idea of 'Te$t of Character' and they want to develop it. They told me they already have interest from a few T.V stations in Europe and even the States. Although he wasn't too sure about the 'Compulsive Masturbators in the Sex Shop' episode. We have organised a meeting for next week. He said there could be big money in this and is dying to meet me. I'm thrilled. Of course it is a complete sell-out of any principles and integrity that I still possessed but I can't afford to look a gift thoroughbred horse in the mouth. What a 40th birthday present!

November 22nd 0 days to go

The big day has arrived. Quite low-key in the end. Kirsten brought me out for a nice meal. Prohibitively expensive, but this is Dublin, after all. Later, in the pelting rain we waited 50 minutes for a bus on Dame Street. We should have hailed a taxi but as stated earlier we're not taxi people. When the bus finally arrived we went upstairs. As we sat down, I noticed a few D.L.T.s smoking at the back. Kirsten told me to forget about it, but eventually I got up and I asked them politely to put out the cigarettes since it was against the law to smoke on a bus. My request was met with a giggle. Then a "Fuck off". Then another giggle.

As Kirsten showered when we got home, I started to think about the Big Four O. I don't feel any different really. It is just a number after all.

However I have come to one conclusion. Aging is the gradual process of accepting your irrelevance and the older you get, you start to see the bigger picture and you realise that the time you were born into, isn't all that important. It's business as usual in the greater scheme of things, only the digits in the years are different. And someday in the not too distant future, your time will be just another bygone era. And maybe you'll be some guy in some random street photograph staring into some anonymous photographer's lens, and the photo will be part of an exhibition in some photographic museum somewhere, and people may wonder, who is that guy, wonder what his story was.

And you'll want to tell them. He was just a guy who sat in a room and conversed with himself in different accents. He derived a certain pleasure from dwelling on the negative yet he did experience the odd spasm of contentment. He believed there was two types of success. Big success and no success. He thought people don't change. They just end up being who they always were. Except with more nasal hair. He was obsessed with the past but realised, like Thomas Wolfe, that you can never go home. He was merely a guy who could sing the odd song. Act the odd role. Write the odd scene. In all honesty, he was nothing special. Just another creative lower being.